ONE MOMENT IN TIME

SHARI LOW

Boldwood

First published in Great Britain in 2023 by Boldwood Books Ltd.

Cover Design by Alice Moore Design

Cover Photography: Shutterstock

A CIP catalogue record for this book is available from the British Library.

Paperback ISBN 978-1-80426-872-8

Large Print ISBN 978-1-80426-871-1

Hardback ISBN 978-1-80426-874-2

Ebook ISBN 978-1-80426-869-8

Kindle ISBN 978-1-80426-870-4

Audio CD ISBN 978-1-80426-878-0

MP3 CD ISBN 978-1-80426-877-3

Digital audio download ISBN 978-1-80426-876-6

Boldwood Books Ltd
23 Bowerdean Street
London SW6 3TN
www.boldwoodbooks.com

To Jan Johnston and Lyndsay MacAlister for Vegas, cocktails, a million coffees and years of laughter...
And to my love, John, and our family - who are everything, always.

PROLOGUE

LAS VEGAS – 19 MAY 1993

Elvis threw his arms out to the side, making the tassels that dangled from his white leather jacket quiver. The Elvis Loves Me Tender Chapel of Las Vegas was his white-walled, plastic-flower-draped stage, and the four people standing in front of him were his audience.

'Do you, Brenda Doris Fulton,' he sang, in a slightly less impressive voice than the man who had actually been Elvis Aaron Presley, '...take this man, Colin Jones...' That set off a flurry of tambourines from the three pink-clad backing singers that the advertising billboard called the Chapelettes, standing to the left of Elvis. 'To be your hunka hunka burning love and husband until your last day on earth?"

'I do,' Brenda whispered, tears falling, and not just because the fluorescent strip lights above them were bringing on a migraine.

Her response set the tambourines off again, and exclamations of 'Praise be,' rang out from the Chapelettes.

'And do you, Colin Jones, take this woman, Brenda Doris Fulton, to be your wife and promise to love her tender until the day you die?'

Colin stared into her eyes and Brenda could see so many things there. Love. Fear. Uncertainty. Discomfort, because the air conditioning in the chapel was non-existent and either the heat or the occasion was making him sweat like a marathon runner. In the midday sun. Wearing a woolly jumper.

'*I do.*'

'*Then, by the powers invested in me by Viva Las Vegas, Nevada and the Lord, How Great Thou Art, I now pronounce you man and wife. May you never be lonesome at night or have suspicious minds. Amen.*'

The opening bars of 'The Wonder of You' soared from a flashing boombox in the corner and Elvis and his Chapelettes sang two verses and the chorus while Colin and Brenda walked back down the aisle.

They'd already signed all the forms and paid for the ceremony before it began – presumably in case they changed their minds and Elvis didn't get his dosh – so they just pushed open the heavy wooden door and stumbled out into the humid, sticky Las Vegas night.

And that's when it hit them both.

Brenda, in a white summer dress, was the first to speak. 'Colin...' she whispered, making eye contact and feeling an unaccustomed shyness. She'd known this man for three years and yet now they felt like strangers. 'What have we done?'

If she was looking for a confidence boost, or an inspirational suggestion, she was searching in the wrong place.

'I've no bloody idea, Brenda. And I've no idea what we do next.'

1

ZARA

March 2023

'How's it going there, Inspector Gadget? Tracked him down yet?' Millie asked, as she floated in from the front shop, bringing three buckets of white hydrangeas for the Miller nuptials centrepieces that night. It was a 6 p.m. wedding at one of the swankiest hotels in the city, so they had to be perfect.

Glancing up from her laptop in the corner of their workroom, Zara took in the oh-so-together vision of her younger sister. Even at 9 a.m. in her standard workout wear (ironic, because she would have to be bribed with cash and wine to go anywhere near a gym), Millie oozed elegance and gorgeousness, all dark corkscrew curls, toned arse and Cheryl Tweedy dimples. Zara, on the other hand, with her blonde hair pulled back in a messy bun held in place by a pencil, her three-month roots, her denim dungarees and Doc Martens boots, was more on the low-key side of the fashion scale. Or, as Millie frequently categorised it, Joiner-Chic.

'Still searching, but I think I've found a possibility.' Zara pulled the pencil out of her hair, and her waves creaked slowly down to her shoul-

ders, reluctantly fighting against the half a can of dry shampoo she'd fired
into it that morning. Usually, it was only Monday mornings that were 5
a.m. starts at the flower market in Glasgow, stocking up for the week at
Blooming Sisters, their flower shop in the West End of the city. But a pre-
dawn Friday run had been necessary this morning to pick up some extra
blooms for this weekend's events, so bouncy locks were bottom of the
priority list. Especially when she'd had to do the run solo because Millie
hadn't come home from wherever she had spent last night.

One of the very best things about their shop was that they also owned
the two-bedroom flat above it. The flat had been a huge plus when they'd
been looking for premises. For a start, it meant they were handy for late
nights and early mornings at work, but also it meant they weren't paying a
separate mortgage or rent for somewhere to live.

Working together and living together might be a problem for some
siblings, but the reality was that out of work hours their paths rarely
crossed. Zara's boyfriend, Kev, would come over, and the two of them
would chill in front of the TV. Millie, at the other end of the genetic pool
party, was a serial socialiser. If there was a shindig anywhere in this city,
then her sister would find herself there, yet, infuriatingly, she still rolled
home at the crack of dawn, had a quick shower, some coffee, then trotted
downstairs looking like she was just home from a rejuvenating week on a
beach. If Zara didn't love her sibling so much, her self-esteem would have
forced her to disown her years ago.

'Ooooh, let me see.' Millie gently placed the blooms down on the
massive steel table that sat in the middle of their back shop, next to the
boxes of lilies that Zara had already deposited there two hours before
when she'd returned from the market.

The workroom slash office had concrete floors, plain white walls and
floor to ceiling shelves packed with tools, trellis, chicken wire, vases and
blooms. The long, steel centre table had been bought second-hand from
an auction of equipment from a food-prep warehouse. The whole room
was a chaotic contrast to the vintage beauty of the smaller front shop,
which had been furnished with shabby-chic furniture and velvet sofas.
Tilly, one of their part-time staffers, was manning the shop, which was just
as well because it was going to take the next five hours to prepare the

arrangements for a three o'clock delivery to the hotel, so they were in for a long day.

As always, Millie couldn't join Zara at the desk in the corner of the room without commenting on her appearance. 'Interesting fashion choice. House of Dungarees?'

Zara ignored her, leaning back so her sister could get full view of the screen. A Facebook page stared back at her. 'Gary Gregg. Do you know how many Gary Greggs there are? Actually, not that many, but none of the ones in the UK were the right age. I tried Canada, Australia and New Zealand, because that's always where Nicky Campbell finds folk on *Long Lost Family*. But zilch. Not even a possible match. This one though is a potential, although he lives in South Carolina.'

'Have you been drinking?' Millie asked. 'Dad's mate came from Paisley. What would he be doing in South Carolina?'

Zara scrolled down further. 'I've no idea, but this guy is roughly the same age as Dad, and look...' She pointed at the screen with all the conviction and triumph of someone who'd just tracked down a serial killer. There were only two posts on his profile. One showing a fifty something, square jawed, suit-wearing handsome bloke smiling at the camera and the other one featuring the same chap in a T-shirt, sitting in a garden.

Millie frowned. 'What? He's got a lawnmower? They're not the sole preserve of Scottish people. He's a bit of a silver fox, though, I'll give you that. Clearly no stranger to a bench press.'

'My talents are wasted on you. Look at his arm.' Zara used the pencil to point at the screen and saw Millie having the same reaction she'd had. Stare. Realisation. Grin.

It was barely discernible to the naked eye, but it was there: the tiny rectangle, with the diagonal lines inked inside it.

'A Saltire,' Millie said, with rising excitement as she examined the Scottish flag tattooed on the gentleman's bicep. It wasn't huge and it looked faded, like it had been done when he was a younger man. 'Oh, you're good. Well done, sis. If the flower shop goes tits up there might be a future for you in private investigation.'

Zara gave a triumphant bow, then held a thirty-odd-year-old photo up next to the screen, a slightly grainy Polaroid pic that showed four people in

their early twenties, two women and two men, standing under the iconic
Welcome to Las Vegas sign. On the white band at the bottom of the photo,
it had four names: Colin Jones, Brenda Fulton, Gary Gregg, Eileen Smith.
And the comment underneath – *Best friends on tour, Las Vegas, 1993!*

'I still can't get over how young they look in this picture. So bizarre that
they got married when they were younger than we are now. What were
they? Twenty-four? Twenty-five?'

Millie nodded. 'Yep. And we struggle to commit to a Netflix
subscription.'

Zara chuckled, because, as always, her sister wasn't wrong. 'I gave up
on Eileen Smith because there are a gazillion of them on social media and
I figured it was a waste of time because she's probably married and going
under a different name now. But this guy... That is him, isn't it?' They both
peered at the man on the far right of the photo, shoulder to shoulder with
their dad, then took their gaze to the image on the screen. 'It's him,' Zara
announced, answering her own question. 'I'm sure of it. Positive. One
hundred per cent. Okay, seventy-five per cent, but I'll go with it if you will.'

Millie puckered her perfect pout, the one that was enhanced by a tiny
bit of filler but still looked natural. 'I think maybe fifty per cent, but it's
worth a shot.'

'Right, I'm doing it.' Zara's burst of decisive action was so abrupt, she
almost knocked over the half-finished coffee that sat to the left of her
laptop and yelped as she caught it. 'Bollocks! That was close. Losing one
laptop to a cappuccino was careless, two would just be...'

'Totally in keeping with your general clumsiness,' Millie finished the
sentence for her.

Zara ignored her. Mostly because she was right. Sometimes working
with someone who had known you your whole life had its drawbacks. The
fact that her younger sister had been there to witness almost every unfor-
tunate incident in at least twenty-seven of Zara's twenty-eight years, and
could not only recall them, but could wrap them up in a story that was
hilarious to everyone except Zara, was the bane of her life. No, Mrs Bassett,
who popped in for a dozen carnations every second Friday, didn't need to
know that ten-year-old Zara had fallen flat on her face at a ballet recital,
fractured her wrist and had been thereafter known as Swan Break. Or that,

as an underage, seventeen-year-old clubber, out for the first time in the bars of the city centre clutching a fake ID, she'd ended the night by falling off her platform shoes and face-planting in a kebab shop. Or – oh, the watery eyes – that her first attempt at losing her virginity a few weeks later had been abandoned after she had somehow managed to snag her boyfriend's penis in the zip of his jeans. He was her ex-boyfriend about three seconds later. It went without saying that Millie hadn't actually witnessed that incident first hand but Zara had blurted it out in a fit of mortification the next day and Millie had responded with her very own brand of sisterly compassion – she'd howled with amusement, laughed until tears streamed down her face, then suggested Zara stick to blokes with button fly jeans in the future.

Moving the coffee cup well out of the way, Zara flexed her fingers and then activated step one of Operation Vegas Reunion. She clicked the friend request button of Gary Gregg's Facebook page, and then the 'message' button.

Dear Gary,

Apologies for contacting you, but I'm hoping you can help with some research I'm doing on behalf of my family. I'm Zara Jones, and I'm hoping you'll recognise my parents' names – Colin and Brenda Jones.

I'm currently trying to track down the guy who was my dad's best mate back in the eighties and early nineties, and who was with them at their wedding in Las Vegas in 1993. We are hoping that person is you?

We're also trying to find my mum's friend, Eileen who was in Las Vegas with them too.

The reason for my search is that my parents will be celebrating their thirtieth wedding anniversary on May 19th, and my sister Millie and I...

Over Zara's shoulder, Millie punched the air. 'Yassss! I got a mention in *War and Peace.*'

Zara ignored the dig and kept on tapping her short, unpolished, nails on the keyboard.

...are planning to surprise them by whisking them back to Las Vegas, so that they can renew their vows on the day of their anniversary, in the same place they got married.

We'd love to surprise Mum and Dad even more by reuniting them with their old friends when we arrive in Vegas. Could you contact me please so that we can have a chat about whether you're the person I'm looking for? My telephone number is UK 141 093 2020.

Hope to hear from you soon.

She pressed send, crossed her fingers and glanced up to the heavens. She was desperate for this to work out. 'Right, romance fairies, do your bit.'

Zara spotted Millie doing that face, the one that flagged up she was about to come out with a smart-arse comment. She wasn't wrong.

'I have it on good authority,' Millie began, 'that romance fairies only listen to people who believe in things of a romantic nature, so I think you might need a backup plan.'

'I do believe in romance,' Zara countered, feigning outrage. 'Kev and I have had a solid eight years of romantic stuff.' Even as she said it, she had to struggle not to laugh. Unless bingeing the latest Netflix series about serial killers was considered the pastime of love's young dream, then she and Kev had probably last been romantic around Christmas... 2016. And even then, it was only because he panic-purchased heart-shaped chocolates in Tesco.

Millie's laser glare went to Zara's denim-clad nethers. 'When was the last time you had a bikini wax? Give me it in years.'

Zara rolled her eyes. Okay, so she had a point. But she'd bet her last ladyshave that Kev wouldn't notice or care if she had enough foliage down there to require a Flymo. No, they weren't swinging from the fluorescent lights, but they were best mates. That's what mattered. He was her favourite person to flake out with at the end of every day and she wasn't taking relationship criticism from a woman whose idea of long-term commitment was a second date. 'Around the same time that you were last in a monogamous relationship.'

'Ouch. Stung,' Millie went full amateur dramatics, clutching her heart for all of two seconds, before her priorities kicked in. 'Right, come on, let's get these arrangements done or we'll never get out of here tonight and I'm on the VIP list for that new club that's opening on George Street. You know, a nightclub. It's where people go to dance and drink and make irresponsible decisions.'

'You can do that without leaving our kitchen,' Zara teased, as she pushed herself up from her chair, squeezing her buttocks in an attempt to restore some feeling to her numb cheeks. It really was time to get a proper office chair instead of the old wooden seat that their gran had donated when they first opened the shop.

Blooming Sisters was their company, their pride and joy, and their reason for getting up at ungodly hours. Zara adored every brick and scent of the place. In the trendy Hyndland area of Glasgow, it had a decent passing trade, but the sisters' speciality and biggest financial earner was event flowers: weddings, funerals, gender reveals, corporate balls, Christmas parties, TV shows... anywhere, in fact that required barrows full of flowers, beautifully arranged.

When they'd first opened the shop, Zara had a very real fear that they'd lose their business loan, their savings and the cash their parents had loaned them in the first six months. Thankfully, she'd been wrong. Now, five years later, the hours were still long, the shop could do with a new boiler, and Zara hadn't yet lost that tiny nugget of fear that it could all go blooms up at any minute, but they were making a healthy profit and – most importantly – in year three, they'd paid back the loan that their mum and dad had given them.

Their parents, however, had refused to accept any interest so that had been the starting point for the Vegas idea. How could they thank the mum and dad that had been so constant in their lives, so loving, so solid, so utterly decent and supportive? Zara wasn't sure if she or Millie had suggested Vegas first, but as soon as it was out there, they'd both jumped right on board, especially when a small inheritance from their lovely granny last year had made it more financially viable. They were about to blow every penny they possessed on this trip, but they both felt it was the right thing to do. Most of the time. After a few gin and tonics, Millie had occasionally announced that the right thing to do was to spend it on a deposit for a Mercedes, and then whack the rest of the payments she couldn't afford on a credit card, but she always changed her mind when she woke up the next morning.

This was, Zara knew, going to be the most special few days of their lives and this was what it was all about. Making lifelong memories. Showing family how much you love them. Going out of your way to create wonderful moments for the people who deserve it most. And earning a lifetime of free Christmas dinners from a mum who would definitely let them off the cooking after this.

For the next half hour or so, they both sang along to Millie's Beyonce playlist while they worked, until Zara finished the first centrepiece, a magnificent glass cube that burst into a cloud of white flowers. It was stunning. Exactly what the bride had settled on, after approximately forty-seven conversations, a dozen changes of mind and at least one hysterical meltdown. 'It's so gorgeous,' she said wistfully, stepping back and walking around the table to view it from all angles.

A sniff came from Millie and Zara's head swivelled round in surprise. Her sister didn't usually do tears or outpourings of sentimentality.

'Are you overcome with emotion?'

'Nope, just bit into this spicy satay stick and it's making my eyes water,' Millie retorted, laughing as she held up the skewer. 'But it is gorgeous. If you're going to enslave yourself to one man for the rest of your life, then I suppose you want to mark the big day with a nice centrepiece.'

'Remind me not to let you write our next promo campaign.' Zara sighed. 'What's wrong with us? Two women, not a romantic bone in your body and not a romantic inclination in my brain. Do you think it's some kind of genetic flaw?'

Millie had already grown bored of the work and had taken a break to check her Insta notifications but she multi-tasked and continued the conversation. 'I think maybe Mum and Dad kept all the romance for themselves. Thirty years. How is that even possible? Especially after a spontaneous Vegas wedding. They're going to be so blown away by this trip. I know it. And if we can get their old pals there, that'll be even more perfect. Although... have you ever asked Mum and Dad why they didn't stay in touch with their mates back then? I mean, they all look really chummy in that photo and yet we've never met them. What if they had a huge falling out or something?'

Zara paused, her fingers intertwined in the stems of two lilies. 'Mum and Dad? They haven't fallen out with a single person in their whole lives. And no, I didn't ask them, because I found the picture in Gran's old photo box when I was clearing out her stuff after she passed, and it didn't seem like the right time. Then we decided to pull this surprise and I didn't want to spoil it. Anyway, the answer's obvious now... it must have been because the other two went off somewhere. Gary Gregg decided to live in America and Eileen Smith must have moved away too. No internet back then. People lost touch all the time.'

'You think?'

Zara caught sight of Millie's raised eyebrow of scepticism. Which didn't happen very often, given her sister's love of Botox.

'Oh God, your forehead moved. Don't scare me like that.'

Millie brushed her fingers across her brow. 'I thought I felt something strange. Anyway, you're probably right. You know I just don't always have your sunny view of life. Relentless optimism gives me a migraine. I'm sure it'll be totally fine.'

Zara pushed down any twinge of doubt. 'It will be. I know it. Any second now, Gary Gregg will reply to my message and tell me this is the best thing that's happened to him in years.'

2

BRENDA

April 2023

Brenda watched as her friend Bernadette's face beamed. BEAMED.

'I think we're going to have to stop being friends until you find a way to wipe that smile off your face,' Brenda told her, as she put two mugs of tea down on the table in the staff room of the Accident and Emergency department at Glasgow Central Hospital. But, of course, she didn't mean it. Bernadette's joy was a sight for sore eyes. A long time coming. The happy ever after. And all the other clichés that anyone could throw at second-time-around, later-in-life love.

Bernadette picked up her steaming mug. 'I don't blame you. If I met me now, I'd think I was unbearable,' she said, her soft lilt bubbling with the warmth that had made her one of Brenda's closest friends. Twenty-five years they'd worked together on the wards at Glasgow Central and Brenda treasured every single one of them.

'Right then, tell me everything. All the details. Leave nothing out,' Brenda demanded. 'Although, I've only got a half-hour break, so you might need to go with bullet points.'

Bernadette chuckled and Brenda thought again how fantastic it was to see her friend's happiness oozing from every pore.

'Okay, bullet points. John and I spent the weekend in Dublin. One of his sons, Tadgh...'

'He's the singer?'

Bernie nodded. 'Yep, but not the one in the band. The solo one.'

Brenda had heard all about Bernadette's manfriend's family over the last few months, since Bernadette had met John during a holiday last summer. The term 'boyfriend' had been ditched because, according to Bernadette, it just didn't seem right given that they could 'both remember the words of songs from the seventies'.

'Well, he had a gig in a concert hall in the city centre, and afterwards, we were all walking home – I told you my Nina and Gerry, and my Stuart and his boyfriend, Callum, were coming with me?'

'You did,' Brenda confirmed, full of anticipation. Bernadette's daughter, Nina, and her son, Stuart, were the lights of her life.

'Right, so we were all walking, John and me, Tadgh and his girlfriend, Hayley, my lot, and we were crossing one of the bridges over the Liffey, and suddenly, John stopped. At first I thought he'd taken a dizzy turn...'

'Occupational hazard,' Brenda pointed out, laughing.

'Exactly. But then, he turned to me and he said, "Bernadette, I'm not one for big gestures, but I reckon this is the only time all these folks will be together for a while and I want them to be here to share this. M'darlin', I never thought I'd have another chance to feel the kind of love I feel for you. This last year with you... well, it's made an old git like me happier than I ever deserved to be and I never want this to end. Bernie, my love, will you marry me?"'

Brenda wasn't usually one for tears, but she felt her eyes welling. 'Oh Bernadette, that's beautiful. And you said...?'

'Well, at first, I didn't say anything, because I was gobsmacked and too choked for words, but when I swallowed the bloody great big lump in my throat, I said, "Of course I will, because I love you too, you gorgeous big sod." And then he picked me up and swirled me around and, honestly, Brenda, we felt like young things again. At least, until he got a twinge in his back and had to put me down.'

A couple of the new junior doctors on the ward wandered in, spotted two clearly emotional women at the table, and then backed out slowly, obviously deciding their microwave cheeseburgers and cans of Red Bull could wait.

'He could barely straighten up the next morning, but it was worth it. The following day we went out and picked this ring...' She flashed a beautiful gold band embedded with three small but perfect diamonds. 'And that was us. Engaged. Soon to be hitched. I still can't believe this is happening to me. We've not decided on all the details, but we're thinking a September wedding in Ireland. Promise me you and Colin and the girls will come.'

Bernadette's cheeks could barely contain her grin and Brenda chuckled with irrepressible delight and joy for her friend.

At least that's what she thought until she heard herself say, 'Yes, of course, we'd love... love...' Her mind froze, she felt herself lose her grip on her smile and Bernadette was now staring at her with a very obvious expression of concern.

'Brenda, ma love, are you okay? Only...' Bernadette's words trailed off and that's when Brenda realised that her face was damp and her laughter had somehow morphed into sobs. Great big fat sobs, the kind that ambush the brain and take over your body and make you tremble and heave with the agony of them. 'Oh jeezus, Brenda,' Bernadette whispered and flew to her friend's side.

Brenda felt the arms come around her, the fingers stroke her hair, but still, she couldn't stop.

'What's wrong? What's happened? Brenda, I'm so sorry if I've upset you but—'

'No!' Brenda managed to blurt, before gathering herself just enough to force out, 'No, it wasn't you, and I'm so sorry.' More sobs. 'I totally spoiled your moment there, Bernadette.' Another sob and a huge sniff. 'I'm so happy for you, I really am.'

Bernadette held her at arm's-length now, pushing back stray strands of hair that had fallen from Brenda's bun on to her face. 'Och, love, what is it then?'

Brenda felt a fizz unravelling in her chest, like a Catherine wheel, sparking everywhere as it let loose until she could contain it no longer. 'I want... I want to leave Colin.'

It was the first time she'd said it out loud and Brenda didn't know if it made her feel better or worse. Strike that. Nothing could make her feel better right now.

The sound of the staffroom door opening again was barely audible until Bernadette yelled, 'Out!' to ward off any potential interruptions. Two young gents in scrubs backed out and the door swiftly closed again. Brenda knew she'd have to go find the nurses later and apologise, but right now she inhaled, exhaled, tried to gather herself. This wasn't her. She didn't do wild bursts of emotion or drama. She was usually the one consoling other people and trying to find a way to sort things out. But there was no fixing this or making it better. She knew that already. That's why it was all so utterly devastating.

A bunch of tissues were thrust into her hands and she blew her nose, while Bernadette sat back on her chair, one hand still rubbing Brenda's arm. 'Right, love, when you can, just tell me what you're feeling and let's see if talking this through can help. God, I feel like a fool. I had no idea you were having problems. You two have always seemed so... fine.'

Brenda blew her nose again. That was it. Right there. 'I know, Bernadette, but that says it all, really, doesn't it? *Fine.* We've always been fine. But I - please don't judge me here - I don't want "fine" anymore, Bernadette. Colin and I... well, the truth is that we've always been great friends, but we got married so young and...' Brenda stopped herself there. There was no point dredging up sob stories from a million years ago. What happened in Vegas when they'd got married... well, clichéd as it was, it had stayed in Vegas. They were young. They'd made mistakes. They'd thought they were doing the right thing at the time. And sometimes she felt like the last thirty years had been one long exercise in making the best of it. 'The bottom line is that I've realised that if I stay with Colin, this is the most I'll ever have. I'll live my whole life without knowing what it feels like to be head over heels in love. Without feeling that special way that I read about in books. Without having that beaming smile that you've had for the last year.'

Bernadette's eyes widened. 'I'm so sorry if I've made you feel—'

'No, no,' Brenda cut her off. 'Please don't apologise. Bernadette, I'm thrilled for you, I really am. You've been through so much and you deserve every second of this happiness and more. But the thing is, I want to know what that feels like too... Is that pathetic? Or selfish?'

'No,' Bernadette shook her head, 'of course not. But... do you think you could talk to Colin? Maybe make him see how you feel? Work on what you've got. I mean, thirty years is a long time to throw away. I'm sure if you told him—'

'I've told him a hundred times,' Brenda admitted, swallowing back a lump of sadness. 'But the thing is, it's just not in his nature. Never has been. He's happy with his life, his work. He's retiring early in a few months and he's already talking about the things he wants to do in the garden. The walks he wants to take. The books he wants to read. And I love him for his laid-back attitude – God knows it's made him a rock of sense all through our lives – but I don't want any of that, Bernadette. I want to travel. To meet new people. To have some excitement. I want to live before I don't have any life left in me. How many people have we lost lately...'

Bernadette nodded her head and Brenda knew she'd understand what she was saying. Another occupational hazard. In A&E, they both saw too much death, too many people taken too soon. And not just anonymous people. Bernadette's first husband, a cardiologist and awful bastard of a man, had dropped dead with a heart attack only a couple of years before. One of their favourite doctors, Noah Clark, had lost his best friend in a brutal car crash only last month. Back at the start of the year, one of the other nurses on the ward, Rosina, a dear friend to them both, had lost her life to cancer. She was five years younger than Brenda and maybe that had been the start of it. The beginning of the wondering, of the fear of what she'd missed in life.

'Too many,' Bernadette agreed, then fell silent again. That was Bernadette's way. Like Brenda, she preferred to listen, to let people talk, rather than try to get her own opinions in.

Brenda picked up her mug and took a slug of tea, hoping the warm liquid would loosen the tight grip her emotions had on her throat. 'That's what I mean. Not to sound corny, or maudlin, but none of us know what's in front of us, or how long we've got, and there's so much I haven't done, haven't felt. While we were bringing up our girls, that was fine. I didn't even notice it. Well, you don't, do you? I was just so happy to have my family and be a mum and I loved every minute of it, but the girls are grown now, living their own lives. And much as I feel sick every time I think about sharing how I feel and telling them that I want to leave their dad, I want to live my own life too.'

Bernadette gave her hand a squeeze, the red fringe of her hair bobbing as she nodded her head. 'Brenda, in all our years I've never known you to make a bad decision, or a wrong move, or to act without thinking, so if this is what you feel is right for you, then I'll do everything I can to help and support you. So what's next? Are you going to talk to Colin about it?'

Brenda nodded, absorbing Bernadette's words and feeling soothed by them. Just to have that reassurance that she wasn't losing her mind, doing something crazy, to have someone telling her to trust her own feelings, it gave Brenda another brick in the bloody big wall of strength that she was going to have to build to get through this. 'I will. Like I said, I've tried already, but he just doesn't get it. He just points out how happy we've been all these years. And he's not wrong. That's what makes it so difficult to explain. He's a good man. He's never treated me badly.'

It was Brenda's turn to squeeze Bernadette's hand now, an acknowledgement of the hell Bernadette went through with her controlling, abusive, narcissistic ex-husband. When she'd found the courage to leave, Bernadette had sworn off men for life, just grateful to have escaped, but then she'd met John and now she was the happiest she'd ever been and engaged to be married to someone who made her giddy with excitement. It gave Brenda hope.

The tea was working, and the words were flowing now. 'I really don't want to hurt him. Any passion we had is long gone, but I still love him as a friend. I just want more than that now. I want more than the same thing, day in, day out. I need to sit him down and make him understand...'

'You do,' Bernadette agreed.

'And I need to tell the girls too. I think that's what I'm dreading most. They'll be devastated. They love their dad and we've always been so close, the four of us...'

'But they love you too, Brenda. Even if it's a shock at first, they'll come round when they understand that you're doing it for the sake of your happiness.'

'But at the expense of theirs and Colin's?' Brenda challenged, repeating the same argument that had raged in her head since she had first contemplated leaving.

'Yes, even then. They're lovely girls and they've got good heads on their shoulders. They'd hate to see you stay in an unhappy situation just for them. I've no doubt they'll be worried about their dad's feelings, but if you all pull together, hopefully you'll be able to help each other through the tough bits.'

Brenda took another slug of tea. 'I hope so. Bernadette, thank you – it's such a relief to talk.'

'I just wish you'd said something sooner. Preferably before I went warbling on about my newfound happy life.'

Brenda shook her head. 'No! That's exactly what I want to hear about. Happy ever afters. Gives me hope that I might get one too. I don't mean a new bloke. I just mean a life where I feel things, have a purpose, where there's excitement and surprises and even bits that bloody terrify me. S'pose telling the girls will be good practice for that.'

'So when are you going to do it?' Bernadette asked, apprehension causing tiny wrinkles on her forehead. 'Just so I know to book a day off and bring wine for afterwards.'

Brenda had already thought this through. 'Not yet. You know it's our thirtieth wedding anniversary in a few weeks, and the girls have planned some kind of family trip to celebrate the occasion. I don't have the heart to tell them before then because it's already all arranged. No idea where we're going. Probably a week in the Lake District – we always took the girls there when they were younger and we loved it. Anyway, Zara told me we were doing something months ago because she knew I'd have to book the time off, so I know it's all organised. I'll wait until after that. And when we're away, I'll put a face on and just enjoy every second of our last trip all together, the four of us.'

'Are you sure you'll be able to keep up the pretence of being happy?' There was an edge of doubt in Bernadette's voice that Brenda understood, but she nodded firmly.

'I've been doing it for years, Bernadette, so I can manage it for a while longer. When we get back from the trip, I'll start looking for somewhere to live, just a wee flat somewhere nice would be fine. Then I'll tell everyone and do everything I can to make it as painless as possible. I'm dreading it, but it's the only way. I want to have a future I can look forward to, but first, heart-breaking as it will be, I need to close the chapter on my life with Colin. You never know, maybe when we're away, he'll realise that he wants more than this too.'

Even as she was saying it, Brenda knew she was clutching at broken straws. She was going to have to be the one to end this marriage. She just had to wait for the right place and the right time to do it.

3

AIDEN GREGG

April 2023

The South Carolina sun was reflecting off the ocean, glinting in the waves that lapped up on the Hilton Head Island sands. The only child of Scottish parents, Gary and Eileen Gregg, Aiden had grown up in Charleston, about a two-hour drive away, but he'd spent every summer and vacation on Hilton Head, so the sands behind his parents' beach house had been his first and only choice for his wedding to Layla. Or, rather, his dad's beach house. His dad had kept the house as part of the divorce settlement and had to pay his mum half the value. He'd be ranting and moaning about that until the end of time. Which was probably around the same time Layla would get here. Punctuality had never been her strong point. It would probably have been a good idea to tell her that the ceremony was taking place an hour before it actually was, because she was already half an hour late and he could see his mom was beginning to wilt in the noon heat. Or maybe that was more down to her proximity to his father.

They'd been divorced for around a decade now, but Aiden knew his mom still found any encounter with his dad a challenge. Especially when, like today, his dad had pitched up with a twenty-nine-year-old nightclub hostess called Mitzy, who was on her third espresso martini and was already threatening to demonstrate that she could do the splits in heels. Right now, Mr Gregg senior and Mitzy were standing over at the bar, shooting back tequila with his best man, Trevon. Trevon was his closest friend, former housemate, entrepreneur, successful owner of a chain of fitness centres and the man he loved like a brother, but still, Aiden made a mental note to disown him if he got wasted and lost the rings.

The string quartet at the other side of the sandy aisle were on their third rendition, or was it the fourth, of the piece of music Layla had chosen. His side of the family had provided the venue and he'd paid for the honeymoon. Layla's mom had been none too pleased at the low-key vibe of her daughter's big day, so she'd insisted on organising the string quartet, a theatrical celebrant, and a buffet that was right now being prepared at the house. And, of course, the dress, which Layla had hinted had cost more than his car.

He wasn't surprised. In the months they'd been together, his bride had made no secret that while she could hang out at the beach and tag along to a ball game, she enjoyed the finer things in life too.

They'd met when she taken the treadmill next to him during one of his daily 5 a.m. workouts at Trevon's gym in the city centre. It was a Monday morning and Aiden had smiled and nodded. On the Tuesday morning he'd said hi. On the Wednesday morning, he'd introduced himself. On Thursday morning they'd chatted while they ran and he had established a brief bio. Layla. 29. Single. Worked in marketing, mainly in the lifestyle and travel sectors. Lived in an apartment just a few blocks from his. Liked to socialise, travel and drink coffee while the sun came up.

On the Friday, he'd asked her out for dinner that night. The dinner had turned into breakfast the next morning, then Saturday night dinner, then Sunday brunch, and they'd both been so intoxicated with each other that they'd had to force themselves not to carry their immediate and intense romance on for several more days, mainly because he didn't think the partners at his law firm would appreciate their top matrimonial lawyer showing up wearing the distracting Aroma De Sleepless Nights, with top notes of Lust and Jack Daniel's.

Yep, despite living in the waste ground left by the battle of his parents' split, there was the boot in the irony bollocks. He was a divorce lawyer. A choice that was no doubt inspired by his parents' marriage dissolution while he was at college. They'd tried not to let any of it affect him, but every time he saw his mom and dad he could read the stress on their faces and a scan of the divorce petition told him that although they were putting amicable faces on for his sake, there were accusations of infidelity against his dad (which were almost certainly true), and plenty of demands and tussles over the division of twenty years' worth of assets. Call it subliminal messaging, but when he'd graduated with his degree from the University of South Carolina School of Law, family law had been the speciality he'd immediately gravitated towards.

Anyway, back to finding the love of his life. Sure, it was the physical stuff that had attracted him at first: the long mane of dark Camila Cabello waves, the huge brown eyes and the perfect smile that – clichéd as it was – had him at hello. She was very recently divorced, which in hindsight, might have been a red flag to some people, but he preferred to disregard that and just call himself lucky.

Layla was stunning, she was smart and she was crazy enough to have fallen in love with Aiden just as hard and fast as he'd fallen for her. Within three weeks, she'd moved in with him, six months later they were engaged, and now, not even a year after they'd met, they were here, on the golden sands, with rows of white wooden chairs under two huge beige tarpaulin shades, an arch of white flowers at the end of the aisle, a celebrant and everyone they loved. Or rather, he was here. Layla was late, as usual. It was her one habit that drove him crazy, but he'd chosen to overlook it and focus on the stunning and smart stuff.

'I'm sure she'll be here any minute,' he told the celebrant, a large gent who was beginning to perspire in the heat. 'Can I get you a drink? Some water?'

'Yes, please. And a bride. A bride would be excellent.'

Aiden had been under the impression that wedding celebrants were supposed to spread joy, but this bloke – a friend of Layla's frankly terrifying mother – clearly hadn't got the memo. Her mother wasn't even here to placate him. Layla was having her one sister as a bridesmaid and both her parents were walking her down the aisle. Aiden loved that choice. He was all in favour of the moms getting centre stage too.

On the way to the makeshift bar at the back of the chairs – it was a laid-back affair with two bartenders serving beer, wine and cocktails – he crouched down beside his own mom, sitting at the end seat on the front row. She'd brought a plus-one of the male variety, Kurt, a guy she'd first mentioned a couple of months ago. This was the first time Aiden had met him, but just on aesthetics he could see why his mom was into him.

'He looks like he could be one of those models in the Macy's Christmas catalogue,' he teased his mom, gesturing to Kurt, who was busy chatting to one of the partners in Aiden's legal firm on the other side of him. It gave him a welcome minute with his mother.

'That's because he probably is one of the guys in the Macy's Christmas catalogue,' his mom replied bashfully.

Aiden's smile was instant. 'Well, get you! A model?'

She flushed bright red and dug him in the ribs. 'He's just a friend. We work in the same office, so he's a realtor and a part-time model as well as being – for today – my very own fake boyfriend. I'll be damned if I'll let your father think I'm here like some sad pity party, on my own, finding him impossible to replace.'

His eyes widened. 'Really? I like your style.' He loved both his parents but he had a special connection with his mom and was more than happy to keep her secrets.

'I'm loving it,' his mom whispered. 'Your father has been breathing in since he clapped eyes on Kurt two hours ago. He could faint at any moment.'

'Okay, so apart from the fake boyfriend, how you doing there, maw?' he asked, knowing that using the Scottish slang for mom always made her smile. He'd never actually been to Scotland, but his mum still had the soft, lilting accent of her homeland. His dad's accent had morphed into something more East Coast USA, except for when he was pissed off, drunk, or delighted and then he'd go full-scale sweary Glaswegian. Going by the loud guffaws (Dad) and the giggles (Mitzy) coming from the bar, he was at least one of those things right now.

His mom must be hearing this too, but, if it was getting under her skin, she didn't show it. Even without Macy's catalogue guy, that was his mom. Calm. Patient. Beautiful. His dad used to say his mom had a wild streak in her younger years, but Aiden had never seen it, except maybe when she'd got heatedly competitive when he was playing sports in high school and college. She was the mom who was on her feet, cheering him on, yelling in outrage if he was fouled in basketball or thumped on the football field. Sometimes he wondered why she could defend her kid until the end of the earth, but she rarely defended herself against some of the crap that used to come out of his dad's mouth.

Until, that is, the day she just upped and left. It was in Aiden's first year at college. His dad had a family home on the day Aiden left to start his freshman year and a bachelor pad by the following summer. His dad had stalled out the divorce, but it had finally been signed and sealed a couple of painful, protracted years later.

Anyway. Bygones. Two parents, with an underlying simmering disdain. It wasn't perfect, but in his line of work, he knew plenty of people who had it worse. He just wished that before grandkids came along, they could get to a place where they could happily co-exist in the same room and be amicable, instead of either acting like a flash idiot (that would be dad) or taking the stonewalling approach (his mum's speciality).

'I'm doing fine, son,' she answered, reaching out to take his hand. 'I think what matters more is how you're feeling. You okay? The worst bit is the waiting, but I'm sure she'll be here soon.' She kept her voice low, so that she couldn't be heard by Layla's guests on the other side of the sandy aisle.

'It's her one flaw. Always late,' he replied, hoping that his smile didn't give away the fact that he was beginning to get more than a little disconcerted. He'd wait for Layla until the end of time, but he was starting to feel bad for his mom, their families, their friends, all of them beginning to flush in the midday heat. He was tempted to text her, but he didn't want to spoil the moment. Besides, she probably wouldn't be checking her phone if she was on the way here. He'd arranged for Layla's entire extended family to stay at a beautiful hotel just a couple of hundred metres along the sands last night. Hotel limos had shuttled most of her relatives here this morning and now they were just waiting for that last trip with the bridal party.

'Were you late on the morning of your wedding then?' Aiden asked his mom, just trying to make conversation to pass these moments and take her mind off the heat and her missing daughter-in-law. His mom would never say anything, but he had a feeling that Layla hadn't quite won her over yet. She had plenty of time to do that. A whole life ahead.

'No, I was bang on time. Probably worried that if I were five minutes late, your dad would move the party to a bar and forget where he was supposed to be.' It could have come out bitter, but her pragmatic smile kept it amusing. That, and the honesty. They both knew it was probably true.

His gaze went back to said father, holding court at, yep, a bar.

His mum reached over and touched his cheek. 'You go mingle with your guests and get ready for your big moment, son. I love every bit of you, you know that?'

She'd told him that every day of his life, even when she was upset because he'd got himself into some kind of scrape. 'I love every bit of you. Except the bit that reversed my car into the garage wall,' she'd said once, when he'd just got his learner's permit and 'borrowed' the car without asking. It wasn't the borrowing that was the issue. It was the putting it back that turned out to be the problem.

'Love you back,' he told her, pushing himself up, then leaning down to kiss her forehead. If Layla was half as good a mom as his was, then they'd have the happiest kids.

He'd just made it back up to a standing position and was about to carry on to the bar for the water for the celebrant, when the ding of a phone broached his consciousness. Then another. And another. Suddenly several of the guests on Layla's side of the aisle were pulling cell phones from their bags or their pockets. That in itself wasn't too worrying, but what was definitely troubling were the nervous glances he was getting after they'd checked their phones.

Shit. Had something happened? Was there a problem? Was Layla going to be held up even longer? He didn't hold out much hope of keeping the celebrant hydrated enough to hold him here if there were going to be further delays. And... wow... why were people still staring at him with those weird expressions?

He wasn't prone to knee-jerk reactions, but a slow, creeping feeling of dread was working its way up from his gut.

'Back in a minute, Mom,' he said, trying to act like nothing was amiss, but he could see by the two tiny frown lines that appeared between her eyebrows that she could sense something immediately.

Smiling at the guests as he passed them, doing his damnedest to act like nothing was wrong, he forced himself to walk at a normal speed up the aisle and over to the bar at the back.

'There's my boy!' his dad roared. 'About to get married. I tried to talk him out of it...' he joked to his audience of Mitzy and Trevon. Although, there may have been a grain of truth in there. A couple of years after his mom had left him, his dad had embarked on another short-lived marriage to the latest in his long line of young, beautiful secretaries. Predictably, it had hit him hard in the finances when it crumbled a year later, so twice-divorced, midlife crisis Gary Gregg wasn't a huge supporter of the institution of holy matrimony.

'Trevon, can you give me my phone?' Aiden had passed his cell to his best man for safekeeping during the ceremony because his suit jacket wasn't tailored to accommodate a handset in his pocket.

'Yeah, sure, bud. You wanna beer first though? Way too good a day to be stressing.'

Trevon's laid-back, South Carolina drawl temporarily slowed the worry that was creeping up Aiden's spine. They'd been friends for years, since Aiden's first week on the job, when Trevon had walked into his office and asked Aiden to represent him in his divorce from the wife he'd married in college. Trevon became his first ever client, mainly because, back then, Aiden had been the only lawyer he could afford. He was still in his late twenties, only a few years older than Aiden, and was working night and day to set up his first gym. When the divorce was finalised, on relatively amicable terms, the two guys had sparked a friendship that had now lasted longer than Trevon's marriage. They'd ended up sharing an apartment for a couple of years, until times, and Trevon's fortunes, had changed.

'Later,' Aiden answered the offer to the beer. 'Just the phone for now.'

'Did I tell you about the time this son of mine...' he heard his dad say to Mitzy, and Aiden knew he was about to dredge up some crazy story from his childhood, one that would invariably end with his dad's words of wisdom on the situation. Mitzy didn't seem to be listening, given that she was still staring at Aiden. He chose to ignore it. He wasn't going to start judging here, but Mitzy was around the same age as him, and he wasn't quite sure what she was doing with his dad. Maybe it was love. Gary Gregg had that big, live-for-today personality that people were always drawn to. What he didn't have in family values or marital loyalty, he made up for in sheer charisma. He was the best company in any bar. The most fun at any party. And the biggest spender in any club.

Come on. Come on, Aiden silently urged the phone, as he waited for it to power up.

After what felt like an hour and a half, it sprang to life, and there was... nothing. Not a single notification. He felt himself relax, felt his shoulders drop back down to normal until...

Ping. Ping. Ping. Ping. Ping.

Five messages. All from Layla. He opened the first one.

Aiden, I'm so sorry, I don't think I can do this.

Fuck. His eyes moved down to the second one, now sitting there in his messages.

I love you so much but it's too soon. I need some space to think.

Fuck. His jaw clenched tight, his natural reaction in times of stress.

I'm not coming today. I just can't. I'm leaving right now. Going... somewhere. I don't know where.

Noooooo.

Please explain to everyone. I'm so sorry to leave all this on you.

Fuck. Fuck. Fuck. All these people. What the hell was he going to say? And how could she do this? He loved her. She loved him. This was supposed to be the start of an amazing life together.

The last message...

And please, please forgive me.

He read them all again, then a third time.

Nope, they still said exactly the same thing. For fuck's sake, how could this be happening? How could she walk away like this?

Panic and disbelief were in charge of his emotions, closely followed by concern for Layla, embarrassment, confusion and devastation. Not anger. Growing up with a dad who was swift to lose his cool had given Aiden a healthy aversion to rage and fury. They solved nothing. Throwing a chair wasn't going to bring his fiancée dancing towards him.

Out of the corner of his eye, Aiden saw that half the guests were now staring in his direction, the other half whispering busily to each other. As for the celebrant, Aiden watched as he finished reading a message on his phone, tucked his book under one arm and set off across the sands in the direction of the nearby car park. It didn't take a genius to guess that someone from the bridal party had sent a few texts to notify loved ones and they were all – with the exception of the master of ceremonies who had already cut loose – watching him, waiting to see his reaction.

And again, fuck. What the hell was he supposed to do? Only one answer was coming to him right now.

'Trevon, I'll take that beer now, bud.'

4

EILEEN

April 2023

Even if the celebrant hadn't been high-tailing it back to his vehicle, Eileen would have sensed that something wasn't right. And it wasn't just an uneasy feeling because for the first time in ten years she was back at the house that held so many memories for their family – some great, a few terrible. Now, she really hoped another awful one wasn't heading straight for them.

She glanced around, caught Aiden's gaze, and a silent conversation passed between them. He shook his head sorrowfully, eyes filled with confusion. Between that, and the flurry of texts that had distracted everyone on the bride's side of the aisle, not to mention the absence of Aiden's soon-to-be wife, Eileen knew immediately what that meant. Layla wasn't coming. Bugger.

Eileen slipped out of her seat and was by his side in seconds, even though it put her within earshot of her ex-husband – a place that she had made it her life mission to avoid.

She wasn't in direct eyeline with her ex, but she did notice that he was pretty ruddy around the face. All that breathing in to keep his stomach as flat as possible in the presence of his latest girlfriend and Eileen's fake boyfriend.

'What's happened, son?'

Aiden turned his phone around and showed her the texts from Layla.

Almost twenty years married to Gary, and then ten years of peace afterwards had taught Eileen that deep breaths, staying cool in a crisis and taking the high road were all good for both her health and her quality of life. However, right now, she wasn't feeling like taking the bloody high road. Right now, she wanted to give that flash tart a piece of her mind for breaking her son's heart.

And yet...

Was it wrong that there was a tiny part of her that was relieved? She'd never in a million years have admitted it, especially to Aiden, but she'd never felt that Layla was the right one for him. Sure, Eileen could spend a solid ten minutes listing all her plus points and it was tough to actually nail down any negatives. It was more of a feeling. Aiden had a warmth about him, a genuine niceness that made Eileen prouder than all the sports championships and career achievements her son had ever clocked up, whereas Layla was colder. Yep, that was it. More calculated. Super sweet on the outside, undeniably beautiful, but a bit too concerned with herself and her image to have that warm humour and all-round niceness Eileen had always hoped she'd one day get in a daughter-in-law.

As soon as this day was over, she was going to google whether Reese Witherspoon was single. But in the meantime...

At her son's side, she was still avoiding eye contact with the ex-husband she only referred to in her head as Gary the Gob. Gary the Gob who had spent the last hour of the preamble for his son's wedding throwing back shots of tequila and feeling up his girlfriend's arse. Sadly, the avoidance strategy was wrecked when his girlfriend reached around Aiden and greeted her with a wave. Aiden took a step back, turning them into a little semicircle of happy families.

'Hi, I'm Mitzy,' the girlfriend giggled.

Gary at least had the self-awareness to look slightly embarrassed. 'All right, Eileen?'

'Just peachy, Gary,' she replied, with probably more disdain than she intended.

He didn't look thrilled. Och well. He could cry into his girlfriend's 34GGs until he felt better. She honestly didn't care. At least, that's what she told herself. Damn, she'd loved that man once. Given up everything for him. Including herself. That was what scared her most. How lost she'd been for so many years, how she'd overlooked things that shouldn't have been overlooked because she was so scared he'd leave. How she still saw him now and felt... It was hard to nail it down. That whole 'love and hate' thing. She loved him for the glimpses of happiness that they'd had. She hated him for throwing it all away and humiliating her time after time. Most of all, being around him gave her a pain in her chest, or perhaps it was her heart, so it was easier to stick with avoidance and hate. And no, not for anything was she ever going to put herself in that position again.

'Nice to meet you, Mitzy.' She wasn't in the business of tearing other women down. Unless she was the bint who had just jilted her son at the altar.

'Mizz Gregg, you're looking fine, fine, fine,' Trevon whistled from the other side of the bar, using her surname to tease her into reacting. He'd always been one to turn on the charm and Eileen adored him. She'd first met him a good few years ago, when he and Aiden had shared a flat, when her son was a fledgling lawyer and Trevon had just opened his first gym. Now he had half a dozen across the state and was a big deal in this town – a well-known influencer and entrepreneur who had long passed his first million, yet he hadn't changed a bit. Since day one, he'd encouraged her and Aiden to work out with him at his cross-fit centre about a mile from her home. Aiden still did the 5 a.m. shift with his mate during the week but Eileen preferred to train at night on her own. Gave her something to fill her evenings. However, she did work out with Trevon most Saturday and Sunday mornings, fearful that if she missed even one session of rigorous training, her arse would slide and her core muscles would collapse in surrender. Being a single fifty-five-year-old woman in a business and a dating scene populated with a whole load of Mitzys demanded effort and discipline.

She saw that Trevon was still grinning at her, waiting for the inevitable comeback. Eileen didn't disappoint. 'And you're looking like you're twenty years too young to be making comments like that to me, son,' she jibed back, making him howl with laughter.

Eileen switched her attention back to the immediate situation. Her son. A beach full of guests. As always, she felt the need to confront the situation head on and to try to fix things, even though she was absolutely at a loss as to how she was going to sort this out. She put her hand on her son's arm. 'Okay, let's all get on the same page. Have you told them yet?' It was typical. She'd tuned into the situation, realised what was happening, confirmed it with a silent conversation with her son, and was already trying to work out a plan to resolve it. Her ex-husband was right there and still hadn't realised that anything was amiss.

Aiden shook his head, then turned to his dad, Mitzy and Trevon. 'The text I was just checking, it was from Layla. She isn't coming. She's changed her mind. The wedding is off.'

'Oh for fu—' Gary exploded.

Eileen shut him down before he could even get warmed up. 'Pipe down there, Rocky,' she said, taking the wind out of his sails. This was typical Gary the Gob. Loud. Alpha male. Solved absolutely sod all.

Weirdly, that's why they'd been such a good team. He was one of those men who lit up a room with his personality, while Eileen had been the person at the back, taking care of every other bloody thing so that he could shine. It had worked for them for years. Until it didn't. Now, every time she saw him switch on the charm, she just wanted to pull out the plug.

Trevon was fully focused on his friend now. 'No way. Damn. What can we do? Name it, bro.'

Eileen cut straight to the pragmatic steps. 'Do you want us to get rid of this lot, son?' she asked Aiden, but he shook his head. The poor man was ashen.

'Thanks, Mom, but I'll do it.'

Eileen watched as this strapping bloke, all six foot two of him, made his way back up to the centre of the aisle. Sure, he was a grown man and an impressive one, but in her gut, he was still her kid, and she was devastated for him. Even if he did now have a chance to marry Reese Witherspoon.

'Hey, folks,' he said loudly, making sure everyone could hear.

Eileen saw her plus-one, Kurt, break off his conversation with Aiden's boss and turn to pay attention.

'I can see from some of your faces that you already know... but just in case you don't, I'm sorry to tell you that Layla isn't going to make it today. She's had a change of heart and the wedding is off. I'm so sorry. I know the effort you all made to come here today, and we appreciate that. If you brought a gift...' he nodded over to the table at the back, next to the bar, where guests had left presents, 'then please take it home with you. Again, I'm so grateful that you gave up your time to be with us and I'm sorry we've wasted it. And thank you to the musicians, you have been great, but you're free to finish up now.'

There was a smattering of applause from the forty or so assembled people and the expressions on their faces were ones of pure sympathy. Or pity. It was hard to tell.

'But hey, the good news...' Aiden went on, facing the crowd again, '...is that Trevon has a banging playlist on his phone that he can feed through a speaker back there and we have a full bar of booze and a buffet that need to be consumed, so please, if you feel like a beach day, kick off your shoes, grab a beer and stay here with us for a few hours while we drown our sorrows.'

There was an almost immediate split. Layla's friends and extended family started streaming out of their rows and, faces full of apology and embarrassment, made their way up the aisle and over towards the car park, many of them stopping to retrieve the gifts they'd brought for the happy couple.

Aiden's mates and work colleagues stayed put, the men cranked off their ties, the women kicked off their heels and several of them made their way to her son to give him a hug and some genuine sympathy. Eileen was grateful for every one of them.

Eileen tossed her shoes to the side, threw her jacket over a nearby chair. 'Trevon, love, can you put on a song that's going to make Aiden feel even a tiny bit better? Extra points if it comes with a beer for me.'

'I've got you, Eileen,' Trevon assured her, pressing a few buttons of his phone, while simultaneously popping the cap off a bottle of Modelo beer.

The intro to an old nineties song, 'Things Can Only Get Better' by D:Ream sounded out from the speakers and Aiden's face managed a sad smile of gratitude when, sympathies and apologies exhausted, he joined them at the bar.

Eileen wasn't surprised that Gary and Mitzy had already headed up to the house, her ex-husband muttering something about asking the caterers to start bringing the food down. The man had a pathological aversion to emotional or awkward situations.

Eileen popped the top off another beer and handed it to her son. 'Did you mean what you said about having a party?'

Aiden sighed. 'Truthfully? Nope. But it seemed like the right thing to say. To be honest, I just want to split and go find Layla and find out what the fuck is going on.'

Her son rarely swore in front of her but Eileen didn't even flinch. If she was ever going to give him a pass, it was today. She could sense his despair and knew that the speech he gave a few minutes ago was inspired by equal parts embarrassment and regret that he'd dragged all his friends here for nothing.

'Well, here's the thing, son. You can go try to track down a woman who has just performed a public ramraid on your heart. Or we can sit here and gaze at the ocean and feel sad. Or we can postpone both those things until tomorrow and go back to your first suggestion – take advantage of the fact that your friends are here, there's loads of booze ad food and I'm in close proximity to your father and, just for you, haven't attempted to kill him yet.' The sheer effort he put into smiling at her joke made a piece of Eileen's heart turn to mush.

He didn't answer though, so she nudged her suggestion along.

'So, what do you think? Want to dance with your aging mother, while she's still got the energy? I could drop dead at any moment and you'd regret saying no.' It was a low blow but right now she just wanted to protect him, to help him get through this, and the best way for him to do that was to stay here, with people who loved him and could take care of him until the sting of this subsided enough for him to think straight.

'Ah, emotional blackmail,' he said, but the corners of his mouth were turning up, so she knew she was making a dent. 'You know you're shame-less, don't you?'

'I absolutely do,' Eileen said. 'Now come dance with your mother before I have to go drag my fake boyfriend over here instead. You really don't want me dancing with him. I think he used to be a Chippendale so there's every chance we'd make a spectacle of ourselves.'

Eileen held out her hand and for a few seconds she wondered if he was going to overcome his urge to go find Layla. Just when she thought she was going to have to pile on some other layer of coercion to keep him there, he took her hand and spun her round.

'You definitely won't kill Dad?'

'Not today,' she promised.

'Then I guess my broken heart can wait until tomorrow.'

5

ZARA

April 2023

Gary Gregg still hadn't replied to Zara's Facebook message.

He hadn't even responded to her friend request. Although, in fairness, as far as Zara could see, he hadn't done anything else on Facebook either, so maybe he was just one of those people who had opened an account and then promptly forgot about it, or decided it was too much work, switched off notifications and then, as before, promptly forgot about it.

'Or maybe reunions with old pals are just not his thing and he can't be arsed,' Kev suggested unhelpfully over breakfast. He was a coder for a software company in offices just a couple of streets away from Blooming Sisters, so he had a regular sleeping-over schedule that generally consisted of five nights a week at Zara's place. She tended to ignore Millie when her sister questioned whether their relationship was love or just a convenient place to stay for Kev, because he could leave their flat above the shop at 7.50, for his whole ten-minute walk to work. Not that Millie actually knew this for sure, because half the time he was gone by the time Millie came home from whatever party or premises she'd ended up at the night before.

The front door banged. Yep, case in point.

Millie staggered in, still in the dress she'd been wearing when she'd headed out with friends the previous evening, holding her heels over her shoulder with one hand, clutching her handbag with the other.

'Ooops. The grown-ups don't look happy,' she joked, her gaze going from Zara to Kev and back again.

Zara tried not to laugh, but she couldn't help herself. At twenty-eight, she almost always went to bed early so she could be up and feeling good to open the shop the next morning. It was nothing to do with any kind of adult maturity. She just liked to be organised. To be prepared. To avoid chaos and panic where possible. Being inherently sensible was her lifelong affliction and there was no getting away from it.

Kev pushed his coffee mug across the table and grabbed his backpack from the floor. 'Right, I'd better go. See you tonight?' He framed it like a question, but it really wasn't. Today was a Thursday. And every Thursday night, Kev stayed here. Just like he did on a Friday. A Saturday. A Monday and a Tuesday. He didn't stay Sunday, because Zara had flower market at the crack of dawn on a Monday, and he didn't stay Wednesday because he played five-a-side football with his mates down at the local sports centre. Every other night? A veritable fizzle of excitement that invariably involved some form of microwave pasta after a long day in the shop, then alternate choices on what to watch on TV, followed by one of them falling asleep first on the sofa.

As the front door banged behind Kev, Millie plonked down on the chair he'd vacated, swaying a little as she reached for Zara's mug of black coffee. 'Tell me you two got naked last night, then had raunchy sex while swinging from our extremely stylish IKEA paper light shade?'

'We did,' Zara deadpanned. 'Twice. If you look closely, you'll see the marks my fingers left while I was clutching on for dear life.'

Millie groaned. 'I really wish I hadn't made that joke in the first place. I'm too close to a hangover to have that image in my brain.' She plonked her head down on the table. 'I will give you all my worldly goods, including my Ninja air fryer, if you make me some toast.'

At the other side of the table, Zara focused back on the laptop. 'I don't want any of your worldly goods and, eh, the Ninja air fryer is mine.'

Millie raised her head slightly and cocked open one eye. 'It is? Then it needs cleaning. Someone – and I've no idea who – tried to make fish fingers in it the other night and it all went wrong.'

Zara had been about to push her own toast towards her sister, but air fryer outrage stopped her and she pulled it back, taking a large bite to emphasise the point.

She checked her laptop again, just in case, by some miracle, Gary Gregg had responded in the last five minutes. Nope.

Sighing, she pulled up her crucial, colour-coded checklist and began running down the items in both the 'To-Do' and 'Done' columns.

With ten days to go until the Vegas trip, the fact that everything wasn't already in the DONE column was making her itch.

DONE:

Flight tickets bought.

Hotel booked.

(Planet Hollywood. Right on the strip).

Request sent for a room overlooking the Bellagio fountains across the street.

Tickets purchased for Celine Dion concert.

(Because that would make her mother's life complete).

Renewal of vows in Elvis Loves Me Tender Chapel booked.

(The same chapel in which her normally conventional Mum and Dad got married – a fact that still surprised and amused Zara in equal measure).

ESTAs completed.

(She'd had to sneak in and take photos of Mum and Dad's passports and apply for their ESTAs using her own email address, which was undoubtedly illegal and they could get arrested on arrival).

> Limo booked from airport to hotel.
> Cover arranged for shop.

Zara had recruited their lovely regular part time worker, Tilly, and her mum, Tina, who'd helped them out before, to work full-time that week. Chances were, with the events side of the business closed down for that period, they'd make absolutely no profit, but they shouldn't make a loss either. Either way, it would be worth it. This was one of those life events that they would look back on until the end of time and that was worth more to her than a week's worth of profit. Besides, she'd taken on more jobs than usual the following week, so hopefully that would go some way to making up for it.

Back to the lists...

> STILL TO DO:
> Buy white dress for Mum for ceremony (Dad can cobble together smart outfit when he gets there).
> Find Gary bloody Gregg. And hope he knows where to find Eileen Smith.

She clicked on to another open page and then nudged Millie. 'Here, look. What do you think of this dress?' Her mum was a size 12–14, slightly smaller than Zara, but a size bigger than Millie, who'd inherited their dad's metabolism and his infuriating resistance to gaining weight, no matter how many calories he ate. Or in Millie's case, no matter how many calories she drank.

Millie took in the white, embellished frock on the Monsoon website. 'Too... floaty. Mum prefers things simpler.' Millie reached over and helped herself to the last slice of her sister's toast. Zara didn't have the energy to maintain her air fryer protest or start a new toast protest. Millie's face lit up, conveying a flash of inspiration. 'Do you know what would be perfect?'

'Tell me,' Zara said, already clicking through a plethora of other frocks hoping that something perfect would pop up, and only half listening, figuring nothing much sensible was going to come out of Millie's mouth when her bloodstream was probably still at least 50 per cent porn star martinis.

'The outfit Gran bought for the garden party at Holyrood,' Millie said triumphantly. And rightly so.

Zara stopped clicking. 'Oh my God, you are so right.'

Their late Granny Ada was a beloved force of nature who had retired, then spent the next twenty years running every association within twenty square miles of her home. The tenants' association. The after-school clubs. The youth club. The lunch club for local senior citizens. The hospital free taxi service. The donation service for refugees. The Christmas boxes for kids who were living in poverty. If there was a great cause, Ada was all over it and it was recognised when she was honoured for her work in the community with an invite to meet the Queen at Holyrood. And oh, what a day she'd had. 'I want a frock that makes me look like Joanna Lumley and a hat the size of a manhole cover,' she'd told Zara, Millie, and Brenda as they'd set off on a tour of every high-end dress store in Glasgow. After a military-level search operation, they'd found what they were looking for in a beautiful little boutique in the Merchant City. A pale cream A-line shift dress embellished with a single strand of pearls around the neckline, and a matching satin crepe shawl, adorned with the same subtle pearls. It was so Audrey Hepburn and so perfect.

Now, Zara knew that, for once, Millie had pulled the fashion rabbit out of the manhole cover hat.

'It would be perfect,' she whispered, feeling a sudden overwhelming wave of emotion. God, she missed Granny Ada. When she'd passed away the year before, it had been devastating for them all, and it was only a small consolation that she'd gone in the way she would have wanted – at the bingo, a heart attack while cheering because her best pal, Rita, had just won a full house. She'd happily lived all her life in a council house, where she knew every single person on the street, so before her home was returned to the local authorities, the family had the heart-breaking job of clearing it out. Most of her possessions were given to good causes but a few things had such sentimental value that the girls couldn't part with them. One of those precious items was her favourite old jewellery box. Most of the contents were costume pieces, given that Ada had no time for fancy trinkets, preferring to put her money to better use, but in between her eighties pom pom earrings and an onyx cocktail ring so big it could take an eye out with a right hook, they'd found an envelope addressed to them. In it was a letter spelling out Ada's legacy for her grand-daughters.

Dear angels,

(She always called them that – said princesses were for losers because they were always waiting to be rescued.)

If you're reading this, then I've popped my clogs. I hope I was dancing when it happened and that my kicks were high and my shimmies ferocious.

You know that you girls are, and always will be, two of the greatest loves of my life. Anything that's mine, is now yours – but the food blender under the sink is on its last legs, so you might want to ditch that.

I have a few requests, because you know, I always like to have the last word. My posh frock. The one I wore to meet Queenie. It's the most beautiful thing I've ever owned, so please keep it, use it if you can, but even if it hangs in your wardrobe forever, you'll know I'm there with you.

I don't have much in the way of jewellery, just my wedding ring and my pearl earrings and necklace. Those are all for your mum, but they'll come to you next and I hope you'll treasure them.

And finally, my loves, there's a few grand in the bank. Not much to show for a lifetime of work, but I wouldn't have it any other way, because money is for spending, not saving. All of it is yours, but you need to know that I will be so disappointed in you if you don't use it in a way that honours me. So let me be clear – do not dare use it for anything sensible! Use it for fun. For adventure. For memories that you will cherish.

And, my angels, take care of your mum. My darling girl. I've a feeling

she's going to need you both and I know that you'll be there for her. Just
as I, wherever I am, will be there for you all.
Love you, angels,
Gran xxxx

Just thinking about the letter made Zara smile. They were doing exactly what Gran had asked. They were spending the whole inheritance on five days in Vegas for their parents. Their wild, hilarious, outrageous Ada would be loving every second of this. Especially now that her dress was coming along for the ride.

Zara moved the 'dress for Mum' task from the TO-DO list to the DONE column. 'I hate it when you're right,' she groaned, but they both knew she was delighted that another issue was solved. 'Since you're so smart, any ideas on my other problem? Gary Greggs hasn't replied to my Facebook message so I've hit a roadblock on that one.'

No answer from the other side of the table.

'Millie? Millie?'

Just the soft murmurs of a sleeping sister, head on the table, out for the count.

Zara consulted the ticking clock on the wall. Half an hour before it was time to open the shop.

Another check confirmed there was still no response from Gary Gregg and, unsurprisingly, staring at his Facebook page wasn't magically stirring up any action.

Okay, another plan needed.

A thought began to form. Gary's Facebook page only had two posts but... Her fingers flew over her mousepad. His friends list. She clicked on it, hoping that it wasn't private.

Yes! There it was. Aware that it bordered on stalking, but telling herself it was for the greater good, she scrolled through the list of strangers hoping for something, anything she could use. His friends list was short, so she'd only gone through about twenty names when something jarred with her. She rolled it back.

Aiden Gregg.

Specs down off her forehead and on to her face, she peered at the guy who filled her screen. About thirty. Handsome. Sharp jaw. Green eyes. Dark hair. Suit. She clicked on his profile and saw that he was a lawyer. Figured. She'd binge watched *Suits* with Kev a couple of years back and this bloke could have come straight from that show.

His profile was private so she couldn't see most of his posts, but she saw enough to spot the very definite similarity between him and Gary. Had to be father and son.

Okay, one last stab at this. Gary Gregg had been a dead end but maybe she'd have more luck with *Suits* man.

Nothing to lose. Zara started typing.

Dear Aiden...

6

BRENDA

Brenda was absent-mindedly staring out of the kitchen window, watching while Colin cut the grass. Since his imminent early retirement from the finance department at the council had first appeared on the horizon, he'd become garden obsessed. Just her luck. Wasn't the male midlife crisis stereotype a motorbike, a sports car or an affair? Apparently not. Colin had shunned all those options for a new lawnmower and a garden that had perfectly symmetrical stripes.

Desperately seeking a diversion from watching the banality of her life play out right in front of her, Brenda picked up the phone and called her daughter. She always tried Zara's mobile first because there was far more chance of her answering than Millie, who was haphazard at best and almost unfailingly forgot to return calls.

They'd always been the same. Even when they were kids, Zara was the one with the good grades, who hated being in trouble and made sure she did everything that was asked of her. Millie, on the other hand, was the ten-year-old who punched Charlie Benson in the face for taking her friend's lunch money. She was the twelve-year-old who refused to do homework because she claimed it was a breach of her human rights. And the fifteen-year-old who was climbing out of her bedroom window at midnight to go meet a boyfriend.

'Mum! Hello there. I was just thinking about you.'

'You were?' Brenda couldn't help but smile. She'd been blessed to grow up with Ada, a mother who'd loved her very much, and now she was lucky to have these two women as her daughters. They were what made it all worthwhile. When all this was done and it was finally the right time to leave Colin, then if all she had was space, peace and her girls, she'd be happy.

'Yeah, I was just thinking about our trip,' Zara went on. 'I'm soooo excited!'

Brenda couldn't admit the truth: she was dreading it. The last thing she wanted to do was spend five days with Colin and she wouldn't even have her work, her favourite TV shows or solitude to read her books to get through it. But at least she'd have her daughters there.

'I am too, pet,' she lied. 'But I'm starting to think about packing and I need some clues.'

'Okay, ask me questions and I'll do my best to answer them,' Zara offered and Brenda could hear the amusement in her voice.

Brenda opened with, 'Okay, is it a week in the Lake District?

'No.'

Brenda tried not to sigh. That would have been her top choice. Not far, very familiar, unfussy, and loads of little cafés for afternoon tea. Back to square one then. 'Right. Is it a beach, a ski resort or a city break?'

'A city break,' Zara conceded and Brenda felt a twinge of relief. It must be London. Or maybe even Paris. At least a city break would be busy, with less opportunities for intimate moments. Maybe she could spend the time visiting galleries, or track down a theatre and go to a show. 'But you'll also need swimwear because there's a pool.'

'Indoor or outdoor?'

'Both.'

Relief gone. An outdoor pool? In a city? Okay, so unlikely to be London. Maybe Barcelona? Amsterdam? She'd always wanted to visit the Van Gogh Museum, so maybe the girls had remembered that.

'It'll definitely be hot in the daytime but it could be chilly at night. Oh, and we're flying there, so you'll need passports and a cabin bag for the airplane.'

'And do I need dress-up clothes or is it casual?' Maybe she'd be able to suss it out that way. If it was all casual, then they were probably staying in an Airbnb and just doing low-key things, which suited her perfectly.

'Definitely a bit of dress-up. You know – for going to bars and nice restaurants. We'll probably do casual things during the days and then some fancy things at night. Definitely heels. Maybe a pair of strappy sandals. How many people get to celebrate thirty years of happy marriage? We need to celebrate this in style, Mum. You and Dad deserve this. Not to mention making the most of the fact that we'll all be together. Anyway, that's all the clues you're getting. Nothing else, so stop snooping. Just let me and Millie take care of everything.'

For a second, Brenda was tempted to just blurt out the truth, but instead she went with, 'Och, you're loving all this mystery. Okay, my love, I'll talk to you later. You have a good day.'

'You too, Mum.'

There was no point in rocking the boat now. The trip was less than two weeks away, so in three weeks she'd be free, and she just had to focus on the positives of that. Especially since the negatives – telling Colin she was leaving, breaking the news to the girls, making plans for a new life – made beads of anxiety pop out of every pore. Was she doing the right thing or would this be the biggest mistake of her life? Maybe this was her midlife crisis. Perhaps she should just jack in her job, get a tattoo and start blaring Cher songs at two in the morning. That would be a far more palatable way to lose the plot, rather than upping sticks and leaving the husband you've been with for thirty years, for no other reason than you're not in love with him any more and you're bored rigid.

Was she just being a daft old fool? And making a horrible mistake?

'Right, that's the garden done for this week,' Colin announced, making her jump. She hadn't even heard him coming in the back door. 'I was thinking about planting some tulips bulbs over by the shed. And maybe putting in some new veggies in the raised bed. Maybe some runner beans. Wouldn't that be grand?'

Brenda had a fleeting mental image of herself picking up the knife she'd used to butter her toast and stabbing herself through the heart. *Here lies Brenda Jones. Died due to boredom-induced hysteria. Leaves behind a husband who is consoling himself by planting fricking runner beans in his raised beds.*

She immediately chided herself for being unkind and over dramatic. Neither of those things were in her nature, but the anxiety and trepidation over this situation were making her mind spin off on a tangent. This wasn't about Colin and his transformation into Alan Titchmarsh in comfortable beige slacks. It was about her and her need for something more.

'Grand,' she managed, before biting her lip to stop herself blurting out anything more. That was the problem. Maybe she should, for the first time on God's earth, actually say what she felt. Actually, it wasn't the first time. He just hadn't heard her before.

She topped up her coffee from the pot on the hotplate and automatically poured one for him too. Old habits. Meanwhile, he slid into one of the chairs at the kitchen table and automatically lifted his newspaper and opened it somewhere in the middle.

'Colin, can we talk for a while?'

The look of alarm on his face would have been comical if this wasn't so important.

'Nothing bad,' she rushed to explain, fearful that he'd make some excuse to flee the room. That was the issue in a real-life nutshell. She felt like she wasn't heard. Like what she said didn't matter. That, basically, she could run through here wearing a thong and coconut shells on her boobs and he'd barely raise his gaze from the *Guardian*. 'I just wondered how you felt about this trip with the girls?' she started gently as she sat down opposite him, no idea where the conversation was going or what she'd have the nerve to say, but somehow unable to say nothing.

He took a sip of his flat white. 'Looking forward to it. Although, I'm going to be outnumbered. I've got a feeling I could be spending a lot of time shopping.'

Brenda felt her teeth grind together at the rank sexist stereotype of it. She hated shopping. Not that there was anything wrong with it but it just wasn't her idea of a good time. Or Zara's either. Millie, on the other hand, probably considered it one of her core skills and greatest talents.

Maybe it was exasperation, or perhaps just caffeine, but Brenda couldn't let it lie. 'Colin, do you ever get bored? I mean, look at us. We have a day off and I'm cleaning and you're doing the garden. Shouldn't life be a bit more interesting than this?'

She deliberately avoided getting personal so that he didn't flee the scene. Instead, he sighed and put the paper down.

'Are you having another one of those days, Brenda?'

She didn't understand. 'What days?'

'Where you're just bored with life and having a moan? Look, I apologise. I'm sorry I'm not this exciting, crazy guy, but this is just real life. The garden needs tidying. The house needs cleaning. I don't see what the problem is.'

She should have held her tongue, as she usually always would, but for once, now that she'd started, she couldn't hold back. 'The problem, Colin, is when was the last time we laughed? Really laughed. Or talked. Or did something spontaneous? Or had wild sex...'

'Oh, come on now,' he began, flushing.

'Answer me,' she demanded, fairly convinced she was having an out-of-body experience. Usually, she'd have shuffled off and dug out her Swiffer to vent her frustrations by giving the living-room blinds a good dusting. Now, all she could think about was that it was her bloody lady bits that could do with the dusting.

'What's got into you today?' he asked, avoiding the question, his fingers still clutching the edges of his newspaper.

'Colin, I can't do this any more,' she sighed, pulling out the seat next to him. Time and time again, she'd planned in her head how she would broach her wish to end their marriage with him, and it was always in a calm manner, after the trip with the girls. Apparently, her brain had taken that suggestion, tossed it in his bloody precious wheelie bin (he'd spent an hour applying number stickers to his bins to ensure they got their own back after they'd been emptied) and come up with a brand new strategy. One that was Operation Blast Off, right about now.

'Listen, I was going to wait until after our anniversary to talk to you about this...'

'About what?' He frowned, the closest she'd seen him to being rattled in a decade.

'About us, Colin. I've never for one minute regretted our lives together, but something needs to change.' She cursed her brain for not having the balls to say it straight but that just wasn't in her nature. And that was the problem. 'I'm fifty-five years old, Colin. I don't want to spend the rest of my life like this. I'm not ready to give up and settle for a thousand more Saturdays like this one. I want something else...'

'You've met someone else?' he blurted, and she wasn't sure if he'd misheard her or jumped to an incorrect conclusion.

'No! Of course not.'

He visibly sagged with relief, and weirdly, in this time of high stress and emotional turmoil, that's when it registered that his sweater was beige. And the walls in the kitchen were beige. The doors on the kitchen cabinets were beige. Even the piece of bloody shortbread she'd pulled out to have with her tea was beige. That was it. Her whole bloody life was beige and she wanted colour. Reds. Pinks. Neon blues. Anything but bloody bland bloody beige.

'Brenda, what exactly do you want?' he asked wearily, as if it were all too much trouble to listen.

'I want a life that excites me, Colin. I want to do new things. To live a little. We've raised the girls and it feels like this should be our time again. Only, I don't feel like you want anything different than what we have.'

'Is it so bad?'

'No, it's not bad at all, but it's not great, is it? Do you jump out of bed every morning, thrilled to be facing another day?'

'No, but who does?'

'I tell you who does – my friend, Bernadette.' It was a low blow and she knew it. She didn't for a second think that Bernadette's life was one that she could have for herself. After decades trapped in a hellish marriage, Bernadette deserved every second of her happiness, and Brenda was thrilled for her, but she knew how rare it was to find love a second time around at their age – especially with a good man who loved you back. No. This wasn't about having a lust-filled affair or a wonderful new relationship. It was just about living.

'Yes, well obviously... Hasn't she got a new man and she's all in the first flush of romance? That's not realistic, Brenda. We've been together for three decades. Of course it's going to get—'

'Boring,' she interjected.

'I was going to say "comfortable". Sorry, if I'm boring you.'

God, he could be so petulant. Strangely though, even this verbal jousting was making her feel more alive than she'd done in months. She smoothed out invisible creases on the beige table cover.

'You're not boring me,' she countered. 'Life is boring me. We're boring each other.'

He didn't bite back. Of course, he didn't. He was far too reasoned and considered for anything that even hinted at emotional spontaneity. He was an accountant, for goodness sake. Not exactly notorious for their wild sides and volatile behaviour.

'Brenda, is... Could this be... Is it maybe... Do you think you could be feeling this way because of...?'

The stuttering gave it away and she suddenly knew exactly what he was going to say.

'I swear to God, Colin, if you say this is down to the menopause, I will get my jacket and walk out that door and you can live happily ever after with your bloody lawnmower.'

He immediately recognised the error of his ways and back-pedalled. She'd been menopausal for a few years now and she was only just coming out of the other side of the hot flushes, the sleepless nights and flares of anxiety, so the topic was not to be trifled with or trivialised.

'No, no, of course not. I wasn't suggesting...' They both knew he was.

'How do you see your retirement, Colin? Don't you want to have a bucket list of exciting things to do? Don't you want to be surprised by life? To be invigorated with new challenges? To wake up excited by your plans for the day? To have fun? To feel passion?'

His shrug said it all. 'I'm happy with my lot. Doesn't that count?'

She didn't have the heart to tell him that 'his lot' didn't bring any happiness to her any more. Her chronic aversion to causing any kind of distress or upset had wrangled control of her mind again and ordered the fleeting bolshiness to bugger off.

They sat in silence for a few moments, before he surprised her by reaching over and putting his hand over hers. 'Brenda, this is nothing that can't be fixed.'

He hadn't listened to a thing she'd said. Or maybe she just hadn't been clear enough.

'You're right,' he went on, trying to placate her. 'I suppose it's just the way life goes after you've been together as long as us. We've just got a bit set in our ways. I'm sorry I didn't see before now that you were unhappy.'

'I should have made it clearer,' she conceded wearily. 'I'm sorry.' Hang on, why was she apologising? She'd dropped hints and tried to have gentler versions of this conversation with him many times before, and he always just overlooked it. Overlooked *her*.

Message to self – stop apologising for everything. It was, she knew, one of her worst habits. If someone bumped into her in a shop, she was the one who apologised. If she had – on pain of death – to complain about something or return something faulty, she apologised to within an inch of her life. When had she become so spineless? She'd spent years encouraging her girls to stick up for themselves and the irony was she was incapable of doing the same.

Newspaper set to the side, he leaned forward in his chair. 'Tell you what. How about I make you a promise to try harder? To inject a bit of fun? I'll make a real effort and we'll have things sorted in no time. Right. Let's start this minute.'

Oh wow. Was he really going to make something happen? Was he going to scoop her up and tell her how much he adored her? Was he going to clear the table with one hand and ravish her right here, right now?

'Let's...' he began, eyes twinkling, '...forget the shepherd's pie we were going to have for tea tonight and phone in some Chinese food instead.'

7

AIDEN

Aiden was lying on the sofa, bouncing a ball in a well-practised, robotic pattern that involved it hitting the floor of his loft apartment, then the wall, then coming straight back to his hand. Throw. Thud. Thud. Catch. Throw. Thud. Thud. Catch.

Trevon came over from the grey concrete kitchen island with two beers – pretty much Aiden's staple out-of-hours diet for the last couple of weeks since the fiasco at Hilton Head Island. What a disaster that had been. That night, his dad and Mitzy had bailed with the rest of the guests – his father never could handle difficult situations – leaving his mum, her fake boyfriend, Kurt, and Trevon drinking long into the night. The next morning he'd woken to find that, yep, Layla was still gone. Embarrassing. Humiliating. But, most of all, excruciatingly sore on the heart.

Even now that he was back in his own place in Charleston, every time he woke up, he was happy for a few moments and then he remembered. Layla had jilted him at the altar and then disappeared off the face of the earth. He hadn't heard a word from her since a text later that night asking him to give her space and time. Until yesterday, that was.

'Are you sure you don't want me to stick around while she's here? I can stay low-key in your room and then be here for you if you need me.'

Aiden shook his head. 'Thanks, pal, but I've got this.'

Trevon took a slug of his beer and then puffed out his cheeks as he exhaled. 'I'm mighty glad you said that because no part of me wants any part of this.'

That made Aiden laugh and for the umpteenth time he wondered what he'd have done without Trevon this last couple of weeks. He'd cancelled his honeymoon leave and gone straight back to work, so that had helped to keep him occupied, but it was the evenings and weekends that were the roughest. Thankfully, his mate had pretty much moved back in with him, sleeping on a pull-out bed in the main area of his loft, making sure he wasn't alone. Heartbreak, rejection and confusion aside, it had almost been like the days when they'd shared an apartment just a few streets away, down near King Street. That had been a couple of years of uncomplicated, endlessly entertaining and totally carefree good times. Maybe he should just have kept it that way instead of introducing adulting, mortgages and grown-up relationships into the equation.

The intercom went and Trevon exhaled again. 'Remember, if it all gets too much...' He took a step forward, then clutched his chest like he'd been shot and fell to the floor.

Shaking his head, Aiden got off the couch and stepped over him. 'At your age, you could break a bone doing that, bud,' he mumbled, but he was struggling to keep a straight face. Even now, Trevon could still make him laugh more than anyone else.

He pressed a button on the receiver.

'Hi, Aiden, it's Pam.'

Speechless, he didn't even reply, just pressed the button to admit the newcomer. Pam. Layla's mom. When he'd got the text from Layla asking if she could come get her stuff today, he'd thought she'd meant in person. That the love of his life, the woman he'd adored, was going to come here and maybe they could talk, get some clarity on what the fuck had happened to their lives together. Apparently not. She'd sent her mother.

'Man, that woman scares the shit out of me. I'll stay to protect you, but I'll be under your bed,' Trevon whistled.

'I'll be right next to you,' Aiden sighed. Layla's mother was the type of mom who called her daughter Princess and thought she could do no wrong, even though she was almost thirty years old and human enough to make the odd cock-up. Like not turning up for her own wedding.

By the time Aiden let her in the door, Trevon had changed his mind about going into hiding, and was sitting over on a stool at the kitchen island, finding some reason to be 100 per cent focused on his laptop.

'Hi, Pam,' Aiden said, deploying every bit of civility he possessed. After all, other than being mildly terrifying, Pam had never been in any way negative to him. In fact, maybe Layla's mom could give him answers.

'Before we start, I'm not here to discuss what happened with you and my daughter. I'm just here to collect her things.'

Or maybe not.

She pulled down the hem of her pink tweed jacket. Aiden knew it was probably Chanel, given that she'd passed her fondness of designer clothes down to her daughter.

'Layla isn't coming?' he asked hopefully.

'No. She's taking a moment to think about things. Practising some self-care. It's been a tough time for her.'

Aiden was desperate to say that it had been two whole weeks – how much thinking did she need to do? He also wanted to throw in that it hadn't been a walk in the park for him either, but he held back on the pettiness. It wasn't his way.

Instead, he went with, 'I understand. Please ask her to give me a call when she's ready. It would be good to talk to her.'

He tried to make it sound as amicable as possible. Wasn't that what he advised his clients to do every day? Stay amicable. Communicate. Work things out one way or another but never block the conversation. He wasn't sure he was achieving that here, and he definitely hadn't managed to facilitate that with his parents. Those two were a war zone that had an occasional ceasefire. Maybe he should give up his career and settle for work in a more appropriate field, one that fitted with his current existence. If you could earn a living moping, drinking beer and bouncing a ball against a wall, that would be the job for him.

Or maybe a doorman, because he ended up, without another word being spoken, grabbing the suitcases he'd filled with all Layla's belongings as requested, and taking them down to Pam's car, where she waved him off with a vague promise that his ex-fiancée would 'be in touch when she has processed everything and feels ready'. Not exactly the kind of news that called for a victory parade and a brass band.

'Thanks for your help there,' he said to Trevon when he got back upstairs.

His mate shrugged. 'You had it covered. I was waiting in the background, ready to go. You know, like my man, Shemar.'

Despite this being yet another low point in his life, that made Aiden laugh. For years, people had compared the two of them to famous names – Trevon bore an uncanny resemblance to Shemar Moore from *SWAT*, and in a dim light, Aiden was a dead ringer for Jamie Dornan from the Fifty Shades movies. Without the controlling nature and the natty leather whips. Anyway, their famous-adjacent looks had earned them many free drinks from inebriated or gullible bartenders over the years.

'Okay, now that you're out of immediate danger, I'm just going to stop by the office and make sure my empire hasn't crumbled while I've been babysitting you,' Trevon told him, picking up his backpack and then doing that whole handshake, semi hug thing. 'The office' was a bit of an understatement. What he was actually referring to was a 40,000 square feet, state-of-the-art fitness complex that was the flagship of his lifestyle brand. His chain of gyms stretched across South Carolina and were hugely popular, training a healthy percentage of the weight-lifting, cardio-busting, basketball-playing, cross-fit-loving population of the city, including – and Aiden thought this was brilliant – one Eileen Gregg, who never missed a cross-fit session in the Harleston Village branch of Trevon's empire.

The loft felt strange when Trevon left. It was the first time Aiden had been alone there since the wedding and he wasn't entirely sure what to do with himself. Work. It was the only thing that was going to take his mind off his shitshow of a personal life. He grabbed another beer, then headed to his home office, a glass-fronted space in the corner of the living area, and fired up his computer. He usually paid no attention to the social media apps on his home screen, but today his eye caught the blue square in the corner. Facebook. He kept his notifications switched off and he hadn't checked it for weeks. Now he opened it to see fourteen new messages. Shit.

One by one, he opened them, not surprised that they were mostly from guests who'd been at the wedding, or people who hadn't been able to make it and who were now probably kicking themselves that they'd missed the drama. Nothing from Layla. He didn't think for a second that there would be and he hated himself for hoping. He clicked on to her profile, expecting to see nothing for the last two weeks, but he was wrong. There was a photo, loaded yesterday, of her naked back, long dark waves flowing down her spine, sitting on a beach, staring out over the ocean. The caption simply said, 'Life'.

Great. Here he was, heart shattered and she was posting artfully taken pics on Facebook. Where the hell had he gone wrong in 'life'? He'd cancelled his honeymoon and gone back to work instead of spending two weeks in the Bahamas with his new wife, yet here she was, lying on some mysterious beach. He gave up trying to make this make sense. The only consolation was that he'd booked refundable flights and hotel on the honeymoon, so he hadn't lost out financially. He just hoped that one day they'd get to rebook it all and this time Layla and her standard six pieces of matching luggage would actually be there too.

He was about to shut down Facebook and get to work, when he spotted a tiny number one next to the Message Request header. Must be someone from the wedding that he wasn't friends with. Maybe someone from Layla's side. Great. More sympathy and reinforcement that he'd been completely humiliated.

He clicked on it anyway. Nope, nothing to do with the wedding. In fact, at first, he wondered if it was some kind of sales spam and was ready to delete it when he saw the picture at the bottom of the message. It didn't take too close an inspection to realise who was in it. His dad. His mum. And they must have been in their early twenties when it was taken.

He went back to the beginning of the message and saw that it had come in a couple of days before.

Dear Aiden,
Sorry if this is the strangest Facebook message you've ever received, but please don't delete it before I can explain the reason for reaching out to a stranger thousands of miles away.
I'm Zara Jones, I live in Glasgow, my parents are Colin and Brenda Jones and I

believe they were friends of your father, Gary Gregg, back in the nineties. At least I think so. I'm rubbish at this investigative stuff, and I only had the photo below to go on. I did try to contact Gary directly but he didn't reply, so I might have got this all wrong.

The reason I'm practically stalking members of your family is that my sister and I are taking my parents (the two people in the middle of the photo) on a surprise trip to Las Vegas, where they got married thirty years ago, to celebrate their anniversary. We'll be there for five days, beginning on 16 May. I think your dad was their best man and I know this is a ridiculous long shot, but it would be incredible if your dad could make it there so we can surprise them with a reunion.

I know, crazy, because the 16th is really soon, and this is impossibly short notice, but how amazing would it be????

Anyway, if you're not totally freaked out by this random woman contacting you, then I'd love to hear from you or your dad. Even if it's not possible for them to meet up, maybe your dad could send a message to my parents? He was obviously part of their lives at a really special time, so I'm sure it would mean the world to them.

Hope to hear from you,

Zara. ☺

PS: my UK phone number is…

Aiden's stare went from the bottom of the message to the picture again and he realised he was smiling. Wow. Look at his dad. And his mum! So young. So happy. So carefree... So different from the bruised, unhappy people that they were now.

Before he could stop himself, he'd picked up his phone and dialled the number. It was answered on the third ring.

'Hello?'

'Hi, Zara? This is Aiden Gregg. You sent me a Facebook message about—'

'Eeeeeeek! Holy shit! I mean, yes. I did. And you called back. Wow. Thank you. Unless you're calling to have me arrested for stalking. Are you?'

The Scottish accent, so like his mum's, the humour in her voice, the enthusiasm, this was the distraction that he hadn't even realised that he needed.

'Well, I'm a lawyer, and I have taken photographic evidence of this...'

A pause.

'You know I'm kidding, right?'

'Oh thank God, because I've seen those American TV shows, and I don't have bail money.'

That made him laugh. 'So tell me... your message...' he prompted.

There was a pause, then, 'Right! Of course. Sorry. Hang on and let me switch off *Strictly*. Actually, you'll have no idea what that is. It's a dancing show.'

'Like *Dancing With the Stars*?' Layla loved that show.

'Exactly! I think.' The music in the background subsided. 'Aaaaw, bugger!'

He recoiled, before she explained.

'Sorry, tripped over the coffee table. Stubbed my toe. Anyway, thank you, again, for getting back to me. As I said in my message, it's my parents' thirtieth wedding anniversary, and we've planned this trip as a complete surprise. The only images I have of their trip is one of them kissing in front of Elvis at the wedding ceremony and this one. And am I right in saying that's your father? Please say yes.'

'It sure is.'

'Amazing! Sorry, my voice went really high-pitched there. It does that when I'm excited. I hope you don't have a dog that can hear me because I've probably killed it.'

Aiden was laughing again. 'I don't, but my neighbour does. I'll check in on it when I hang up.'

This might be the strangest and most amusing call of his life.

'So, the thing is, I know it's a terrible imposition, especially since I've now checked and seen that you're in Charleston and that's the opposite side of the country from Vegas, but do you think that there's any way at all that you might join us there? Just saying that out loud, I can hear how crazy it is. Please feel free to say no and tell me I'm deluded.'

His first thought was... well, it was to say no. But then, there was another thought right behind it. Why not? He'd booked time off for his honeymoon and then not taken it, so he had vacation time and a relatively light schedule this month. And he hadn't spent one-on-one time with his dad in years. It would be great for them. And for him too. Get his mind off the missing wife and his chafed heart.

'You know, crazy as it sounds, I could ask him. He hasn't been in Scotland in at least thirty years and I'm sure he'd love to meet an old buddy.'

'Yaasssss! That's brilliant.'

Another thought was coming together too. 'Although, my mom—'

'Of course! Bring your mum too. She'd be so welcome. I'm sure my parents would love to meet her.'

That confused him, until he realised his mom hadn't been part of the discussion yet. 'That's the thing – they've already met her. My mom is in that photo too. She's the lady on the opposite side.'

A gasp. 'You. Are. Kidding. Me.'

'Not kidding.'

'You. Are. Bloody. Marvellous.'

'Definitely that, though,' he chuckled.

'I've been trying to track down Eileen Smith too, so this is a full house. Yaaaayyy! So your parents are married too and now we've got the opportunity to get all four of them back together again. Oh, I'm giddy. That's amazing.'

He'd walked right into that one. 'Not exactly. In fact, there might be a slight issue there. My parents are divorced...'

'Ah, I'm sorry...'

'And they're not great at being in the same room.'

'Ouch. Understood. Och, well – so close.' The disappointment in her tone was palpable, and strangely, that gave him an overwhelming urge to help her.

And there were other factors in play here – the biggest one being that he was absolutely over his parents hating each other. Jilted situation aside, the most uncomfortable aspect of the wedding was that his parents couldn't even be in the same place without all that bubbling tension. This could be the perfect opportunity to broker some kind of peace deal between them, to remind them how much they had loved each other once, and to build, if nothing else, a new friendship between them. He was a trained mediator – surely this wouldn't be beyond his skills? Throw in old Scottish friends and this had all the makings of an amazing life experience for them all. Except... there was no way they'd agree. None. So he was going to have to get creative.

'Look, leave it with me. I've just replied to your Facebook message with my email and phone number. Can you send me all the details? I promise you, I'll do everything I can to make this happen.'

'Yes! Thank you. I owe you a cocktail. Ten cocktails. A kidney. I'm so grateful. This will shock the life out of them all, it really will.'

'I can safely say you're not wrong,' he told her.

They swapped goodbyes and he hung up, still smiling.

This, he decided, was either a really great idea or the worst one he'd ever had. There was only one way to find out.

He picked up his phone again and dialled.

'Hey Dad, it's me. Listen, I've just been thinking... how d'you fancy getting out of town for a few days week after next?'

8

EILEEN

Eileen was toying with the idea of going to cross-fit at the gym, but she couldn't quite motivate herself. It was so unlike her, but she'd felt this way for a couple of weeks, since the non-wedding catastrophe at Hilton Head. It was that old saying that you're only as happy as your unhappiest child. Well, she only had one, but she was pretty sure Aiden was mighty unhappy at the moment. Not that he'd wallow in it or lean on her for support. They were as close as any mum and son could be, but somewhere along the line – around the time of the divorce, if she remembered correctly – he'd begun handling all his own issues without her. She had never been sure whether it was just natural maturity or whether he didn't want to add any more problems to her pile.

She sighed as she stretched up, then went to the office fridge for a smoothie. Normally, other than her regular vinos, she stuck to a Keto diet pretty religiously, but today was her cheat day. Actually, yesterday had been a cheat day too. And most of last week. Urgh, what was the point?

It wasn't just Layla's cowardly no-show that was irritating her. If she were completely honest, breathing the same air as Gary had left her pretty discombobulated too. That man was the bane of her life. Prior to the wedding, she'd trained like a demon, eaten completely clean, and done face yoga – BLOODY FACE YOGA – for three months, just to try to keep all her bits in the right place and for what? So that arse could parade around with his twenty-nine-year-old girlfriend and make her feel about 102. Yes, sure, she knew that she won in wisdom, experience and character, but what good were redeeming qualities when Mitzy could do the bloody splits. In heels. Even – and Eileen was embarrassed to admit it – her fake boyfriend, Kurt, hadn't made up for the dent to her confidence from that whole interaction.

It wasn't that she wanted Gary back, because she truly didn't, but working out and getting herself in the best shape possible was a pride thing on two counts: the first was that she wanted him to look at her and realise that he'd let a bloody good thing go, and because he was a shallow, surface-level, trophy-girlfriend sporting dickhead that notion would be largely dependent on how she looked.

And reason number two, she'd done it for herself because she wanted to feel good. To be her best self. To keep her confidence high, both at work and, God forbid, for the slim possibility that she might actually build up the inclination to get serious about meeting someone again.

Eileen sighed and sat back in her chair, stretching up to the ceiling, then swearing as a button popped right off her shirt and shot across the room, narrowly avoiding taking Kurt's eye out. She hadn't shared all the details of Kurt's background with Aiden on his should-have-been big day, but her fake-for-the-day had joined her realty firm and was crushing it, pulling in huge numbers, especially in the islands and coastal areas of the state. He was also killing it in his personal life, dating a dashingly hand-some real estate mogul who was a major presence in the flip market. She loved a gay wedding, so she was hopeful it would go the distance.

'Do you want this back?' Kurt asked her, and she knew he'd have one eyebrow raised in question if he wasn't obsessed with minimising facial movements to avoid wrinkles.

'Keep it. It's a down payment on all the beverages I owe you for coming with me to the wedding.'

'Wouldn't have missed it. I had the best time. Apart from, you know, the bit where no one actually got married,' he said, and even though that should sting, the cool, matter-of-fact way that he said it made her love him even more for his attempt to inject some humour into the situation. If this man wasn't only attracted to other guys, in the 30–60 age bracket, with a median income in excess of $500,000, she'd be seriously smitten by him. Not that she'd do anything about it. That ship had well and truly sailed. The HMS Gary Gregg. Off it went, carrying a full cargo of her self-esteem, her confidence and her desire for a future relationship, and it hadn't been seen since. Right now, the only way she was going to find a romantic partner was if she got stuck in a lift with some unsuspecting bloke for at least a week, or if Amazon started sending out boyfriends with her monthly subscription of age-defying moisturiser.

In the early years after the divorce, there had been odd dates here and there. A few relationships that lasted three, four, five months, but lately she just didn't have the energy for the politics of it all. There was dating. Which was basically a free for all. Then there was exclusivity, which meant you wouldn't date other people. Then there was monogamy and commitment, but she hadn't got that far with anyone else yet. How would that even happen? There was no point denying it – it was near impossible for a woman of her age to meet decent guys these days. She didn't have the stomach for the online stuff and the dating apps – all that swiping left and right gave her a migraine. Also, in her experience, most of the single men out there of her age wanted to date thirty-year olds. The Mitzys of this world pretty much had the market sewn up. Jesus, what a depressing thought. And if she wasn't careful, she knew a whole load of other depressing thoughts would flood in too – what was she doing with her life? Was this all there was – just work and working out and friends that didn't come with benefits other than a great line in chat and the willingness to act as a fake boyfriend?

Sometimes she wondered if she should just pack everything up and go back to Scotland, but that was a romantic, ridiculous notion. She had no-one there to go back to. Her mum had passed away when she was in her early twenties, and she'd never known her dad. She'd only been back to her homeland twice since she'd put down roots in the USA, and those trips were over fifteen years ago, for her grandparents' funerals. Both times, she'd gone alone because Gary was too busy to go with her and they'd been flying visits. No looking up old friends. She'd burnt her bridges with the people that mattered in her homeland thirty years ago and nothing good would come from reopening those wounds.

'Right, I'm going to go work out, then set up for my open house tomorrow,' she said to Kurt, who immediately perked up his ears.

'What's the spec?'

'Five bedrooms, 2400 square feet, colonial-style down by the water – $6 million, so it's a steal.'

'If you have six million lying around,' Kurt said playfully.

'And if you do, I'll help you spend it,' Eileen quipped.

It was the biggest property of her career and she knew that, right now, Kurt was working out how much commission that would be. A dollar or two short of $240,000. Okay, so tax had to be deducted, but it would still be an eye-watering amount of money. It would be enough for her to take a break, but what would she want to do? Travel? Remodel her apartment? Buy a flash car? Nope, nope, and hell no. Urgh, she was actually beginning to annoy herself with all this negativity now. Enough.

Reaching behind her, she pulled her purse from the back of her chair and brought it round to her desk, then snapped her laptop shut, giving herself an internal talking-to as she did so. *Right, Eileen, get it together. Let's do this. Go set up this house, then you can take the rest of Saturday off, lie on the sofa and watch old romcoms.* The Proposal. The Holiday. *Maybe throw in a* Pretty Woman *or a* How To Lose A Guy In 10 Days. *Then tomorrow? Arse out of bed, an early morning workout, then over to the open house, get this pad sold and bank a lovely cheque.*

Satisfied that she had a semblance of a plan, she was just about to go when her cell rang. Trevon.

'If you're calling to moan at me because I'm not in the gym, spare your breath. I'm a middle-aged woman on the edge today and only carbohydrates and laziness are going to help me.'

To others, Aiden's best mate was a thirty-something, successful, strikingly impressive health and fitness entrepreneur, a self-made man, an influencer and a catch, with – at the last count – about a million followers on Instagram. To Eileen, he was just Aiden's friend of many years, the guy who made her laugh, and her fairly regular weekend training partner. There was no fixed routine, but she always took the same cross-fit class at one of his gyms on a Saturday and Sunday, and more often than not, he showed up and either did the classes with her or shared a drink at the juice bar afterwards.

'Oh damn. Let me guess – *The Holiday* or *How To Lose A Guy In 10 Days*?'

'I hate that you know me this well. How's Aiden?'

'Hanging in there. I'll let him tell you the latest. Anyway, gotta go. I'm on my way to the gym – was just checking if I'd see you there.'

'Only if someone forces me at gunpoint.' A beep. She checked the screen. Incoming call. 'Trevon, Aiden is on the other line.'

'No worries. Catch ya.'

'Catch ya back.' She sounded ridiculous and felt even worse when she tried to use modern lingo, but at least it made Trevon laugh as she hung up. She switched the line. 'Hi, honey, how are you doing?' she asked, hoping that the answer wasn't going to be 'drowning my sorrows in a case of beer on a Saturday afternoon'.

'Hey, Mom, I'm good.'

He actually sounded quite positive. Oh bollocks, had Layla come back? Was the damn wedding back on? Because if it was, Eileen wasn't sure she could face that woman, at least not without giving her a piece of her mind.

'Glad to hear it. So, what you up to?'

'Nothing much – just got something that I want to run past you.'

She couldn't keep it in any longer. 'Does it involve anything to do with Layla, because, son, I know you're a grown man and it's your life, and of course I'll respect any decision you make, but I had a dream last night that I fed her prawns that had been lying in the midday sun for hours. Don't judge me. I'm an imperfect human being.'

His laughter warmed her heart. 'I'm not judging you. I think I might have had the same dream. Must be genetic.'

She idly twirled her pen in her free hand. After worrying about him pretty solidly for the last fortnight, it was good to hear him sounding like his old self. Whatever had made that happen, she was grateful for it.

'Probably best that we stay away from seafood so we're not tempted,' she said. 'Have you heard from her?'

'No, her mom came by and collected her stuff this morning, so I think that's pretty much done for now. Still don't get it, but I'd drive myself crazy trying to figure it out, so I'm just going to let it ride until she's ready to talk.'

How did he get so sensible? His father would have been in there like a bull in a china shop, and she would be... well, she still liked the prawns idea.

'Good idea. What was it that you wanted to run past me then? If it involves eating, drinking or making bad choices, I'm in.'

'Well, actually, maybe all of the above.'

'Really? I don't think I've ever been prouder. I thought I'd lost you to decency and maturity,' she joked, loving the sound of his laughter on the other end of the line. 'Tell me more.'

'I've decided to get away for a few days week after next and thought maybe you could come with me? You know, do that trip we've been saying we were going to take for years but never got around to?'

If general surprise could make more of her shirt buttons pop off, they'd be shooting across the room like bullets. A few years ago, she'd floated the idea of a mum/son trip but it had never happened, and then he'd met Layla and the idea had faded.

'You know what, son, I'd love that. In fact, it would be amazing. Where and when? Not that it matters because we'll have a great time wherever we go.'

'I'm, erm... just working some stuff out. I'm looking at the sixteenth of May...'

She quickly checked her calendar. Less than two weeks away, but she could do it. Even if there had been a clash, she'd have made it happen. 'Good for me,' she agreed. 'And where? New York will be just heating up. We could catch a Knicks game. Or maybe Miami? We haven't been there since that time your father fell overboard trying to take a selfie on a boating dock.'

The memory made her smile more than it should. It was a few months before the divorce. Before everything happened. Before she'd found out what he'd been up to. In hindsight, the clues about his latest antics had all been there. Selfies? That alone should have started the alarm bells ringing. There he was, posing like an absolute eejit in front of swanky yachts and then sending the photos to his mates. At least, that's what she'd thought he was doing. Turns out the truth was very different.

An involuntary shiver ran down her spine and she shook it off. Why was she thinking about that waste of space now when her son was on the phone planning something wonderful? Excitement pushed the dreaded memories out of the way and took centre stage again. With a bit of jazz hands for extra effect. This was going to be sen-fricking-sational.

'Can I get back to you on the destination, Mom? Here's the thing, I want it to be a surprise, so I just need you to trust me.'

She definitely did. Even if the very thought of that made her inner control freak – the one that found life after she was forced to pick up the pieces after her divorce – want to lie down in a dark room.

'Fine by me, son. I'm just happy to be getting the chance to do this.'

'Me too, Mom. It's going to be great. I have to go just now – plans to make and things to arrange.'

'Okay. Dinner this week some time?'

'Sure. I'll come over Wednesday. I'll bring some wings. The Lakers game is on at eight, so we can catch that.'

That had always been their thing. No gender stereotypes in their house. She was the one who'd always watched sport with him, gone to games, made it a priority to be involved in the stuff that interested him. Dinner this week and then a trip with her son. Her smile was making her cheeks hurt.

She picked up her cell and texted Trevon.

Change of plan. On way to gym. See you there.

The Holiday, The Proposal and *How To Lose A Guy In 10 Days* could wait. Life wasn't so bad after all.

9

ZARA

16 May 2023

The minivan they'd ordered to take them to the airport turned up bang on time. At the shop window, Zara gave a cheer as she watched it coming down the street at 8 a.m. – mostly because, at the very same time, a taxi was arriving containing her sister.

Zara wrenched open the front door. 'I swear to God, you're going to give me a heart attack. I was leaving without you,' she told Millie, watching as she pulled herself out of the cab, still in the bright red minidress she'd worn to go out the night before. Although, it now appeared to be partially covered by a man's shirt that was tied at her waist, and she was wearing hotel slippers on her feet. Her fake tan, eyelash extensions and dark wavy weave were still, however, looking spectacular.

'You worry too much,' Millie told her, blowing her a kiss as she passed her at the door. The only consolation was that Zara had insisted her sister fully pack the night before, so Millie's cases were sitting, ready, waiting to be loaded into the van. 'Let me just go brush my teeth. I've showered, so I promise I'm peachy fresh. And then I've got the best story to tell you. I think I'm in love.'

Zara was already multitasking, pushing cases out of the door to the minivan driver while discussing Millie's romantic life. 'With the same guy you were in love with last week?'

'Nope. I'm over that one. He wears socks with small animals on them.'

In fairness to the van driver, he didn't bat an eyelid at this information.

Zara got the van loaded, taking extra-special care of the case containing Gran's dress. It was one of those folded-over suit-carrier thingies and she was taking that in her hand luggage. The very thought of it going in a suitcase that could potentially get lost made her stomach lurch. Millie said she felt the same about the bag containing her make-up.

'I'm back. How do I smell?' Millie asked her, before exhaling in her face.

'Minty,' Zara confirmed, relieved to see that Millie had also lost the red dress and slippers and changed into cream leggings, a matching crop top, white trainers and a sexy long oatmeal cardigan. On mere mortals, cream was a brave colour choice for travelling, but Millie liked to stand out. Zara couldn't help but compare it to her own travel wear: jeans, black boots and a navy blazer over a white T-shirt. Unremarkable, bordering on boring. Sometimes she was fairly convinced that she and her sister had never shared a womb.

Zara stopped Millie at the door of the van. 'Passport?'

'Yes.'

'Purse?'

'Yes.'

'Phone?'

'Yes. I've also got an uptight sister who keeps checking stuff. Do I get extra points for that?'

'Nope, you just get to count your blessings.'

Millie climbed in first and then Zara clambered in behind her.

'Hang on,' Millie put her hand up. 'Where's Kev? Didn't he come to snog the air out of your lungs in a long, passionate goodbye?'

Zara gave the van driver their parents' address before answering. 'No, he's doing t'ai chi at the park this morning. Says it'll balance his zens. Or his chakras. Or... I've got no idea. I got to t'ai chi' and switched off.'

'You know, it's truly amazing.'

'What is?' Zara asked, mentally running through her own checklist, while clicking on her phone's Maps app to make sure there were no traffic jams on the way to the airport.

'Every time I think that guy can't get any more boring, he climbs to a whole new level of snoozeville. He's like the gift that keeps on giving.'

Zara, very maturely, flicked Millie on the thigh and gave her the pursed lips of disapproval. Although... okay, maybe she had a point. Kev wasn't exactly a thrill a minute but at least she knew what she had with him. He was kind. And safe. And they both just let the other person be themselves. Then there was the fact that she'd been with him for pretty much her whole adult life. She'd take that kind of stability over Millie's rotating door of conquests any time. No judgement, but she couldn't maintain that level of effort or expenditure. Millie's monthly hair bill cost more than their mortgage.

Her sister's head flopped down on to Zara's shoulder and Zara ruffled her hair. 'You're a fricking nightmare, you know that?'

'I do,' Millie agreed. 'But you love me.'

'Only sometimes. Eeeek, I'm so excited. I can't wait to see Mum and Dad's faces when we announce where we're going. This is going to be amazing and I'm not even going to tell them that their old pals are coming. I'll save that until we get there. Keep the surprises coming. I spoke to Aiden again last night – he's managed to get both his mum and dad to agree to come, although, he did say it was slightly complicated because they are divorced now. I think he's looking at this as an opportunity to improve their relationship. Must be so difficult to be in that position. You know, I never take for granted how lucky we are that Mum and Dad are still happy. Thirty years. It's just amazing and—'

Millie's snore made Zara jump. Brilliant. She'd been talking to herself like a complete diddy for the last five minutes.

She distracted herself by checking the traffic again. Still fine. Then she ran through all the details from all her holiday lists in her mind. All done. And the shop was in the safe, capable hands of her trusted part-timers,

Tilly and Tina, who were working the full week to cover for them. They were good to go.

When they reached their parents' house, the van slowed at the kerb, and Zara reached over to open the door, letting Millie's head fall and earning a dramatic 'Ouch!' from Sleeping Beauty.

'We're going on holiday,' Zara announced, throwing her arms wide, then hugging first her mum, then her dad.

This was amazing. Brilliant. One of the best days ever. Time and time again, she'd imagined in her mind how all this was going to play out today – the excitement, the surprises, the beaming faces of her parents when they learned what was in store for them. Now that it was all happening, she felt like the total cliché of a kid at Christmas.

'On you go into the van, Mum – we'll get the luggage.'

Her dad helped her load up their cases, while Mum climbed in and sat next to Millie. By the time they got back in, Millie had replaced Zara's shoulder with her mum's and was sleeping soundly again.

'Let me guess – she stayed out all night and got back ten minutes before you left this morning?'

'Yes, she did, but it was one minute, not ten,' Zara confirmed, matching her mum's grin.

'Thought so. I wish I had half of the energy she's got, I really do. At least her life's never dull.'

It was a throwaway comment and normally it wouldn't have registered, but there was something in her mum's tone that jarred. Was she okay? Come to think of it, her eyes were a little puffy and she looked a bit drawn and there was a bit of a defeated slump across her shoulders. It wasn't that Zara expected her mum to come cartwheeling out of the house, but she wasn't giving the vibe of someone who was about to go on an all-expenses paid celebration with her family. Even Dad was looking chirpy, staring out of the window and humming something upbeat but indecipherable.

'Are you okay, Mum?'

That immediately changed her mother's whole body language and she broke into a smile. 'I'm so sorry, love. Just a bit tired, that's all. Did a couple of double shifts this week so the others on the ward could get some time off.'

Ah, that explained it. Her mum worked way too hard and Zara had been suggesting for ages that she cut her hours down, but Brenda was having none of it. Maybe with Dad taking early retirement next month, Mum would slow down so they could spend more time together. They deserved to take it easy and enjoy life more. And this trip was the perfect place to start.

The van was on the M8 heading towards Glasgow airport now and Zara couldn't see any traffic issues ahead. Excellent.

'Are you going to tell us where we're going then?' Mum asked, and much as Zara was bursting to tell her, she shook her head.

'Not yet. We'll tell you at the airport when Millie wakes up. This is a gift from both of us, so it's only fair.' Zara decided not to mention that they were using every penny they'd inherited from their gran – she knew that Mum would only object. Like Zara, her mum had always been uncomfortable when anyone made a fuss of her or made her the centre of attention, and she definitely wouldn't want to know that Gran's money – intended for her granddaughters – was being diverted to this. It was going to be worth it though, to show their parents how much they meant to them, and how delighted they were that Mum and Dad were reaching such an incredible milestone.

Traffic slowed over the last mile or so to the airport but they still got there in plenty of time. Zara mentally ticked that off her potential pitfall list for the journey.

'Millie, come on. We're here,' she nudged her sister's leg with her foot relentlessly until Millie woke up.

'Is it just me that wants to sing Elvis songs and have a wee dance?' Millie asked, and Zara shot her daggers, fearing she'd give the game away. Thankfully, Mum and Dad were both too busy climbing out of the van to notice.

They piled their luggage on to two trollies, paid the driver, and then, excitement bubbling, Zara led them into the terminal, heading in the direction of the British Airways desk. She saw her mum register the destination - London Heathrow - on the screen above the counter and watched as she smiled and all the tiredness dropped from her face.

Wow. If Mum was this happy when she thought they were only going to London, wait until she found out where they were actually headed.

Before they joined the queue, Zara stopped at a pillar about twenty metres from the check-in desks. It was now or never. She knew the ground agent would mention that they were transferring on to Vegas, so it was time to get in there first and then enjoy every second of their parents' delighted reactions.

She gave Millie the subliminal signal and they launched into an unrehearsed explanation of their gift and what was to come.

'Mum, Dad, you know that – apart from me – we're not really a big gesture kind of family...' Millie began, and Zara rolled her eyes. Trust her sister to point out the obvious. 'But thirty years of marriage, well, that's pretty much a miracle and it deserves a really special celebration.'

Okay, she'd redeemed herself, Zara decided, and took over the reins. 'And we know you've made so many sacrifices for us over the years. Millie's acting classes alone could have bought you another house.'

'Two houses if you add in my dancing classes, but I'm great at a nightclub, so it was money well spent,' Millie piped up.

Zara glossed right over that. 'And then, helping us to open the shop... well, we wouldn't be where we are today if it wasn't for you.'

'Working long hours and smelling faintly of soil,' Millie interjected.

Honest to God, why couldn't she have a normal sister? Although, not that Zara would ever admit it, but this one was worth it for the amusement she provided.

'Anyway,' Zara said firmly, 'as I was saying, we want to repay your love, your support and your general brilliance. So we're taking you to—'

'London!' her mum blurted, beaming, as she gestured to the information screen. 'Och, girls, I'm thrilled. I was hoping it was there. I can't wait to go tour the galleries, maybe see a show...'

'Well, you'll definitely see a show, but it's not London, Mum. It's somewhere a bit more exciting than that. You see, we thought it would be perfect to take you back to where this all began, so we're going to...' A pause, then a conspiratorial glance, beaming faces, and a synchronised screech from the two sisters.

'LAS VEGAS!'

Zara was frozen in the moment, arms thrown wide, smile on face, unable to comprehend why her mum was just staring at her like she couldn't compute what was going on. Had they actually said Las Vegas out loud? She was sure they had, yet their mother's expression was more stunned horror. Had mum been so desperate to go to London that she was now disappointed they were going to the entertainment capital of the world? What the hell was going on? And why did her body and facial expression refuse to change until she got some kind of reaction from her parents?

When it came, it was even more confusing. She was sure her mother whispered, 'Oh no,' and her dad, not untypically, said nothing, just glanced at her mum with a face that conveyed something between uncertainty, anxiety and horror.

Millie regained her powers of speech first. 'Okay, we were expecting a response that was very slightly more enthusiastic than that one. We did just tell you that we're taking you to Vegas, right? Or did we accidentally confess some dark secret that ends with anonymous tests in a clinic? Kidding, Dad.'

Zara shook her head, trying to make the synapses in her brain fire up in the right direction. This wasn't on the list. It was supposed to be pure joy and wild excitement at this stage, not paralysed shock. 'Mum? You are happy about this, aren't you?'

There was an excruciating delay that was only a few seconds, but felt like a week and a half, before her mum finally forced – and Zara was sure that was the only way to describe it – *forced* a smile. There was another pause before she managed to add actual words.

'Of course, we are, darlings. It's just a bit of a shock, but thank you so much. This is... this is... this is wonderful.'

For the first time in her life, outside of Santa, the tooth fairy and the risk of your vagina falling off if you wore miniskirts in sub-zero temperatures (that last one was directed at Millie, aged fourteen), Zara was fairly sure her mother was lying to her.

10

BRENDA

This. Was. A. Nightmare.

Las Vegas.

The one place on earth that she'd quite happily go the rest of her life without revisiting.

How could this possibly have happened? Actually, she didn't even need to question that. Her lovely, thoughtful, sentimental Zara and her wild, party animal, Millie. How could she not have considered that Vegas could be on the cards? In hindsight, it made perfect sense. Brenda just wished she'd seen it coming so that she could have reacted better. The girls had looked shocked and crushed by her reaction and she didn't blame them.

She'd somehow managed to slap on a smile, put one foot in front of the other and get on the plane to London. Sitting on the tarmac at Glasgow, she was mortified to admit it, but she'd prayed the domestic flight would get delayed, cancelled, anything at all that would mean the second leg of the trip was off and they could just head for a London hotel and revert to her original hope of finding a way to get through the next few days with Colin by filling the hours with shows and wandering around the tourist spots.

Unfortunately, she hadn't been that lucky. The Glasgow flight was on time and they'd sailed through Heathrow Terminal Five and made it in plenty of time for the second leg of their travels. Now they were soaring towards the end of their ten-hour flight to Vegas, sitting four abreast in the front row of premium economy. If this was any other trip, to anywhere else on earth, she'd be relishing the treat. The comfy chairs. The lovely meals. The regular top ups of her wine glass. She'd never flown premium economy in her life. They definitely hadn't travelled this way last time they'd gone to Vegas. The cheapest economy seats. Right up the back. They'd been too excited to care that the wall behind them vibrated every time someone flushed the toilet. The very thought of that trip stirred up a whole juggernaut of emotions, and she slammed the door shut on them before they could enter and take up residence in her mind. There was not one single cell in her brain that wanted to relive any moment of her last visit to Vegas.

On the screen in front of her, the flight tracker told her they had an hour to go until they reached their destination. An hour. The butterflies in her stomach were launching a full-scale offensive now. An hour to work out how she was going to get through a trip to a city that was the location of a marriage that should never have happened, to a man she was now planning to leave, and all of it in the sightline of her two daughters, who thought they were doing something wonderful for her. Brenda could actually feel her heart racing in her chest at the very thought of it. Why couldn't she just be happy? Why wasn't this enough? If only she could make herself content with what she had, then no-one would get hurt and she wouldn't have to live with the guilt of breaking up her family. But... at what cost? The rest of her life spent unfulfilled and miserable? How could she possibly keep this façade of happiness going for a lifetime when right now she was struggling to see how she could make it through this week?

To her right, she saw that both Zara and Millie were sleeping, so she nudged her husband, on her left.

'Colin, I don't think I can do this,' she whispered.

He paused the show he was watching on his TV screen – some lifestyle thing about (shoot me now, was Brenda's first thought) historical gardens across the world – and took off his earphones.

'Did you say something?' he asked her.

'I said, I don't think I can do this. The trip. This is awful.'

He shared her pain by taking a sip of his red wine and adjusting the position of his lower limbs on his foot rest. 'Och, Brenda, it'll be fine. I don't think there's anything to get too worked up about. Let's just take it a day at a time and try to enjoy it.'

Brenda wondered what the punishment would be for suffocating her husband at 30,000 feet with an airline pillow.

He pinged his headphones back on and Brenda took a deep breath and tried to focus her thoughts on something less homicidal.

This was exactly what she hadn't wanted to happen between them. She'd wanted to leave while there were no hard feelings, while they were still friends who could say goodbye, without castigation or resentment on either side, but that was getting harder and harder to do. And it was her fault. When she'd let him persuade her to give them another chance, when he'd said he'd make more of an effort, that he would take steps to lift their relationship out of terminal decline, she should have refused and pointed out the obvious – if they hadn't managed to build something wonderful in thirty years, they were hardly likely to do that now.

He'd made a nominal effort in the first couple of days. They'd even gone to the cinema on the Sunday night, after a lovely dinner in a little trattoria just off Byres Road. On the way home, they'd held hands and when they got back to the house, and it must have been the wine, she'd kissed him. In the kitchen. Without giving him prior warning. Just a spontaneous kiss. Then she'd then taken him by the hand, led him upstairs, and for the first time in months, they'd even had – pass the smalling salts, Mavis – sex. And it was... decidedly average and over in ten minutes. Maybe fifteen, if you counted the time it took him to get undressed and fold his clothes beforehand. Afterwards, he'd given her a triumphant, 'See! I knew we could get back on the horse,' and then gone to sleep.

Every minute of that night, and every minute since, her affection for him had eroded just a little bit more, and even though she hated herself for letting that happen, she didn't seem to be able to stop it.

The lights in the cabin suddenly pinged on and there was a simultaneous announcement from the crew.

'Ladies and Gentlemen, we are now commencing our final service before landing in Las Vegas in approximately fifty minutes...' They then went on to say something about breakfast, but Brenda missed it because, beside her, Zara had woken up and was grinning at her now, her face so full of anticipation.

'Has it all sunk in yet, Mum? I'm sorry we shocked you. Honestly, though, you gave me the fright of my life. I thought for a few moments that you were horrified and we were going to have to chase you through Glasgow airport and drag you back to the check-in desk.'

Brenda had never been much of an actress (except a week ago last Sunday, when she did what she hoped was a fairly convincing job of portraying someone who was enjoying having swift and silent missionary position sex with her husband), but her daughter's happiness depended on this, so she went full-scale Meryl Streep. 'I'm sorry, sweetheart. It's just... well, you know I'm rubbish with surprises and this is such a huge, amazing one. It just threw me. I'm so grateful though, and so is your dad. This is the loveliest thing anyone has ever done for us.'

Zara stretched over and kissed her cheek. 'You're so welcome. You deserve it.'

'Urgh, is there a whole emosh-fest going on with you two? Only they're about to bring breakfast and you'll put me right off my sausages.'

'There are so many jokes in my head right now, but every one of them is really immature and Mum will be horrified, so I'll keep my mouth shut,' Zara told her sister, making Brenda chuckle.

If they'd done one thing right, it was raising their daughters to love each other. They couldn't be more different, and yet, somehow they managed to overlook any flaws and just focus on the good stuff. But then, maybe they'd learned that close to home. Wasn't that what Brenda had been doing in her marriage all these years? Overlooking the problems? It was a behaviour that worked well with siblings, but not so well if you wanted a fulfilling marriage that would deliver a lifetime of happiness.

Breakfast was served, and still Brenda had no clue what was ahead, other than an ominous promise of, 'We've got so many surprises lined up, Mum. You're going to have the best time.'

'I'm already having a great time. Just being with you two is such a treat. You know how much I love you both, don't you?'

It was Millie who replied. 'Mum, you really need to stop with the soppy stuff. You make it sound like the plane is going down and we're delivering last messages of love. And let me tell you, if we're crashing, I love you both, but you'll find me up in the cockpit with the pilot that gave that last announcement. His voice is the sexiest thing I've ever heard.'

It was probably just as well Colin still had his headphones on and if he wondered why they were all laughing, he didn't ask.

'You know, Millie, when I grow up, I want to be just like you,' Brenda joked, realising there was a grain of truth in there. There was no denying the personality traits that Brenda had passed on to Zara, or how proud she was of all the other lovely facets that made her elder daughter such a lovely soul. But Millie? Maybe the learning was supposed to go the other way with that one. The fearlessness. The openness. The absolutely unapologetic determination to enjoy life. That was the kind of person Brenda wanted to be.

'Oh great. Smashing. Because one irresponsible nightmare with no shame isn't enough in the family,' Zara teased.

'I'd argue, but she's right,' Millie concurred, draining her coffee cup.

The cabin crew cleared their trays, and after visits to the loos to freshen up, the sexy captain announced it was ten minutes until landing. Brenda's butterflies had another fly around her abdominal cavities. Las Vegas. She was here again. She was here again. She was here again. And her brain couldn't quite get off that loop. Dammit. She was here again.

The plane landed with a thud and some people around them began to clap. Brenda didn't join in. Instead, she channelled Meryl Streep again. 'How long are we here for, sweetheart?' she asked Zara, knowing her daughter would have the itinerary memorised. There was probably a laminated paper copy in her carry-on case too. That trait came down from Colin. He never went anywhere without the full schedule encased in a waterproof, wipeable folder. Brenda had taken a week off as directed but she just wanted to check what day they'd be leaving so that she could brace herself for the mission of maintaining a cheery demeanour at all times.

'We leave on Saturday, that's the day after your actual anniversary. I know it seems crazy coming all this way for just five days, but at least it'll be memorable.'

It would definitely be that.

Millie swooped in with some words of wisdom. 'And the best cure for jet lag is just to stay awake, so maybe we can get you to walk on the wild side with us, Mum. All day activities and all night dancing and drinking.'

Brenda would usually laugh that off as she'd never been much of a drinker. In fact, she hadn't been drunk since she was in her twenties, apart from that one work night out where the young nurses on the ward had introduced her and Bernadette to apple-flavoured shots. The last thing Brenda remembered was asking if they counted towards her five a day. But that said, right now it was sounding like a healthy plan for surviving the next five days.

They gathered up their belongings, waited patiently in line for the passengers in front of them to move forward, then eventually followed them along the aisle to the door.

'Goodbye. And welcome to Las Vegas,' the smiley flight attendant chirped.

'Thank you,' Brenda replied, because even in times of emotional turmoil, she was nothing if not polite.

When she took her first step in to the Las Vegas terminal, she felt her hands begin to shake and shoved them in the pockets of her cardigan.

'This is awesome!' Millie cheered, slipping her arm through her mum's. Brenda prayed that she wouldn't feel her trembling. 'This must be so different from last time you were here, Mum.'

Brenda gazed around at the white walls of the terminal building but recognised nothing.

'It sure is,' Meryl Streep answered with a wide smile.

'I've never asked you before. When you came here last time, were you and Dad planning to get married? Or was it a spur-of-the-moment thing?'

Not even Meryl could handle this one. Conflicting answers ricocheted across her brain, but she couldn't quite nail one down. It was all too much. The memories. The fractured marriage. Even making her way, right now, to a place she really didn't want to go, either physically or emotionally. Yes, she wanted more excitement in her life, but not this kind, because this was the equivalent of a marital death row and she was a dead woman walking.

This city held so many secrets, so much that she wished hadn't happened.

She blamed herself. She blamed Colin.

And more than anything, she absolutely blamed the other two people who had landed in Vegas with them back in 1993.

11

AIDEN

The text message beeped into Aiden's phone just as he was leaving his apartment. He checked the screen, every time his first thought going to the possibility that it could be Layla. Of course, it wasn't. Other than the text about collecting her stuff, he still hadn't heard a word from her since the no-show at their wedding. And no, that still didn't sting any less. Although this whole Vegas thing had been a welcome distraction, as had the couple of calls he'd exchanged with Zara and her sister, Millie. In fact, they'd had a FaceTime call a couple of nights ago that had lasted an hour, mainly because Millie was regaling him with stories about the social life in Glasgow. He already had an open invitation to visit and he hadn't even met them in person yet.

They'd discussed all the different ways to let the reunion play out and they'd come to the conclusion that keeping it a surprise for everyone would make it even more special when they all came together. Hopefully, his mum would have got over the fact that his dad was there by then – or, if not, at least meeting Zara's parents again after all these years would cheer her up and give her something to make the trip worthwhile. Reuniting with old friends – that had to be a special moment for her and his dad too. He couldn't wait to make that happen for them. And it went without saying that if the four of them got together again, then maybe his parents would remember why they had once liked each other. It could definitely be the catalyst that rekindled their friendship.

That's probably why he smiled when he saw that the text was from Zara.

The eagle has risen. Or at least, we'll be taking off in about ten minutes. I'm hopeless at this spy stuff. Mum was so shocked, I thought she'd keel over and she still doesn't know the best bit! Can't wait to see our mums' faces when they meet each other after thirty years. Dads too. It's going to be epic! Have a safe flight and see you soon (feels really weird saying that!). Zx

He was getting used to Zara and Millie's habit of putting an x or two at the end of every text. It was kinda endearing.

He fired off a reply.

Just leaving for airport now. See you on the other side. A

Then he remembered and changed it to 'Ax'.

He slipped his phone into his pocket as he rode the elevator down to the lobby of his apartment block, running through the plans to make sure he had everything covered. His dad was spending the week down in Hilton Head, so he was making his own way to Charleston airport. Aiden had planned to pick up his mom on the way, but she'd called to say she had a showing on a house she was selling, so she'd meet him there. In truth, it was probably the best way for this to play out, because if he told her on the way to the airport that his dad was coming with them, he was pretty sure she'd demand that he stop the car and let her out on the freeway, whether it was a life-threatening situation or not.

Whenever he felt a twinge of anxiety about the duplicity of this whole situation, he reminded himself of three things. The first was that this had all started as a plan to reunite his mum and dad with old friends on a special occasion. The second was that the relationship between his mom and dad couldn't get any worse, so there was nothing to lose. And the third was that he was one of the most respected and successful divorce lawyers in the city, so he should be able to negotiate some kind of peace agreement between his own warring parents.

Oh, and there was a fourth thing. He had adequate health insurance, so if one or both of his parents tried to murder him for this, he had a fighting chance of recovery.

'Ready, bud?' Trevon asked him when he reached the swanky car, fired up and waiting outside the door of his building. His mate had offered to drop him at the airport and pick him up again on his return. Aiden wasn't going to argue. It meant he could have a beer on the plane on the way back and stay in holiday mode just a little bit longer. Or block out the chaos if his parents were still at war by then. Also, Trevon drove a slick Maserati, and Aiden's childhood love of flash cars had never left him, so he'd take any excuse to ride in it.

It was a twelve-mile drive from downtown Charleston to the airport and traffic was light, so it only took about twenty minutes.

'You know, I almost want to come with you so I can be there to rescue your ass when your mom finds out your dad is coming along for the ride.'

'You think it's a bad idea?' Shit. He'd spent days convincing himself that this was for the greater good, but Trevon was hinting otherwise.

'Man, it's a terrible idea. Your mom hates him.'

Okay, maybe more than hinting.

Aiden offered the case for the defence. 'But don't you think she'll get over it if they can just sit down and talk?' He was willing his buddy to agree but Trevon wasn't getting the memo.

'Hell, no. She's going to be so pissed off, I reckon I'll get the invitation to Christmas dinner instead of you this year. And you can kiss goodbye to Thanksgiving too.'

'I'm glad my pain is amusing you, bud. Thank you for being here to give me confidence and words of wisdom.'

'Any time. And you know... I'm trained in all that first aid shit, so give me a call if it gets messy at the airport.'

Trevon was still chuckling when they drew up in the drop-off zone at the terminal building.

Aiden reached over and hugged him. 'Thanks, man. You're an asshole, but you're my favourite asshole.'

'Right back at ya. If this doesn't work out well, it's been good knowing you.'

Aiden shook his head, laughing, as he got out of the car, then grabbed his bags from the trunk. He gave his mate a wave as he drove off, then headed inside.

The check-in line was short, so it only took half an hour or so to check in his main case at the baggage drop, before heading over to the small café bar area in the corner of the departures lounge.

The space was half full, mostly with people in business attire, or Gen Zs with three devices plugged into the myriad sockets at each section of the counter. He'd just found a tall table with four high chairs around it when he got a text from his mom.

Arrived! Where are you?

He scanned the terminal and saw her by the door. He texted back.

Look to your left

He watched her read it, follow the instruction, then smile when she saw him waving to her. As she walked towards him, he thought, not for the first time, how great she looked. She worked hard in the gym – sometimes with Trevon, other times at spin classes or boxercise, or cross-fit, or whatever else was going on down there. She also took good care of herself and dressed impeccably, just like today. Ripped jeans, high-heeled grey suede boots, a white blazer and her highlighted blonde hair falling in waves over her shoulders as she pulled a cream suitcase. She was in her fifties, but could easily pass for someone in their thirties or early forties. He only knew the bullet points of why his parents had split up, but it wasn't pretty. Much as he loved his dad, he knew he had a short attention span, a fragile ego and a wandering eye. His mom, on the other hand, was funny, she was smart, she had a core of absolute decency and any guy would be lucky to have her. What a fool his dad had been to let her go. Maybe this trip...

Aiden stopped himself. No, he wasn't going to get his hopes up for some romantic happy ending because he knew better. Especially after the recent events in his own life. He'd settle for a ceasefire between his parents and anything else was a bonus.

'Hey, son,' she smiled breezily, kissing him on the cheek, then climbing on to the stool beside him.

'How did the showing go?' he asked, sensing that she seemed happy.

'Great. Qualified buyer. All cash. He had a couple of other options, so I just have to wait and see. It would be the biggest sale of my career, so cross your fingers.'

'Crossed,' he told her, holding up his hand to prove it. 'Can I get you a drink? We've got plenty of time before we have to head to security and there's no queue. I just want to talk to you about something before we go through.'

'Eh, sure,' she replied hesitantly, with a definite edge of suspicion. 'Gin and tonic, please.'

The barman reached him right at that moment and put two coasters in front of them. 'What can I get you folks?'

'A gin and tonic and a beer, please.'

The drinks were in front of them in a couple of minutes. His mum took a sip of hers first. 'I needed this.' She put the glass back down on the bar before she went on, 'I'm so glad we're doing this, but the curiosity is killing me. So spill. Where are we going and what do you want to talk to me about?'

He wasn't going to spoil the surprise about meeting Zara's parents, but he did want to give her the heads-up about his dad coming. He'd debated whether to wait and tell her where they were going when his dad arrived, but decided against it. One shock at a time would be enough.

'What would you say if I told you we were going to Vegas?' he asked, full of enthusiasm and hoping she would have the same reaction.

She didn't.

His job had taught him how to read people and right now he was reading a whole range of emotions on her face. Confusion. Disappointment. Deflation. And something else that he couldn't quite put his finger on. Maybe disapproval? Or alarm? But typical Mom, she didn't vocalise any of that. Instead, she went for, 'I'd say that I'll have a good time anywhere because I'm getting the chance to hang out with you.'

Okay. Not great, but he'd take it.

'Have you been before? I've never heard you mention it.'

Of course, after his conversations with Zara and Millie, he already knew the answer to that question, but he didn't want to give that away and spoil his other surprise.

'Once. A long time ago.'

'Did you love it?'

'It was... different.'

Shit. She really wasn't going for this idea. He felt himself beginning to experience a slight cold prickle of dread. Maybe he'd misjudged this whole situation. Maybe there was a reason she'd never mentioned that she'd been to Vegas or expressed any desire to return. Perhaps Trevon was right and this was a really bad move. And he still hadn't told her his dad was coming. Tell her now. Tell her. Just say the words. Or... maybe just ease into it a little more with casual conversation and a slice of avoidance.

'Different how?'

She brushed off the question. 'Oh, it was a million years ago. Back when I didn't need to dye my hair to cover the grey. It was the first time I'd ever been to America, and it was only supposed to be for a holiday, but I never left.'

'I'm pretty glad about that,' he said. That information was new to him though, and for the first time, he realised that he had no idea why or exactly when his parents came to this country. All he knew was that they'd been in their early twenties, and he'd assumed that they'd come from Scotland for work because he remembered them telling him that back in Scotland his dad was a DJ and his mom had worked in a club. However, if they'd originally landed in Vegas, then how had they ended up in South Carolina? Why hadn't they stayed in Vegas, where there were plenty of jobs in the hospitality and tourism industry for young people? Why had they remained in the USA, yet their friends, Zara's parents, had gone home? And why had he never asked any of this before? He realised that these were all questions he should know the answer to, but now probably wasn't the best time to drill down into his family history. Not when he was still working up to telling her about their travel companion. First things first. He had to make sure that she would get on the plane, before revealing the little nugget of turbulence that he was adding to the occasion.

'So, are you good with this?' he checked. 'I've never been either, so I'm totally up for experiencing it for the first time with you.'

She took a sip of her drink, then flashed a smile. 'How could I possibly refuse you? Yep, I'm up for it. Let's do it.'

He saw her shoulders drop, as if she was relaxing, and he knew it was going to be okay. At least until she went on...

'It'll be cool for me to experience it properly too. Last time I was there I was with your dad, and not to speak ill of fools, but you know... I'm glad I'll be in better company this time.'

Oh crap. He had to tell her, and it had to be now because when his dad arrived he was going to have to do some explaining to him too. Best to tackle them one at a time, and do it now. He could wait until they were through security for this little reveal, but that was way too shady. If they both agreed to come after they found out all the facts, it had to be of their own free will and with the best intentions – not because federal law restricted their right to backtrack through security to the freedom of the outside world.

'Actually, Mom, that was the other thing I wanted to talk to you about. You see, I had this crazy idea that—'

'Aiden?' A booming voice from behind him cut him off and two things happened at once. His dad thumped his back in greeting and his mum visibly paled.

'What the...?' was all she got out, before his dad's gaze went to Aiden's right and he realised that the blonde sitting next to his son was his ex-wife.

Now he had two parents, frozen in time, staring at each other, then slowly, ominously, both moving their steely gaze to settle squarely on him.

'Aiden...?' his mum started, but obviously too slowly for his father, who cut her off with, 'Do you want to tell us what the fuck is going on?'

12

EILEEN

For once, she was on the same side as her ex-husband and that wasn't a place she ever wanted to be. Eileen couldn't remember being this pissed off with her son since the day that he had wrecked her car as a teenager. Even then, he had the excuse of youth and immaturity. What was his bloody excuse now?

'Okay, bear with me and let me explain,' he said, two hands held up in surrender.

'Did you know about this?' she demanded of Gary the Gob, who, in fairness, was uncharacteristically short on words and giving a good impression of someone who had absolutely no idea what was going on.

'Not at all,' he said, his Scottish accent the one of their early years together, before he'd become Gary Transatlantic and adopted an American twang and several thirty-something girlfriends. He wasn't exactly in Leonardo DiCaprio territory, but he was close.

Eileen believed him and turned her steely gaze back to Aiden.

'This had better be good, son,' she warned, in a voice that she hadn't used with him since somewhere between puberty and graduation.

'It is, I promise,' he countered, then took a slug of his beer for fortification. 'Right, here it is. At my wedding... by the way, am I too late to play the sympathy card? You know, the jilted at the altar, life left in ruins, one?'

'Way too late,' Eileen told him, unwavering in her demand for some kind of reasonable excuse for putting her in this position.

'Thought so. All right, so at my wedding, before the whole desertion-broken-heart bit, I was bugged by the fact that you two don't get along.'

'There are good reasons for that,' Eileen heard herself say and she wasn't proud, but it was the truth.

Still, Gary the Gob was keeping that gob shut. And was it just her, or had it suddenly got really hot in here? If she had a heart attack brought on by unexpected exposure to an ex-husband, she was going to be even more raging than she was now. She had just about managed to stomach that they were going to Vegas and that she'd be setting foot in that city thirty years after she last went there, but to be going with her bloody lump of an ex in tow? No. No way. She loved her son, but this was too much.

'I don't doubt that, Mom. I know you both have your reasons. But the thing is, they're nothing to do with me...'

'Exactly!' she agreed, then realised that he wasn't finished.

'Yet I'm the one who always has to deal with it.'

Oh.

He was on a roll now.

'It's a nightmare. My wedding was supposed to be the happiest day of my life, until, you know... the bit where she didn't show. And all I was worried about was whether you two were going to get in a fight, or ignore each other all day, or just generally hate every minute of it because you were both in the same place at the same time. It's an impossible situation to be in.'

Eileen felt a minor twinge of guilt. She could see what he was saying, and she hadn't realised it had affected him quite as much as it clearly had. They'd divorced after he left for college, so he'd never actually lived with them as two single people, or – maybe more accurately – two warring factions. He'd just got on with his life and split his time, his birthdays, his Christmas, between the two of them and he'd done it all without complaint, so she'd had no idea that their aversion to each other bothered him.

'And the thing is...' He was still going and Eileen could see the cool, articulate professional lawyer coming out in him. No wonder he was so good at his job. 'It made me think about the future and the fact that if we don't change something, then it's always going to be like this.'

The bar was filling up now and she was embarrassingly aware that the couple at the next table were listening in on their conversation, riveted to the drama.

'How's that going to look? If I ever get someone to actually show up when they're supposed to be marrying me...'

Ouch, that stung.

'And if we have kids, then what's that going to be like? Every family event and occasion, are we going to have to deal with you two avoiding each other and throwing daggers across the room? *Sorry, honey, you can't have both Grandma and Grandad at your fifth birthday, because your friends might get in the way of their passive-aggressive disdain for each other?* I'm not having it, so you two need to sort it out and get over it.'

Eileen still resolutely stared straight ahead, but in her peripheral vision she could see Gary glance at her with an edge of uncertainty in that way too handsome face. If only he didn't look like that, his life would have been very different. There was no way he'd have got the attention that followed him everywhere if he didn't give off 'older but still irresistibly attractive dad in a romcom' vibes.

That thought, however, was being pushed out of the way by her son's very pertinent and beautifully articulated point. She felt a wave of guilt make her flush in a way that hadn't happened since the menopause. Or perhaps she'd just downed her gin and tonic too quickly? No, it was definitely guilt. And a little bit of shame thrown in for good measure.

'Do I need to keep going, because I was only at my imaginary kid's fifth birthday. I have a whole load more birthdays, first days at school, proms and graduations still to pull out of the bag.'

Eileen sighed. 'Dear God, no, make it stop. We hear you. And I don't know about your father...'

Aiden gestured to his dad. 'He's right there – you can include him in the conversation.'

'Baby steps, son. Don't push it,' she cautioned him. He might have a point, but she wasn't going to back down completely just yet. 'I was going to say, I don't know about your father, but for my part in this, I apologise. I suppose I hadn't really thought about it from your perspective because you were already an adult when we split, and you've never shown that it bothered you before now.'

Eileen had a small suspicion that he was slightly milking it, but at the end of the day, he was right. Also, it was more than a little embarrassing that he was, in effect, pointing out that the only adult in this conversation was the one she'd given birth to.

'But I can see what you're saying. Much as it pains me. Although there might have been better ways to handle this. You know, maybe a coffee in a random Starbucks. Or a walk in the park.' She wasn't letting him off too easy. 'Five days in Vegas could be construed by some as being a tad excessive.'

'We're going to Vegas? Shit, if you'd told me that I'd have brought better suits,' was her ex-husband's intellectual, erudite response.

'If it helps, we're staying at the Bellagio. And yes, I realise I'm trying to sway you with that.'

It wasn't working. Eileen really needed another gin and tonic. Vegas. This was all kinds of wrong. Their history with that place. Everything that had happened there. The effects that it had had on their relationship and on...

Nope. Not going back there. What mattered was that it was probably the worst place on earth that Aiden could have chosen to reunite his parents. Especially as one of them would undoubtedly run wild and spend the whole five days in casinos and clubs, trying to recapture his youth with women who'd yet to experience the joys of a hot flush or a stretch mark. Yep, even in her head that sounded toe-curlingly bitter. Time for an internal pep talk. *Come on, Eileen, you're better than this.*

'Okay,' she said.

The couple at the next table gave away their serial eavesdropping when her agreement elicited simultaneous air punches and a silently mouthed, 'Yes!' She chose to ignore it.

'Okay?' Aiden asked uncertainly.

'Okay. I'll come, and I'll make an effort, because you're right. Life is long, we're a family and it's not your fault that your dad is a tit.'

Her son shook his head, but she could see he was trying to contain a smile. Gary, not so much.

'And it's not his fault that his mother is a smart-mouthed, unreasonable git either,' her ex threw in for good measure.

Aiden resorted to more beer. 'It was going well for about five seconds there,' he chided them. His exasperation was clear, so she stepped in with a conciliatory gesture.

'I'm sorry. Please apologise to my future imaginary grandchildren for that momentary lapse. I'll try not to let it happen again. Like I said, I'll come to Vegas and I'll make an effort. And so will your father. Won't you, Gary?'

For the first time since they'd arrived, she let her gaze sit on her ex-husband and read his face and, to her surprise, she saw what looked like genuine happiness there. Although, that was probably the Vegas thing. He was easily swayed by hedonistic endeavours.

'Yeah, I'll go with it. We'll make it work.' He met her eyes and they came to an unspoken agreement. This wasn't about them – this was about their son and his happiness, so it was time to put all the bullshit to one side, let bygones be bygones and sort their issues out, at least on the surface. Gary held out his hand. 'Deal?'

The gesture threw her, and she hesitated. The first time she'd touched this man, she'd felt an irresistible pull that that been almost visceral, an electricity that had set every cell in her body on fire. The last time she'd touched him, she'd felt nothing but pain and disgust as she'd punched him square in the face for breaking her heart.

Realising this was a 'put up or shut up' moment, and her son was watching, she forced herself to respond and shook his hand. This time she felt... confused. Angry. Cornered. But something else too. Hopeful? Relieved? It had been so long since she'd dipped into any kind of emotional place with her ex, that she was wasn't quite sure.

'Is it wrong that I want to order champagne and celebrate this moment?' Aiden joked, but Eileen could hear the relief in his voice and she was glad. He'd obviously put a lot of thought into this and his intentions undoubtedly came from a good place and a need to make this situation better for all of them, so she wasn't going to spoil it.

'I'll have some of that, but let's go check in first before I change my mind,' she said, grinning. She needed to walk, to think, to come to terms with this moment and shore up her inner resources to deal with it. She'd spent the last ten years hating Gary, and that had been a comfortable place for her. It had allowed her to shut down her emotions, to close off any part of herself that could be vulnerable. Now Aiden was asking her to take the lock off the door and let his father in, just a little bit. Problem was, she wasn't sure how to do that or how far the door should open.

They picked up their bags and climbed off their chairs, and to her surprise, just like countless trips before this one, Gary automatically reached for her suitcase and began to pull it.

'Hey!' She put her hand out and stopped him. 'I can get my own case.' As soon as it was out, she heard how churlish that sounded, so she immediately followed it up with a more conciliatory, 'But you can buy the champagne when we get through security.' She accessorised that one with a smile and heard a sigh of relief from Aiden.

As they walked towards the check-in desk, Eileen pulling her own case, she nudged Aiden with her shoulder.

'Well played, son. But just promise me something...'

He threw his arm round her shoulder. 'Anything, Maw.'

'Promise me there's no more surprises.'

'Only good ones, Maw. Only good ones.'

She had no idea why, but she had an eerie feeling that might not be true.

13

ZARA

Las Vegas. Sin City. Zara had spent the whole, chaotic, horn-beeping, music-blaring, traffic-crunching, incredibly slow, thirty-minute ride from the airport with her eyes wide, taking in the sights and sounds of a city that was like nothing she'd ever seen. It was like an out-of-body experience and, right now, that body was on the set of *Ocean's Eleven* and delighted to be there.

Millie's wide smile and twinkly eyes left Zara in absolutely no doubt that her sister was waiting for George Clooney and Brad Pitt to wander past at any moment too.

Her mum and dad, however, were... she struggled to pin down the word. Underwhelmed? Uneasy? Especially her mum. Zara knew her well enough to see underneath the veneer of her fixed smile and fake enthusiasm and she just didn't get it. Maybe she was still tired. Yep, that must be it.

The limo dropped them at the reception on the ground floor at the back of Planet Hollywood, and they checked in using an interactive machine in a lobby that was busy with a crowd that was a bizarre cross between Primark and Prada on the first day of the January sales, only with more sequins and bigger hair.

After three false starts and the firm conviction that they'd be lost forever, wandering between the casino tables and the restaurants on the ground floor of Planet Hollywood until the end of time, they found the lifts and made it to their rooms on the thirty-fourth floor of the hotel. Zara and Millie went to their parents' suite first.

'Swanky,' Millie commented, scanning the huge king bed, with the grey padded headboard, and the punkish artwork on the wall above it. There was a barn-style sliding door into the huge white marble bathroom, with a shower that had more bits on it than Zara's car. There was also a gorgeous fruit basket and an anniversary congratulations card, as per Zara's request. But it was when she threw open the curtains, they all gasped. The Bellagio fountains were directly ahead and in full flow and, wow, it was a breathtaking sight. As the four of them stood watching, Zara spotted a tear running down her mum's cheek and leant over to give her a hug. Finally! Tears of happiness.

'Does it feel different from last time, Mum?' Millie asked.

'Completely. Last time we were so... young. We stayed in a hotel off the strip. I couldn't even tell you where now.'

Zara decided to chance some curiosity.

'Was it just the two of you?' The photo Zara had found at the bottom of Mum's old box of photos had been the only clue that they weren't alone, but that was because, as far as Zara could remember, neither of their parents had ever talked about their wedding, or their time here, other than to say this was where they'd got married. End of story.

Their dad got in first with the answer. 'No, we had a couple of, erm, friends with us.'

'Really? Who? And what happened to them?' Millie was pushing it, but Zara was intrigued to see what they said.

'Och, they were just pals we knew back then,' their dad shrugged. 'No idea what happened to them. It was such a long time ago.'

Zara exhaled. For a horrible moment, she'd had a fear that he was going to say there was some big fall-out. She should perhaps have considered that a little more deeply before now, but other than one passing conversation with Millie, it hadn't crossed her mind, probably because her parents hadn't had a single disagreement with anyone in living memory.

'Right, why don't you get showered and freshen up and we'll go next door and do the same.' She checked her watch. It went without saying that her body was confused, given that it had left Glasgow a million hours ago, and yet now they were in Vegas and thanks to the eight-hour time difference, it was only mid-afternoon. 'Let's say, meet here at five o'clock. That gives us a couple of hours if you want a nap, Dad.'

'I could definitely do with that. Quick forty winks, eh, Brenda?'

'Sounds fine.' Their mum hugged each of the girls in turn. 'And thank you both so much for this. It's an amazing gift and we're so lucky to have you,' she said, reinforcing what she'd told them on the plane.

Zara gave her a squeeze and decided to stop worrying. It was ridiculous. Of course her mum was happy. Just because she wasn't doing cartwheels across the room didn't mean that anything was wrong. Positive outlook. It was great. Grand. Smashing.

They were only in their own room for ten seconds when her resolve snapped. 'Do you think Mum's okay?'

Millie had already flopped on the bed and now she was rolling over and picking up the handset on the phone. She put her hand up to shush Zara. 'Hello? Yes, this is room 34056. Can we have a bottle of Prosecco please? And cake. What kind do you have?' A pause. 'Yes! Two of those. Thank you.' She replaced the handset and pushed herself up on one elbow to contemplate Zara's question. 'You know, normally I'm an emotional vacuum and I'd completely miss any hint of a problem unless it was pasted on a billboard outside my window...'

Over on the other bed, that made Zara grin, mostly because it was absolutely true.

'...But even I can see that something's a bit off. Look, it's Mum. She's the most low-key, understated person we know and she hates being the centre of attention. A bit like myself,' she added, with her perfectly outlined pout, while fluffing up her fake lashes and then bending over to pull off the Prada boots that had cost her a month's salary. 'It'll just take her a minute to get used to this and then she'll be great. I'm sure of it. They're probably next door right now having wild, wanton sex and recapturing their youth.'

'That's a mental image I could probably do without, but thanks, Mills.' Occasionally her sister's endless optimism and aversion to fretting came in handy, while her ability to brush things off was a masterclass in emotional positivity.

Millie was already over the conversation and had picked up the remote control to switch on the TV. In seconds, she'd located her happy place with *The Real Housewives of Beverly Hills* and was lost to the real world.

Zara checked her phone. There was one text message from Aiden that was just pinging in now that she'd connected to Wi-Fi. Bugger. She'd forgotten to switch on her data roaming.

Hope you had good flight. About to take off. Both parents on board. It was touch-and-go for a minute but deployed full-scale guilt to get them here. Will text you when we land. Ax

She felt a flurry of excitement that went straight from the pit of her stomach to her cheekbones and made her grin. This was going to be great. Amazing. Time to bin the doubts and just focus on how brilliant it was going to be.

Pushing herself off the bed, she pulled up her suitcase and began unpacking. Millie would live out of her case but Zara liked things to be organised. The first thing she did was open the folded-over suit-carrier, take out Gran's dress and hang it up, sending up her usual, silent, 'Wish you were here, Gran,' to the heavens, just in case Ada was watching. Zara chose to believe that she was. Her gran was the type of woman who would hang out of her window to get a good view of any drama, so there was no way she was missing this.

The doorbell rang, and Zara was the closest, letting in the room service waiter, laden with wine and cake. She signed the check, then fished a ten-dollar bill out of her back pocket and handed it over, hoping that was enough. She was one of those people who over-tipped everywhere because she didn't want anyone to think she didn't appreciate them. The waiter didn't seem offended and closed the door behind him without slamming it, so she figured that was a good sign.

She poured two glasses of vino and handed one over to Millie, who managed to take it without even looking up. On the TV, the housewives were in full-scale screech mode over some perceived slight, and Millie was engrossed, even as she mused, 'Do you ever think you want a life like that?'

Zara climbed on to the bed beside her sister. 'Like what?'

'Like that,' Millie gestured to the TV.

'What, fighting with all my pals and spending obscene amounts of money on clothes and handbags, while struggling to form an expression because my entire face is pumped full of Botox and fillers?'

'Exactly that,' Millie replied, with almost religious reverence.

Zara popped a spoonful of red velvet cheesecake in her mouth, then had to wait until she swallowed before she could speak and... oh dear lord, that tasted amazing. 'Nope. Can't think of anything worse. Tell me you wouldn't want to leave the life we have and live like that instead.'

Millie shrugged, made a weird face.

'Millie! Honestly?'

'Not that, exactly. But, Zar, don't you ever think there's more to life than what we do? I mean, it's great and all, but I don't want to arrange flowers for the rest of my life.'

If Clooney and Pitt wandered out of their bathroom right now, Zara wouldn't have been any more astonished. She'd never seriously considered that Millie wouldn't want to keep on doing what they did now. They had a lovely life. Great jobs. Earned a decent living. And they got to do all that with each other. She'd never really thought about it, but she just assumed that they'd always do this, perhaps even expand the business, maybe open another shop or two eventually. Clearly that wasn't Millie's vision.

'Oh no,' Millie drawled, and Zara saw she'd finally dragged her eyes from the TV and was looking at her. 'I've never said that out loud before, have I?'

Zara put her spoon down, suddenly not feeling much like cake. 'No. I mean, I didn't know you'd even considered doing something else. Have you got plans? Is there something you want to tell me?' Her voice was a few notes higher than normal, but she couldn't help it.

Millie rushed to object. 'No! No! Definitely not...'

Okay, that restarted her cardiovascular system and let her breathe again, until Millie added a sheepish, 'Although... maybe?'

Zara just stared at her, open-mouthed, until Millie buckled and spilled.

'I don't mean I want to leave right now. I just think... Look, it's right for you. You're good with boredom...'

'Millie!'

'Sorry, I didn't mean it like that. I just meant that you don't like change. Adventure. Crazy shit. But I do. I'm happy with what we're doing just now but I don't want to do it forever.'

Zara tried to get her head around that. 'So, you mean like some time in the future you'll maybe want to try something else. Not in the immediate future?'

'No, of course not. Definitely far in the future. A long way off. Ages away.'

Okay, so she wasn't saying she was leaving her right now. Huge relief. But... Zara couldn't leave it alone. She had to know.

'So when, roughly, are you thinking? When's ages away?'

Millie shrugged. 'It depends.'

'On what?'

'On whether you want me to lie or be honest.'

Oh. Bollocks.

'Honest.'

Millie shrugged apologetically and pushed the words out like she was delivering the worst news ever. Which she bloody well was. 'Maybe next year?'

Zara couldn't speak. Thankfully, she was saved from having to find a way to form words by the ping of an incoming text on her phone.

Aiden.

Landed. On way to hotel now. What's the plan?

14

BRENDA

It had almost been a relief when the girls left and – for the first time since the minivan had picked them up at the house this morning, Brenda could breathe. Las bloody Vegas. Never in a million years would she have guessed that the girls were planning this and if she had, she would have stopped them. What a waste of money. Worse than that, she felt like such a complete fraud. She eyed the king-size bed, and it wasn't lost on her that this should be a time of excitement and maybe a bit of naughtiness in Sin City. She wasn't feeling either of those things.

She sat on the edge of the bed. 'Colin, we have to tell them. We can't keep doing this.'

'Doing what?' he asked, going over all the touchable objects with an anti-bacterial wipe. He'd always done that. As soon as they got into any hotel room, out would come the wet wipes, and he'd be off, cleaning away, protecting them from germ-induced certain death. He once spent a whole hour disinfecting a Blackpool hotel room, only for the front desk to call up and tell them they were in the wrong room and had to move, so he had to do it all over again. It wasn't a compulsion – he wasn't in the least bit bothered about stuff like that at home. No, it was just a habit. Like the fact that he had a single Scotch after dinner most nights, smoked a pipe in his shed or only ever listened to Radio 2. It had never irritated her more than it did right now. Even when the little nurse angel on one shoulder told her it was a valiant step in the eternal war against bacteria, the little wife angel on her other shoulder wanted to set fire to his wet wipes.

'Letting them think that everything is fine,' she answered his question with a touch of exasperation. 'That *we're* fine. The girls have brought us all this way to celebrate our anniversary. Doesn't that seem so wrong to you? Not just the money they must have spent, but also all the thought that's gone into this.'

He finally stopped bloody cleaning. 'Honestly, no, Brenda, it doesn't. It seems kind. Thoughtful. Like something you would do for the people you love.'

Urgh, now he was making her feel even worse. She could see there was a touch of gaslighting going on here, and that she should probably just ignore him, but for once, her emotions got the best of her.

'I bloody know that! And I agree on all those things, but that isn't the point. Have you forgotten our conversation a couple of weeks ago? Colin, we're here and making a pretence of celebrating a marriage that's on its last bloody legs.' She hoped the walls in this place weren't too thin, because she'd be mortified if the girls next door could hear this.

He popped the cap back on his wipes. 'I thought we were giving it a go. Getting things back on track? I mean, last week we had...'

Brenda closed her eyes. 'Please don't say sex.'

'I wasn't going to,' he countered. She breathed a sigh of relief, until he added, 'I was going to say "great sex".'

He topped that off with a wink and Brenda wondered how long she'd have to bang her head against the wall until she was rendered unconscious.

If anything, his relentless and unequivocal optimism were just making her feel weary now. She didn't want to fight. It went against every grain of her non-confrontational, drama-avoiding soul and the anxiety of it made her sweat.

She rallied and came back with a more conciliatory tone. 'Colin, we shouldn't be here. It feels dishonest. And, let's face it, we don't have the best memories in this city.' She didn't have to spell it out. They both knew what had happened here and they'd both chosen never to discuss it.

His sigh made his shoulders sag. 'What's dishonest is acting like we haven't had a good marriage all these years.'

'I never said that!' she objected. Why couldn't he hear her? 'We were happy. I admit that, Colin, but people change. They grow. And we've grown apart.'

'But you're the only one who thinks so,' he argued. He even did that calmly. Passive-aggressive bickering. That's what they were both reduced to now. Brenda wasn't sure whether it was making her loathe him or herself more.

This was pointless. She went into the bathroom, locked the door, turned the taps on in the bath and then sat on the toilet and FaceTimed Bernadette. It was almost 11 p.m. at home, but Brenda and Bernadette shared the same rota, so she knew her pal would only have got home a little while ago, and she'd be showered, pyjamas on, and lying on the sofa with a coffee in hand. If they'd had a particularly challenging shift, they often spoke after they got home, no matter the hour. It was their way of processing. Of decompressing. Of supporting each other. This wasn't a life-or-death situation, but Brenda could do with hearing her pal's dulcet tones right about now. She was relieved when Bernadette answered on the second ring.

'I was hoping you'd call! Well? Was it London? Are you in some flash suite in the Savoy that's going to make me unbearably jealous?'

'It's not London.'

'Hang on, hang on, let me guess. That looks like a marble bathroom, so it's definitely flash. Paris? Monaco?'

'I'm running a bath and I'll have flooded the room by the time you get the right answer, so I'm going to have to tell you. It's Vegas. I'm in Las bloody Vegas.'

Bernadette's jaw dropped. 'And that isn't a good thing?' she asked weakly, sensing Brenda's displeasure and reacting with understandable surprise and confusion.

Brenda got it. To most people, this would be an absolute dream. Or at the very least a brilliant adventure. But those people hadn't been here before. Now that she was looking at Bernadette's raised eyebrows of puzzlement, she realised that she'd never told her friend what had happened here. Once again, the whole 'what happens in Vegas stays in Vegas' thing had never been more apt.

She was desperate to tell her pal the full story, but not only would the bath be stone cold by the time she'd finished, but she also didn't want to risk Colin overhearing her. Things were bad enough.

'This is where we got married...'

'No way! Why do I not know that?'

'It's a long story,' Brenda sighed. 'And not one I ever want to tell. But the girls knew and now they are so thrilled because they think they've done something wonderful by bringing us here to celebrate our anniversary.'

Bernadette was catching on now. 'Oh sweet Jesus. You still haven't told them?'

'I can't, Bernadette. It's bad enough that I've told Colin several times, and he doesn't want to hear it. Or accept it. I don't know. I just broached it with him and he reminded me that we had great sex last week.'

'Oh my God, did you?'

'No! My nightdress and my slippers were on the whole time. How great could it have been? My mules barely trembled.'

'Oh, Brenda, I... I... that's... I mean... that's...'

At first, Brenda thought the Wi-Fi was playing up, then she clocked on that the disruption to Bernadette's speech was caused by her friend trying desperately to control the urge to laugh.

And it was utterly contagious. Before she could even think about it, Brenda was creased over, absolutely howling with giggles. Tears began streaming down her cheeks, she was gasping for air, and there were points where she didn't know if she was laughing or crying. Laughing. Definitely laughing. But with a dash of hysteria thrown in.

She barely heard the knock at the door. 'Brenda, are you okay in there?'

That sobered her up. 'Yes, I'm fine. I'm just on the phone to Bernadette. She was telling me a joke.'

That set the two of them off again.

'Ah Bernadette, you've no idea how much I needed that,' she spluttered, when she regained the power of speech.

'Me too, pet. I know we're laughing, but I feel for you, I really do.

Keeping up any kind of pretence is tough.' Bernadette knew that more than anyone. She'd stayed in a marriage with a controlling arse for decades, while pretending to the world that she was happy. That took guts. And then it took more guts to leave him. 'You know you can call me any time if you just need to chat, or to let off steam.'

'Thank you. I'll take you up on that.'

'Good. So what's your plan for the rest of the trip then?'

Brenda turned the taps off and dipped her toes in the water. It was perfect.

'I'm going to pretend I'm having a great time and make the best of it. I think the girls have got some sightseeing planned and maybe a couple of shows. I saw an open-top bus on the way here, so I might give that a shot to kill a couple of hours. I mean, in this heat it'll probably kill me, but that might be a mercy. Death by open-top bus.'

'Glad you're being so reasonable about this,' Bernadette matched her joking tone.

'Absolutely. Only thing for it. I just need to go with the flow.'

'I think that's the best plan, I really do. But can I just ask one thing, Brenda?'

'Of course. Anything.'

'If those mules get a tremble, can I be the first to know?'

'I'm hanging up now.' Brenda ended the call with a chuckle.

After stripping off, she climbed into the bath and rested her head against the cool white surface, letting the memories that had been biting at her all day ease their way into her mind. She'd been twenty-five last time she'd been here. And Colin wasn't being completely honest when he'd dismissed the couple they'd been with as just old friends that they'd lost touch with. There had been so much more to it all than that.

Eileen Smith. Gary Gregg.

The four of them had been inseparable. Joined at the hip. They'd met a few years before, when they all worked together at the Beat House, a night-club in Glasgow's city centre. Gary was the DJ, Eileen worked in the ticket booth, taking people's cash as they came in the door, Colin and Brenda both worked behind the bar. Initially, for them, it was an extra job to supplement their student grants while he was at Glasgow uni studying to be an accountant and she was in her second year at the College of Nursing. But even after they'd graduated and started working, they still kept their club jobs for extra cash.

Brenda closed her eyes and she could see a snapshot of the four of them when they first formed their little clique of four. Gary was a couple of years older than them, and so tall and handsome that half the girls in the Beat House would make doe eyes at him while he was up there blasting out the latest Simple Minds or Duran Duran tune. And oh, Gary knew it. He loved the attention, lapped it up, dancing in the DJ booth with his white vest and his shirt over the top of it, tucked in to his acid-wash jeans, his dark hair barely moving because he had a fringe flick that was solidified by half a can of hairspray before he climbed up on to the stage at night.

Colin was shorter, but he had his fans too. He wore little round John Lennon glasses and came across as the smart guy that he was. Kind, too. If there was a crisis – and there was at least one a night in the club – then Colin was the one with the cool head that went out of his way to make sure everyone was okay. And he noticed things. When Brenda had got her first perm, the one that was the size of a beachball, he'd told her it looked great and she would be a shoo-in if they ever needed a fourth member of Bananarama.

Eileen was the last to join the gang, but it felt like she'd always been there. Brenda had adored her on sight. This gorgeous tall blonde, who had no idea how pretty she was so she was always getting into relationships that were wrong for her.

The four of them had formed a merry band. What was it that they called it these days? A framily. Yep, that's what they were – a framily that stuck together for the next few years, a clique that laughed, that lifted each other up, that swore they'd be friends for ever... Until they weren't. Ouch, that still stung.

The last time she saw Eileen Smith was right here in this city, in a hotel not too far away. In the horror of that moment, Brenda had told her that she never wanted to set eyes on her again as long as she lived.

Now, back there in her mind, Brenda felt her chest tighten and her brow furrow and she realised that sentiment hadn't changed.

15

AIDEN

The check-in process at the Bellagio was pretty seamless and Aiden had spent most of the time at the desk scanning the reception area in wonderment at the absolutely over-the-top spectacle of it all. A massive multicoloured glass sculpture hung from the ceiling in the centre area of the lobby, above marble floors and walls embellished with ornate gold décor. The whole place looked like a kaleidoscopic acid trip for people with buckets of money to spend.

If he'd been travelling on his own, he'd probably have gone for somewhere like the Aria or the Cosmopolitan, a bit less ostentatious than the most grandiose hotel on the strip, but he was cognisant of his audience. His dad liked everything flash and larger than life, while his mum liked classy with a large slice of glam. This suited them both and maybe went a small way to making up for all the duplicity and subterfuge required to get them here. Besides, he'd managed to wangle a full refund for his honeymoon to the Bahamas, so he was cool about spending that money and a bit extra for them all to stay somewhere iconic. Maybe – even before she realised the true purpose of the trip – his mum would forgive him if she saw the effort he'd put in to make this truly special. Although, he wasn't betting on it. She'd been perfectly nice on the five-hour flight here, but she was also quiet, with an undertone of low-key, well-concealed fury.

About halfway into the flight, so probably somewhere above Okla-
homa, his dad had gone to the loos, so he'd leaned over to his mom. 'On a
scale of one to ten, how mad are you at me right now?'

She'd sighed, and he could see the resignation in her face. 'Much as I
love you, probably a solid eight. This is going to cost you a sensational
Mother's Day present next year.'

The fact that she was still joking gave him hope. It also made him feel
absolutely crap.

'I know, and I'm sorry. I promise it was done with the best intentions.
Maybe it won't be so bad,' he'd said hopefully. 'It might even give you two a
chance to start building a friendship.'

'I get that. I guess I was just looking forward to a trip with just me and
you. We haven't done that in years. It'll take me a minute to get my head
around the new plan, but it'll be fine, don't worry.'

He'd spent the next two and a half hours feeling smaller than the
packet of pretzels that came with his beer. It wasn't helped when his dad
sat back down on the other side of him, leaned in and said, 'Good move,
son. If your mom calls it a night early, I'm up for hitting a couple of clubs.'

The man didn't help himself, he really didn't.

Fear that he'd say something else stupid had made the flight feel twice
as long as it actually was, so now it was a relief to have checked in and be
heading for their rooms.

As he'd requested, they were all on the tenth floor, overlooking the
fountains. Aiden and his dad were sharing a queen suite with two double
beds and a sitting area, while his mom was next door in a king suite.

'I'm just going to grab a quick shower,' his mom said, when they got to
their doors.

'Want some company, Eileen?' his dad offered, thinking he was
hilarious.

His mom delivered a deadpan retort of, 'Not even if I were drowning
and you were the only one that could save me.'

Aiden was pretty sure he could feel his inner soul curl up and wish for
a quick death.

In the room, he rounded on his dad. 'What are you doing? Are you
trying to provoke Mom, or have you just generally lost your mind?'

Before he got an answer, the doorbell went, and he let in the concierge, who had brought up their suitcases.

His dad went to the minibar, pulled out two beers and tossed one to him.

Aiden tipped the bellman and then went back to his original question. 'Well?'

His dad put his hands up. 'Look, I know. I get it. I hear this stuff coming out of my mouth and I want to punch myself in the face, I really do.'

Aiden sat down on the orange velvet bucket seat by the window and put his feet on the matching footstool. 'Why do you do it, then? Because honestly, Dad, it's not landing well with Mom, and nothing is getting better while you're coming out with crap like that.'

He felt bad going in on his dad like this, but it was warranted. If his mum called it quits and left early because she couldn't put up with his nonsense, then they'd have achieved nothing and the whole purpose of the trip would be blown.

'I think...' His dad went quiet and for a moment Aiden thought he was going to come out with some profound theory of self-reflection. 'I'm just trying to make her laugh.'

'Really? Because I'm pretty sure she isn't next door splitting her sides right now.'

His dad lay back on the bed, one arm behind his head, his beer balancing on his taut abdomen. Aiden had no desire to inherit his pop's sense of humour, or his self-awareness, but he wouldn't mind his abs.

'She used to find me funny. Back then. Before the divorce. And don't even say it, because I know that was on me too.'

'What was? What actually happened? You've never told me and I guess I didn't want to rock the boat by asking.' Aiden couldn't contain the urge to understand the details of their split. Sure, he knew there were allegations of infidelity, but nothing had been confirmed and he'd never learned the ultimate reason behind his parents' divorce. They'd just shown up at college at spring break, sat him down and said they were calling time on their marriage. Irreconcilable differences, they'd said. When he'd tried to delve deeper, his mum had just insisted that they'd grown apart and that was all she'd ever said about it. He respected that she didn't want to bad-mouth his father to him, or force him to take sides, but at the same time, it would help him to broker a resolution to the cold war between them if he actually knew the specifics. His dad wasn't for giving them up then or now though.

'We were going through a rough patch, I didn't handle it well, did something that I shouldn't have and that's all I'll say about it. But that was almost ten years ago and I'm still paying for it. I guess I think that if I come out with the stuff that used to amuse her, then maybe there's a chance—'

Woah. What? Aiden sat forward in his chair. 'A chance of what, Dad? Are you saying you want you and Mum to get back together?'

Shit, this couldn't be true. His dad had positively embraced single life. There had been the holidays, the flash cars, the long stream of girlfriends twenty years younger. He had never given the slightest hint that he regretted his divorce. In fact, the opposite. He acted like it was the best thing that ever happened to him.

His dad shrugged. 'No! At least... no. I don't think so. Okay, maybe. Sometimes. Yes. Making a right arse of it though.'

'No arguments here. What about Mitzy?'

'Yeah, she's great, but come on... do you think she'd be with me if I had zero in the bank? I'm not naïve, son.'

'So why stay with her then? Why not look for someone who loves you, not the lifestyle?'

'She keeps me young and shallow as it is, I like having a beauty on my arm. Mitzy certainly gets us noticed and if I'm not with your mum...' he let that trail off, with a shrug. 'Look, son, I've no idea what I'm doing. There's this fallacy that you get to my age and you have it all sussed out. Utter bollocks. Your mum cut me dead after the divorce, so, yeah, like a right tit, I've probably been trying to get her attention. The jokes. The women...'

'That was to make her jealous?'

'No, not at first. That was just to have a good time, see what I'd been missing. But, son, it's a shitshow out there. Do you know the effort it takes to keep all that dating stuff going? I mean, it's all fun and games at the start, but then it's serious work. Sometimes I just wish I could go back to being married and settled and... you know, maybe go a couple of nights without having to go to the gym and batter this old body into any kind of shape.'

'You're not old. You're two years younger than Brad Pitt.'

'Yeah, and he should have stayed with Jennifer Aniston. Look at the royal cock-up he's made of things. There's a lesson in that. Just wish I'd learned it.'

Aiden had never seriously considered the possibility of his mum and dad getting back together – a ceasefire had been the most he'd hoped for. But maybe... Nope, he wasn't getting his hopes up and he wasn't interfering. At least, no more than a bit of unsolicited advice.

'You know, Dad, if you really do want any hope of reconciling with Mom, first thing you'd have to do is drop all the other women, drop the fake jokes and the big gestures and just be consistent, be real.'

'Be boring?'

'Nope, not what I said.'

'Yeah, but that's what I heard, son. Look, we'll see how the next few days play out. I'm just gonna be me, and hope she sees that life with me could be a lot of fun again. And if she doesn't... well, that's her loss.'

Aiden sighed. He'd never learn. There was no hope. 'You know, Dad, for a smart guy, you're hiding it well.'

His dad pulled another can from the minibar. 'Yep, son, but that's why there's beer.'

Aiden caught the Bud that was tossed in his direction, laughing as he shook his head. There was no point trying to change this man. This was who he was and whether Aiden approved or not, if he wanted his dad in his life, he just had to roll with it and try to soften the edges. But if he ever had a son, the kid was getting nowhere near Granpa Gary and his messed-up perspectives on life.

His dad picked up the remote for the TV and switched on a ball game, putting an end to what was probably the most open, honest and emotional exchange they'd ever had. Gary didn't do depth. He didn't do feelings. He only did living in the moment and planning the next good time.

Aiden sighed. Great. One parent bailed out to another room. Another one watching football. It was going so well. He really hoped Zara had a plan to get them all together soon, because otherwise this was going to be the longest, most stressful few days of his life. And that was coming from someone who had been jilted on his wedding day.

His dad's focus on the TV gave Aiden the opportunity to check his texts. Just one from Trevon.

Did your mom knock you out?

Aiden typed back a quick answer.

Not yet, but still time. If I stop replying, come identify my body.

He sent it then checked his WhatsApp, his emails... nope, nothing from Layla. He wondered what she'd think about all this. She hadn't had a chance to get particularly close to his mum, but they seemed to like each other, and she'd only met his dad a couple of times. How weird was that? He was getting married to someone who barely knew his parents. But then... they'd only been together for ten months, and he tended to go to sports events with his dad, or drop in on his mom alone, so it wasn't a huge surprise. Layla hadn't really been into the whole family gathering thing. It was something that he'd hoped would grow over time.

Aiden felt his jaw start to tighten at the thought of her. Where was she? Was she sitting somewhere right now thinking about him? Was she ever going to give him an answer as to why she'd ditched him, why she'd bolted at the last minute? Was there ever, in any world, going to be a way to come back from this? And was it pathetic that there was a part of him that still wanted her, that would listen to her and try to forgive?

'Yasssss! British football. Son, I might be here all night,' his dad joked, settling back now that he'd found a channel with his favourite sport. His mum used to say his dad would watch anything that involved kicking, throwing, catching or chasing a ball, although, she and Aiden weren't far behind him. That said, when it came to participation, his dad enjoyed reminding him that it was the saddest day of his life when Aiden chose to focus on basketball instead of soccer. His mum said it was the happiest of hers. Much as she enjoyed all sports, it thrilled her that she got to spend the next few years sitting on bleachers in the sports hall instead of standing outside in the heat all summer.

He was about to toss his phone to the side and watch the game with his dad, when a new text popped up. Zara.

Welcome to Vegas! How's it going your end? All okay here I think. My parents are knackered though – jet lag – so was thinking we should wait and ambush them with the surprise tomorrow? Me and sis going out for drink later though. Want to meet and hatch a plan? Zx

It wasn't the worst idea. His mum wouldn't be up for a late night and there was no way he was going to hit the Vegas clubs with his dad. Everything he did over the next few days had to be with the objective of making both parents happy, not favouring one over the other, or doing anything that would piss one of them off or make either of them feel excluded. This must be what parenthood felt like. Right now, it was like having two kids and trying not to show favouritism, even though one of them was mad at him, and he wanted to put the other one in a time-out.

That would all change tomorrow, though. As soon as they met their old friends, hopefully all the petty bullshit between his mum and dad would be forgotten and they could just all enjoy every minute of the rest of their trip.

He began typing.

All good here. Tomorrow perfect for getting the olds together. Drink tonight sounds good. Just let me know where and when. Looking forward to meeting you both in person. Ax.

16

EILEEN

This was going to be the longest few days of her life. Eileen let the power of the water jets pummel her body, while she contemplated what the hell she was doing here. This was like one of those reality shows where you got dumped on an island with your ex and there was a chance of survival if you chewed your own arm off.

The worst bit about it all was the disappointment that it wasn't the mum-and-son trip that Aiden had promised. She'd been so looking forward to that, so into the thought of taking Aiden's mind off the wedding disaster by making new memories. How many more times would they get to do that? Even if he did manage to sort things out with Layla – and Eileen was not, under any circumstances, supportive of that scenario – then they weren't exactly going to invite his mother along for a natty wee weekend break. No, this was it. Her one chance to have some one-on-one time with her son. Gone. Sabotaged by that bloody man she used to be married to.

And Vegas. Of all places. The one city she would quite happily go the rest of her life without revisiting. Looking over to her right, she caught her reflection in the mirror and wondered what she'd say to that twenty-five-year-old who was here last time. Other than *'turn around right now and run because you're about to make the biggest mistake of your life.'*

In some ways, she could still see that young woman. The blonde hair was still exactly the same shade, only now it came from bottles in the salon, slapped on to cover the grey. She was still exactly the same weight too, mostly thanks to Trevon, who was merciless when they worked out together. The boobs were lower and the arse was flatter, but with a good bra and the right jeans she could turn back time – while singing the words of every other Cher song too. Being a teenager in the eighties had many plus points but the wonder of Cher was definitely in the top ten, somewhere between shoulder pads, Malibu and pineapple, and the joys of getting your first Walkman.

The thought of Malibu and pineapple was like a portal that took her straight back there. That had been Brenda's favourite drink. Eileen had been more of a vodka and fresh orange girl, with an occasional Dubonnet and lemonade for some variety. When they worked in the Beat House, Brenda used to sneak drinks out from the bar to the ticket office for Eileen, and she'd knock them back before the entrance doors closed and she was redeployed to help the cloakroom staff return jackets at the end of the night. After a few of Brenda's generously proportioned drinks, it was a miracle anyone went home with the coat they'd come in with.

Brenda. How long had it been since she'd thought about her? After they'd been here last time, Eileen had put her right out of her mind, slammed the vault of Brenda memories shut and refused to open it again. She was probably sitting in Scotland right now, surrounded by grandchildren and loving her life. She'd probably still be nursing, because even when she was in her first year on the wards, Brenda loved her job and everyone could see that it perfectly suited her personality. Yep, Brenda would be happy. Fulfilled. Would have found a way to overcome a rocky start and make a brilliant success of her life. Eileen hoped that was true, because then maybe, just maybe, it would prove that they'd all made the right decisions back then, even if it didn't feel that way at the time.

Climbing out of the shower, she dried off her body, then unclipped her hair, letting her blonde waves fall over her shoulders. Without even thinking, she opened her Chanel No5 body lotion and began slathering it on. Gary had bought her that cream every single year at Christmas because he knew it was her favourite. She'd never have predicted that her love of Chanel would outlast her love of her husband.

Body lotion on, teeth brushed, and fresh make-up applied, she threw on jeans and a black shirt, then slipped her feet into black Louboutin ankle boots. Now it was a different woman that stared back at her in the mirror. This one was accomplished. Sexy. Confident. Eileen wasn't sure if that made her good at playing dress-up or a fraud.

Okay, time to go. She could do this. *Stay calm. Don't rise to him. Ignore him if he's being a dick. Remember why you're here. Stay calm. Don't rise to him. Ignore him if he's being a dick. Remember why you're here. Stay calm. Don't rise to him...*

No matter how many times she repeated the mantra in her head, she wasn't sure it would stick.

It lasted until Gary whistled when he opened the door, and followed that up with, 'You scrub up not too bad for an old bird.'

'And it's amazing how you managed to get to this age but avoid wisdom or class.'

Ding ding. Equal points at the end of round one.

Gritting her teeth, she reminded herself why they were there. This was for Aiden. It was important to him that they got along. *Make it happen, Eileen. Focus on the positives.* Right now, the only one of those she could see was that there was no denying her ex looked handsome. Charcoal shirt and black trousers, his salt-and-pepper hair brushed back to emphasise his piercing blue eyes, and just enough stubble on his face to be sexy but not scruffy.

Holding her breath, she waited to see if her body reacted. That was the problem with Gary Gregg. Towards the end of their marriage, when it was clear they were in a rough spot, her brain could be telling her he was an arse but her body still found him deeply attractive. When he turned around to head back over to the chair at the window, she scanned him from head to toe and waited for an internal response from her erogenous zones. Nope, nothing. Clearly her libido forgot to get on the plane back in Charleston.

'Hey, Mom, you look gorgeous,' Aiden said as he came out of the bathroom.

'Thanks, son. So what's the plan?'

He sat on the edge of the bed and pulled his black boots on. With his black jeans and T-shirt, most people would be hard-pressed to guess he was a lawyer. If Eileen saw him in the street dressed like this, she'd go with country singer or Tim McGraw's younger brother. If only he'd stuck at the guitar lessons she'd got him for his tenth birthday.

'I thought we'd go downstairs and eat in Jasmine, that's the Chinese restaurant here. I've heard really good things about it and I know Asian food is your favourite.'

Eileen wasn't going to object. Growing up in Scotland, the Saturday night treat had always been a trip to the local Chinese take-away to pick up dinner. Chicken curry. Boiled rice. Spring rolls. That was in the old days, when they didn't deliver to the house, and anyway, her mum would never have dreamt of wasting money by paying extra for someone to bring it to them.

An unexpected wave of sadness brushed her heart. It had always just been her and her mum, so when an undiagnosed heart problem took her way too early, not long before Eileen came to Vegas last time, she remembered not being able to explain how she felt. Now, looking back, she could see the right word was 'untethered'. It still brought a twist to her gut when she thought about how she'd already lived ten years longer than her mum, taken before she could love again, or have some adventure or travel to experience anywhere as beautiful as the lobby that Eileen was walking across right now.

When they reached the restaurant, Eileen saw it was busy, but not uncomfortably so. They were seated straight away, and of course Gary Big Bollocks ordered a bottle of champagne. He couldn't help himself, Eileen decided. When the universe was putting together his genetic code, someone took their eye off the ball and doubled up on the hedonism and flash twat genes.

When it came, Gary proposed a toast. 'To us. First time together for dinner in... what? Ten years?'

'And thank you for coming,' Aiden added. 'As far as parents go, you two are not too bad.'

Laughing, Eileen raised her glass, reminding herself yet again that this was for their son. And besides, all those Instagram self-help posts always said that letting go and forgiving was the key to moving on to a happier life. Maybe it was time to ditch all the resentments and just play nice.

'To us,' she echoed.

If anyone at another table had glanced over at them, they'd have undoubtedly assumed this was a happy family here on a trip. Or maybe a birthday celebration. Perhaps even an anniversary. Or a... hang on. Rewind. Her brain double checked the thought that had just nudged its way to the front of her mind.

'Mum, you okay? You look like you're in another world.'

That snapped her back to reality. 'I'm fine, it's just that...' Flustered, she stumbled over her words a little. 'I've just realised the date. It's the sixteenth of May.'

Gary's face remained a picture of nonchalance, so she knew he didn't remember. Not a surprise. This was the man who'd forgotten their wedding anniversary on at least ten of the twenty years they were married. In fact, on their tenth anniversary he came home late from an impromptu paintballing trip with his mates and couldn't work out why she didn't speak to him for a day and a half.

'Last time we came here, we landed on the sixteenth of May too.'

Gary reacted with something between wonderment and puzzlement. 'We did? How do you remember that stuff?'

'Because it was exactly six months after my mum died. It always stuck in my head. Still does. And that makes it...'

'Exactly thirty years ago,' Gary finished for her. She wouldn't have been more surprised if he'd said it in Cantonese. He remembered when her mum died. There was no one else in this whole world who would have known that. To Eileen, someone with no other family, and no friends from her younger life, that suddenly mattered. Someone knew her. All of her. All her history. She'd been on her own, totally independent and fighting her own battles for so long, she'd forgotten what it felt like to have someone who knew where you came from.

Tonight, it felt like that mattered. She didn't know why. But she did feel the swing of a wrecking ball to the wall she'd built up since the divorce, just enough to take down some of the bricks, to see a ray of sunlight through the hole and temporarily stun her resentments and furies.

Enough bricks were down to make her relax, allowing them to spend the next couple of hours eating fabulous food, chatting about a whole load of neutral subjects, laughing and generally having a good time. It felt... great. Familiar. Almost a relief. Hating someone as much as she'd loathed Gary was exhausting so it was lovely to suspend hostilities, even for a brief moment in time. Eileen had no idea what was in that champagne but she was taking a bottle of it back up to her room. Although, her memories of the last ten years hadn't been completely erased, so she was definitely putting it on Gary's tab.

'Right, chaps, I'm exhausted, so I'm going to call it a night,' she announced, and got a tiny fizzle of pleasure that Gary's brow betrayed a flinch of disappointment.

'Yeah, I think I'll turn in too,' he said.

Another surprise. She'd have bet her last fiver that he'd stay out most of the night and party like a man half his age.

'What about you, son? Turning in?'

Aiden shook his head. 'No, not quite yet. Think I'll go out for a walk. Clear my mind. Get a bit of exercise.'

It had been so long since she'd seen it, that she almost missed it. The slight flush of the face. The split-second glance to the right. Both tells when he was younger that he was being slightly economical with the truth.

They were in Vegas. Her ex-husband was here. Her son was hiding something, and the bricks were suddenly jumping right back up onto her wall.

She had no idea what Aiden was up to, but she had a sinking feeling that she was going to find out. And if it was anything like his last surprise, she'd really much rather that he kept it to himself.

17

ZARA

'I really need a drink,' Zara announced, blowing out her cheeks for uncharacteristic dramatic effect.

'I need the whole bottle,' Millie countered, completely characteristically taking the dramatic effect one stage higher.

Zara was so discombobulated that she didn't even notice the gorgeousness of the ivory padded chair that she'd just plonked herself down on at the Chandelier bar in the Cosmopolitan Hotel. The bar had come up loads of times when she'd done her research on the best venues in the city, and it was just across the road from Planet Hollywood, and next to the Bellagio, so it had seemed like the perfect place to suggest for their rendezvous with Aiden.

A waitress who could very well have just sashayed off a catwalk was by their sides in seconds to take their drinks order, temporarily suspending their conversation.

Zara didn't even have to look at the drinks menu, given that there were only two options for her – a gin and tonic or a glass of Prosecco. That was as far as her alcohol tastes went. Tonight, circumstances narrowed her choice to the hard stuff. 'I'll have a gin and tonic, please.'

Millie read from the menu. 'And I'll have a Whiskey Business.'

'What's that?' Zara asked, intrigued.

The waitress's Southern drawl was perfect for this one. 'Knob Creek bourbon with bitters, Amaro Meletti, that's a caramel and chocolate liqueur, and "Old Time Rock 'n' Roll" syrup.'

'Wow,' Zara exclaimed. 'That sounds like it would either knock me out, or I'd require hospitalisation to have my stomach pumped. Cancel the gin and give me one of those too please.'

'I have no idea who you are, but I like you a whole lot more than my usual sister,' Millie decided.

Zara feigned disdain and sat back in her chair, exhaled and tried to bring her heart rate down to normal, which was no mean feat in the corset dress Millie had insisted she borrow for the night. It was bright red, showed a fair crack of cleavage, cinched in like a vice from hips to under the bosom, and made her walk in six-inch wiggles because the below-knee skirt was way too tight. Zara had no idea how Millie could wear outfits like this for a whole night. She'd only changed into it after dinner and already her cardiovascular system was shutting down in protest.

Thankfully, she had a prime subject to take her mind off the lack of oxygen.

'Is it just me or was tonight the weirdest night ever?' she asked, already knowing what Millie's answer would be.

'Definitely weirdest night ever. And I once had a date with a bloke who wore a gimp mask and told me his safe word was garlic mayonnaise.'

'That's two words,' Zara pointed out.

'Exactly! Weird, right?' Millie agreed, but her mischievous grin gave away the joke.

The waitress reappeared with their drinks, and Zara threw at least an inch of it back in one go.

Millie watched her, eyes wide. 'Yep, I definitely like you better than my other sister called Zara.'

'Don't judge me,' Zara warned. 'I'm feeling highly thrown by this whole bloody thing. I mean... I don't know where to start, really.'

'The cardigan. Let's start with the cardigan,' Millie suggested. 'And yes, I know that's shallow, so you can judge me all you want.'

Zara would usually give Millie the 'don't form judgements about people because you don't know what they're dealing with in life' speech, but that didn't necessarily apply here, because the only thing that her parents were dealing with was an all-expenses trip to Las Vegas.

Yet her mum had celebrated that fact by showing up at the restaurant in the kind of cardigan she'd wear to walk the dog. If they actually still had a dog, that was. Their beloved old golden retriever had passed away about five years ago. Maybe Mum had been saving that cardi since then.

'I mean, in fairness we didn't tell her exactly where we were going before we left home this morning. Was it only this morning? It feels like a week ago. Thing is, though, she knew it was somewhere nice and I did emphasise the glam nights, but it's like she absolutely doesn't care.'

'Would a bit of lippy have killed her? Or, you know, a brush.'

Zara ignored that, naturally resistant to criticise any woman on the basis of her appearance, even if Millie was right. However, that wasn't even close to being the strangest thing about the night. That acclaim was awarded to both parents, for their performances as a couple who pretty much couldn't stand the sight of each other. When had that happened? True, it was a couple of months since they'd all sat down for a family dinner, but the change was so palpable that only three possible explanations came to mind. Either they'd been pretending that everything was fine back then, or they'd had a huge fight today, or...

'Do you think Mum has discovered Dad is, like, a serial killer or something?' Millie adjusted the neckline in her pink, off-the-shoulder minidress.

'It wasn't my first thought, but you might have something there. I just feel like...' Zara paused to try to put it into words. 'This isn't turning out how I thought it would so far. I honestly expected Mum to be thrilled and excited. I thought we'd blow her socks off, but I've never seen her so absolutely fed up. Am I overreacting? And, yes, I get the irony of asking you that question, given that you haven't *under*-reacted to anything since we were in primary school.'

Even as she asked, Zara knew that she wasn't imagining anything. Her mum really had come down for dinner in PF Chang's, the Asian restaurant on the ground floor of Planet Hollywood, in trousers and a cardi. She really had struggled to raise a smile. Her eyes had been red-rimmed and she had played with her food but not eaten more than a couple of mouthfuls. She'd barely said anything despite both Millie and Zara trying to start a dozen conversations. And for the first time in living memory, she hadn't so much as glanced at their father from the minute they got there until the minute she said she was tired, excused herself and went back up to bed, leaving Dad to throw back what was left of his beef and broccoli and follow her ten minutes later. It was bizarre. Their parents never fought. They never acted strangely. If Mum was ever upset with Dad, she never showed it. She was always just... well, Mum. Happy. Calm. Reliable. Dependable. Mum.

Zara didn't have time to ponder it further, because she heard a low murmur of, 'Holy crap, is that him?' from her sister.

Looking up, she saw that her sister's powers of observation had been, as always, spot on.

It was indeed Aiden Gregg and the hint of surprise in Millie's tone was warranted. They'd had a couple of FaceTime calls, so they both knew what he looked like – dark hair, green eyes, that all-American, preppy thing going on, which had to be an environmental influence because both his parents were very definitely Scottish. However, it was something else seeing him in person. Zara hadn't realised he was this tall, for a start. Well over six feet. And his shoulders were the width of a skip. He was just wearing black jeans and a V-neck T-shirt, but he had a walk that oozed confidence and, now that he had spotted them, a smile that it was way too easy to stare at.

The waitress clearly thought so too. She was already back at their side to take his order of a Jack Daniel's and Coke. They'd exchanged pleasantries by the time she returned with that, and two fresh cocktails for Zara and Millie. Zara couldn't even remember what was in it, but it was obviously really potent stuff because she was already beginning to feel a bit giddy.

'We can't thank you enough for doing this,' she told Aiden, as she lifted her drink and somehow managed to miss her mouth. Wow. It was even stronger than she thought. A few drops spilled in her lap and she casually brushed them away, hoping it wasn't too obvious.

'It's no problem, it really isn't. In fact, I think I need to thank you guys. Tonight was the first time since I was in college that I've managed to get my parents at the same dinner table. I chose Chinese so there would be no sharp knives on the table, but they actually got on pretty well.'

'We had Chinese food too, but it wasn't as chipper.' Zara clamped her mouth shut, horrified that she'd admitted that to a virtual stranger, then fumbled for an excuse. 'I think our parents are just jet lagged, though. Anyway, back to your mum and dad. So they didn't stay friends after the divorce?'

Aiden shook his head. 'I wish. Those guys are the worst advert for my practise. I spend all day every day preaching to my clients that they should try to keep things amicable and move on in a positive way, while my mom and dad can't stand the sight of each other. Seriously, tonight was like a miracle.'

Zara reconsidered sharing more about how they'd had the opposite experience, but it still didn't feel right to discuss her mum and dad's private business with someone they barely knew, even one that had flown thousands of miles to meet them here. Instead they spent the next couple of hours swapping stories, comparing notes about their very different childhoods. 'I can't believe you don't actually own a puffer jacket,' Zara told him at one point. 'I think that means you can't claim Scottish heritage, no matter what your DNA says.'

Every time he laughed, she saw the perfection of his white smile. This man was clearly no stranger to an orthodontist.

'Have your parents ever mentioned ours, or talked about how they were all here together?' Zara asked him.

He shook his head. 'Never. But then, I guess it was a long time ago. My dad has been here for a couple of conferences over the years, but I didn't even know that my mum had ever been to Vegas. I hadn't really thought about it much before, but now I've realised that I can't remember her ever talking much about her past. I know she has no family left in Scotland, but I never figured to ask about friends.'

'Yep, our mum kept this all pretty close to her chest too. I can't imagine her being here, never mind getting married here. She's more of a "morning service in a country church" kind of person. I honestly struggle to accept that we're related sometimes,' Millie smiled, leaning forward in her chair.

Zara could see the signs. Millie was tucking her hair behind her ears, keeping eye contact with Aiden, throwing out all her best lines to make him laugh. Oh, she was definitely smitten. This poor guy had no idea what he was in for, but she wasn't going to third wheel them any longer. Time to go. She needed sleep and maybe Kev would answer her this time when she called him. And no, she wasn't going to contrast Millie's existence, sitting in a five-star hotel in Vegas, flirting with an absolutely gorgeous man, who was interesting, charming and great company, to the fact that Kev had worn the same old jeans for the last fortnight and they'd spent an hour last weekend debating whether to risk a microwave chicken meal that was a day out of date, or go for the deluxe option and toss a deep pan margherita into the oven.

She did that stretch-up-and-smile thing that people did when they were about to announce they were calling it a night. 'Sorry to be such a lightweight, but I'm going to leave you two to it. I'll just pay the bill and—'

'No, let me get it. I insist.'

Zara hesitated at Aiden's offer, then, 'Okay, but we're buying lunch tomorrow and don't argue – jet leg could make me a total battleaxe and you wouldn't win.'

Laughing, Aiden immediately interjected with, 'I wouldn't dare. At least let us walk you back to your hotel.'

Zara gently but firmly brushed him off for the second time. 'It's literally across the road and it's like Sauchiehall Street on a Saturday out there. I've just realised you don't know where or what Sauchiehall Street is. It's in Glasgow, it's really busy and that's just a saying.' What was wrong with her? Those bloody drinks were making her talk nonsense.

Thankfully, Aiden didn't notice her blush to the same colour as her dress, as he was already standing up to say goodbye.

Zara hugged her sister and when she was close enough that only Millie could hear, she whispered, 'You're welcome.'

Millie's squeeze of thanks told her everything she needed to know. Millie was absolutely into this guy.

Zara stretched up to hug Aiden next. She wasn't usually one for doing all the tactile stuff with people she'd only just met, but this felt absolutely natural. 'Okay, so tomorrow at noon at Lago restaurant in the Bellagio.

Honestly, I'm so excited. I can't wait to see their reactions. It's going to be the best thing ever.'

That thought, and the happy buzz of too many of those cocktails, kept her smiling as she crossed the road to her hotel.

The trip hadn't exactly evoked the joyful surprise and giddy excitement she'd expected so far, but tomorrow was another day. Her parents were going to meet their old friends and nothing was going to spoil it.

Only the loud beep of a taxi horn alerted her to the fact that she might be daydreaming.

18

BRENDA

17 May – Two Days Until The Anniversary

'Room service!'

The voice at the door woke Brenda up and it took her a minute to make the fog clear and remember where she was. Vegas. That's right. Yesterday, she'd woken up in her semi-detached bungalow in Glasgow and today she was waking up on the other side of the world. This was the most unexpected thing that had happened to her in her life. Or at least, since the last time she was here.

Her subconscious obviously thought so too, because she'd tossed and turned all night, slipping in and out of a dream that was so vivid that at one point she woke and could actually feel her heart racing. It was thirty years ago. She was here in this city. Excited. Happy. Colin was here too. And Gary and Eileen. They were in a nightclub just off the Strip. They got separated and Brenda was searching everywhere for her friend. Couldn't find her. Panic. She wondered if maybe Eileen wasn't feeling well, had left, gone back to their hotel. Brenda raced back to check and... That was when she'd woken up, heart thudding, and had to put the air con on because she was sweating.

Colin had, of course, then awakened to object to the cold air. Said it always made him congested the next day. The snoring coming from the other side of the bed proved that he had a point. She wanted to nudge him, to roll him over on to his side, but she was afraid it would wake him up and then she'd be faced with the possibility of having to talk to him and that wasn't a risk she wanted to take. Not yet. Not when he seemed incapable of hearing what she was saying.

A loud knock on the door and a second call of 'Room Service' reminded her of what had woken her.

Stumbling out of bed, Brenda made her way to the door, trying not to yelp when she stubbed her toe on the end of the bed. Lights would probably have been a good idea before moving. The blackout curtains had the whole place in darkness. It didn't even cross her mind to wonder who'd ordered the room service. Colin had still been awake when she'd fallen asleep last night, so she just assumed it must have been him.

She barely had the door open when Zara and Millie breezed right in past her. Millie flicked the light on, and Brenda saw that Zara was carrying a tray loaded with coffees and pastries.

'Morning, Mum,' Zara chirped, managing to kiss her on the cheek on the way past. 'Time to get up and get going. We have plans. Lots of them.'

Despite wanting to crawl right back into bed and pull the duvet over her head – preferably without the snoring husband by her side – Brenda chuckled. She adored these two beyond words and their enthusiasm was contagious.

Plans. She liked the sound of that. The busier they were, the faster the time would pass, and the less room there would be for awkward moments with her husband, or desperate moments of thinking too much about what she was going to do with her life when they got home.

Over at the window, Millie threw open the curtains, letting daylight flood the room. In bed, Colin groaned, while Brenda squinted against the sun. 'What time is it?'

'Ten o'clock, Mum! Time for action. Or at least, coffee and doughnuts. I'm on the maple one. My hangover demands it.'

Now that her vision was clearing, Brenda could see that Millie had plonked herself down on the chair over by the window, was still wearing last night's make-up and her hair was close in size and shape to the topiary balls she'd bought in B&M for either side of her front door.

She took the coffee that Zara was holding out to her, and joined Millie, sitting on the matching chair on the other side of the small bistro table between them. Colin finally managed to get an eye open and pushed himself up in bed, to be rewarded with a large cappuccino and an apple Danish from Zara.

'Morning, my darlings,' he croaked. 'Sorry, I'm a bit congested this morning.'

Of course, he had to get the dig in about the air conditioning. Or maybe he was just stating a fact, but why did everything he said and did annoy her now? Every. Damn. Thing.

That thought immediately invoked a wave of remorse. Why was she being unkind? This wasn't her. Yesterday wasn't her. Last night definitely wasn't her. Another twinge of regret. She'd behaved terribly at dinner. Barely said a word or eaten a morsel. It had just all been so overwhelming, so claustrophobic, and she'd been too tired to pull herself up and put the act on. Well, not today. This morning she was absolutely utterly sick and tired of her inner moaning. Of her worry. Of listening to her own mind fret and complain. Today she was going to be back on her game. Happy face on. Positive energy. Nothing was going to spoil this time with her daughters.

Colin took a slug of his coffee and then got up and headed to the bathroom. 'I'm just going to grab a shower and wake myself up.' At home, he'd have been out in the garden by now, pruning things, checking plants, or sitting gazing over his kingdom, plotting his next task.

As usual, Millie was the one that got straight to the point. 'Right, Mum, first of all, are you okay? Have you and Dad had a fight? You were miserable last night and my hangover can't take the emotional suspense.'

'I'm fine, my darling, and I'm really sorry about last night. I was jet lagged, exhausted, and just a bit out of sorts. I'm feeling much better today, so go on, boss me around and tell me what I'm doing.'

Zara took that as permission to open her backpack and dump a whole load of toiletries and brushes on the desk. 'Beautifying. That's what we're doing this morning, and then we're taking you and Dad out for a very special lunch. We've got about an hour to get ready. Do you want to have a shower before we get started?'

'No, that's okay – I had a lovely long bath last night before we went out for dinner and then another one when we got back.'

She didn't add that she'd only gone for a second bath so that Colin would fall asleep before her, or that she'd had a third bath in the middle of the night, between two bouts of fitful sleep.

'Okay, I'm all yours. Do whatever you have to do.'

Zara's thumb made a few clicks on her phone, and Michael Bublé was suddenly in the room with them. Oooh, he was Brenda's favourite. The sound of his voice, the calming effects of breakfast, the chat from her girls… in only a few minutes she was relaxing into this whole situation and thoroughly enjoying it. She closed her eyes while Zara sprayed her hair with some coconut-smelling liquid, then opened them when she felt her begin to wind huge rollers into it. Millie, meanwhile, was giving herself an overhaul – she had a packet of cleaning wipes out and was scrubbing her face.

'Did you stay late in the restaurant, or did you go out?' she asked them, curious to hear what they'd got up to. Two young women, out in a new town – they deserved to have a bit of fun.

A glance passed between them that Brenda knew well. It was the 'answer the question but don't tell her everything because we'll get in trouble' glance. They'd been sharing it since they were toddlers trying to avoid taking the blame for there being two slices of jammy toast in the dog bed.

'We just went to the bar across the road in the Cosmopolitan Hotel. It was amazing, Mum, you'll love it. It's definitely on our list of places to take you to,' Zara was too busy winding in another roller to look her in the eye.

Millie's hangover and general evasiveness and Zara's chirpiness were definitely signposting that either she or both of them had been up to no good, but Brenda tried not to sound suspicious. 'Sounds great. Did you meet anyone nice?'

Another glance of conspiracy crossed the room. Ah, so there was definitely a story there.

'I know exactly what happened,' Brenda told them, laughing.

Beside her, Zara froze and Millie stopped moisturising her face. 'You do?'

'Absolutely. You both went out for a sisterly drink, but then Millie, you spotted someone you liked, and you ended up going dancing while you,' she turned to Zara, 'came home and phoned Kev for a blether.'

Zara's laughter was instant. 'Mum, honestly it's like you're psychic.'

Another look passed between them, but this time it was one she didn't recognise. She was going to have to brush up on her skills.

'You're almost right,' Millie admitted, now patting concealer on the dark circles under her eyes. 'Only there was no dancing. I just met a guy from South Carolina and we sat up chatting for a couple of hours, before he, very gentlemanly, walked me back to the lobby downstairs and then went off to his hotel.'

'Sounds lovely,' Brenda replied. 'And will you see him again?'

Millie and Zara both nodded, but it was Millie who answered. 'I've got a feeling I just might.'

Brenda spotted the cheesy grin and the twinkle in Millie's eyes that gave it away – she liked this one. Brenda was pleased for her. Not that she thought for a second that Millie should settle down, but there was no doubt her youngest liked to burn the candle at both ends.

'And you're almost right about Kev. I did call him, but we didn't have much of a chat, because he was just waking up and he's not a morning person. I'll try him again later.'

Brenda kept her thoughts to herself, just as she'd done for years on the subject of Zara and Kev. He was a lovely boy. Kind. Easy-going. But sometimes Brenda worried that Zara would wake up one morning and wonder why she'd spent her whole life with one man, and one who wasn't very interesting at that. It was the relationship version of apples and trees and Brenda held a latent fear that she was responsible for that. Had she taught her daughters that bland mediocrity was what a successful relationship looked like? Was that what Zara was settling for and Millie was rebelling against?

She didn't have time to ponder it further, because behind her, Colin came out of the bathroom wearing a white fluffy robe.

'Can I have my orders please? Dress code and time schedule,' he requested, getting into the swing of things.

Much as she moaned about him, Brenda couldn't argue with his general loveliness and caring heart as a father. He'd always been the strong silent one, left most of the front line parenting to her, but he was there when it mattered, he loved his girls and they knew that they could always count on him. It showed now, in how much they both loved him to pieces.

Millie scanned his current outfit. 'That suits you, Dad, I'd go with the robe.'

'I was thinking the same thing,' he agreed, chuckling.

'Or maybe, smart casual, something for a lunch in a nice hotel,' Zara suggested.

Colin took that on board. 'I suppose the robe would be a bit warm in this heat,' he conceded, grabbing a few things from the wardrobe and heading back into the bathroom to change. Brenda heard the sound of his electric shaver, then a while later, he came back out of the bathroom, fully dressed and smart in his navy chinos and white polo shirt. After his garden, his second love was his golf, so he perpetually dressed like he was about to step on to the first tee.

'Wow, check out big handsome there,' Millie teased him. She already looked nothing like the woman who'd walked in here an hour ago. Her old make-up was off, and in its place was a more natural face that took the same amount of time, but made her appear fresh-faced, younger, and more like her sister, who, like today, barely went with more than a quick brush of mascara and some lip gloss.

'You look great, Dad,' Zara agreed, getting a bashful smile in return.

'Thank you, girls. I'm just going to head on downstairs and get a bit of fresh air. I'll wait for you by the front door.'

Twenty minutes later, Brenda, Zara and Millie found him there and he joined them. If he noticed Brenda's makeover, he didn't say, but she didn't care. Zara had worked wonders. Her curly shoulder-length bob that spent most of its life scraped back into a bun at work, was in a semi-updo, with wavy tendrils falling down each side of her face. Her eyes were a smoky light grey, not too much but enough to make them stand out against the nude lip. And she had no idea what miracles had been worked, but she appeared to have cheekbones for the first time since her twenties. The girls had picked her outfit too – a plain pale blue shift dress, that they'd accessorised with one of Millie's long gold chains and small gold hoops at her ears. For someone who spent most of her days in scrubs or comfy clothes, feeling frumpy, weary and unattractive, this was a revelation. She hadn't felt this lovely in years.

An internal voice piped up, expressing the wish that she'd lost the twenty pounds that the last few months of emotional eating had added to her hips. She blocked the thought. Not today. Today, for the first time in recent memory, she was just going to feel good about herself.

'Tell me we don't have far to go, because this heat will have my make-up off in no time and all your amazing work will be wasted, Zara.'

'Nope, not far. Just across the road, actually.'

Brenda felt her excitement rising. The Bellagio. It was stunning and last time she'd been in this city, she remembered standing not too far from here, gazing up at the frontage and thinking to herself that one day she'd be able to afford a cocktail in there. Well, today was that day and the bonus was that she was here with her two gorgeous daughters. What a treat.

They crossed over, then walked two abreast – Millie and Colin in front, her and Zara behind them – up the sloped entrance to the hotel and made it to the lobby without, thankfully, breaking a sweat.

Brenda's eyes were on stalks as Zara asked a concierge for directions, then led them to a wonderfully opulent restaurant. It was gorgeous. Sumptuous. Lavish. Oh, she couldn't wait to tell Bernadette about this.

'We have a table booked under the name Zara Jones.'

The maître d' at the podium checked his screen. 'Right this way. Your guests are already here.'

That threw Brenda just a little. Guests? They must be meeting Millie's new man friend this morning after all.

Millie and Zara were in front now, and Colin was at Brenda's side behind them, as they all followed the maître d'. Brenda was still scanning the room, taking in every detail, gasping at the huge windows with views out to the fountains and the strip, until several things happened at once.

The maître d' stopped at a table that was tucked into a corner.

Millie's smiley dimples came into full force as she said, 'Mum, Dad, this is Aiden.'

Zara gleefully added, 'And we think you already know his parents.'

That was the moment. The horrible, stomach churning, heart-stopping moment that Brenda realised she was looking straight into the faces of Gary Gregg and Eileen Smith – the only two people in this entire world that she truly detested.

19

AIDEN

Aiden's eyes were watching what was going on, but his brain was struggling to process it. This was almost like an emotional rerun of his meant-to-be-wedding day. The anticipation. The joy. The absolute conviction that you were doing something wonderful that would delight your family and make everyone happy... only for it to all fall apart in an anticlimactic crapshow of unexpected developments.

He could see that Zara and Millie were watching with the same abject confusion, especially when, like him, they spotted their mum's laser-focused stare going between his mom and his dad, then back again, her jaw dropped, her fists... oh man, her fists were clenched. And she didn't appear to be the type of lady who clenched her fists in fury on a regular basis.

His mother was staring back, but there was something in her expression that he didn't recognise. Horror? Dismay? No, it was something else. Embarrassment? But why?

As for the men, Zara's dad was giving off the vibe that he'd rather be anywhere but here and his own dad had puffed up his chest, the way he always did when he sensed he was about to face an uncomfortable situation and was preparing to go on the offensive. It was like a standoff between two rival gangs, but with less weapons and more Bellagio napkins to wipe up any bloodshed.

What was going on? This was supposed to be a joyful reunion between four old friends. What were they missing?

Zara found her voice first and she went for the obvious move in a situation that wasn't unfolding as expected. He'd been just about to do the same, but she got in there before him, her words oozing uncertainty and unasked questions. 'Mum? Dad? Aiden's parents are—'

'I know who they are,' her mum assured her. 'Hello Gary. Eileen.'

Shit. She looked like a lovely fifty-something lady with a kind face and comfortable shoes, but she sounded like a mob boss.

A suited waiter approached, immediately sensed the tension and kept right on walking. The atmosphere here was so ice cold that Aiden was kind of wishing he could bail out with him.

'Hello, Brenda.' His mum this time, and she sounded rattled. But this wasn't 'Dad has shown up with a twenty-nine-year-old' rattled. This was something much more than that. This was rattled to the core. It was also the first time in living memory that his father had stayed silent for more than thirty seconds. Aiden had been pretty sure his pop would have been pumping hands, slapping backs, hugging everyone and ordering champagne by now. Instead, he was just staring at Zara's mum, waiting for the next comment to come and very obviously not looking forward to it with giddy glee.

Aiden caught Zara's gaze, saw his own confusion reflected back at him, and decided it was his turn to try to navigate his way through this. For the umpteenth time in the last few weeks, he found himself in a situation that his training and career experience should have equipped him for, yet he was at a loss as to how to handle this. He decided to start slow, test the waters, make sure he was picking up the right signals.

'Okay, this isn't how we thought this was going to play out.'

His mum spun round and now she was challenging him. Crap. What were the chances that some form of divine intervention would strike in the next five seconds and divert attention from this catastrophe – a meteor shower, alien invasion, hell, a fire alarm would be enough.

'What do you mean "we"? You planned this, Aiden? How do you even know these people? I don't understand.'

Zara spoke up to rescue him from that one. He'd expected that Millie would be the more forceful one in this situation, given that she seemed bolder, more up front. In all the video calls they'd had over the last fortnight, Zara had been funny, thoughtful, warm, but when he'd met them last night, he'd realised that Millie was the wilder of the two, the more vocal, the one who liked to dance until dawn. She reminded him of his dad. Always seeking out the party. At 2 a.m. this morning, she'd been up for dragging him to a club and he was having such a good time, he almost went. Now he was glad he hadn't. Doing this on no sleep would have crushed him.

Zara was still acting as his witness for the defence. 'Erm, no, it was me who planned all this. I just roped Aiden in, but, like he said, we didn't expect—'

'What did you expect, Zara?' her mum asked her very calmly.

Aiden noticed Millie was waiting in the background, just taking in everything that was going on.

'I thought...' Zara paused.

'*We*,' Millie interjected, taking her share of the heat. 'We thought...'

He watched as Zara took a deep breath, threw a grateful glance at her sister and bolstered by the need to explain, started again. 'Okay, first of all, Mr and Mrs Gregg, I'm Zara, and this is my sister, Millie – we're Colin and Brenda's daughters and despite this being a very strange moment, it's lovely to meet you.'

'Ah, Mr and Mrs Gregg – so you two got married. Shocker,' Zara's mum murmured, making both her daughters' heads swivel to stare at her with undisguised astonishment. This was all very obviously out of character and a complete surprise to them.

'Brenda, let Zara tell us...' That came from Zara's dad but withered before it was finished under a death stare from her mother, who, thankfully, had at least unclenched her fists.

Meanwhile, Aiden was, at all costs, avoiding glancing at his mum in case her expression suggested he was about to be put up for adoption.

Zara started again. 'As I said before, this was all down to me.'

'*Us*,' said Millie, with a supportive nudge.

'Yes, us. Me and Millie. Aiden honestly had nothing to do with it, other than go along with what we thought was going to be a lovely surprise for our parents. You see, it's my mum and dad's thirtieth wedding anniversary in a couple of days and I... *we* thought it would be amazing to bring them back to the place they got married.'

'You got married here? When we were here last time? You're bloody kidding me. Didn't waste time, eh, Colin?' This was the first time his dad had spoken, but it wasn't making any more sense than the last ten minutes.

'Pot and kettle there, Gary,' Zara's dad spat out a challenge, and now Zara's eyes were even wider.

The waiter came back in for another approach, realised things were no better, and made a second retreat.

What the hell was going on? Were people just blurting out random statements and passive-aggressive digs for the fun of it? Were they being pranked?

Zara kept ploughing on, like someone being consumed by quicksand and desperately hoping she'd say something that would make one of the bystanders throw her a rope and pull her out. Aiden was standing with the lifejacket, but he just wasn't sure when the best time was to throw it.

'I'm going to go back to the beginning,' Zara announced, as if returning to the start could somehow change the outcome of where they were now. If nothing else it might buy them enough time to suss out what the hell was going on. 'A few months ago, my gran died, and I was going through old photos at her house when I found a picture taken here, back in 1993.'

There was a sharp intake of breath from Zara's mom, but she didn't say anything, allowing Zara to carry on.

'I thought... well, wrongly by the looks of things... but I assumed you'd all come here together and Mum and Dad got married on the spur of the moment. Your names were on the back of the photo – although it was your maiden name, Mrs Gregg, so I didn't make the connection at first because I didn't know you were married until Aiden filled in that piece of the puzzle. I actually thought that you, Mrs Gregg, were probably a bridesmaid, and that you, Mr Gregg, were the best man. Like I said, I'm beginning to realise that I may have got that wrong.'

'I'm afraid you did,' his mom cut in, before adding a conciliatory, 'but I can understand why you'd think that. We weren't a couple back then.'

'Weren't you?' That came from Zara's mom again, but got no reply from his side of the trenches.

Time for Aiden to weigh in and take his share of the responsibility. 'After she found the photo, Zara tracked me down through Facebook. She actually tried to contact you first, Dad...'

'I don't know how to work that thing. Never use it.'

'He's more of a Snapchat guy. Like the young things half his age,' his mum barbed, and Aiden sighed. When it came to his dad, she just couldn't help herself.

'Anyway, Zara found me and sent me the picture. It was just after everything happened with my wedding...'

'Your wedding? What happened with your wedding? I thought you were single,' Millie blurted.

'That's another long story. I'll get this one out of the way first,' he replied, with a rueful shrug. 'Anyway, it was around then, and I thought this could be a really good idea to cheer everyone up and do something cool. Zara and Millie and I have been communicating back and forward, planning what we thought would be an awesome reunion. Sorry, Mum, Dad, the stuff I told you at the airport wasn't strictly true. This wasn't me just trying to get my divorced parents back on friendly terms...'

'Ah, so you're divorced,' Zara's dad said, with a hint of triumph. 'We're still married. Thirty years.'

Fricking hell, this had turned into some kind of warped competition.

Aiden ploughed on despite beginning to feel that he was sliding into the same quicksand as Zara. 'Like Zara and Millie, I figured you were all old friends who'd lost touch over the years, and this would be a really cool thing. I'm sensing not.'

'Definitely not,' his dad countered. 'And, son, next time you want to plan any kind of surprise for me – anything at all – do me a favour and ask me first.'

'Copy that,' he retorted. An excruciating silence descended again and Aiden wondered if he should just call a halt to this, usher his mum and dad out of here, then make a run for it, but he felt so sorry for Zara that he waited for her to take the lead.

'I'm sorry. To you all. Obviously, there are things in play here, a history that we don't know anything about.'

'That's okay, love,' her dad said, and Aiden saw the relief cross her face. Just those three words changed Aiden's opinion of him. Going on the friction between the two fathers, he'd instinctively taken his dad's side, but he wasn't sure why – it wasn't like Gary had a solid history of wise choices and good decisions. Maybe there was at least 50/50 culpability here. It would help if one of the older generation actually took a shot at explaining what had happened between them.

Millie was obviously having the same thought process, because she signalled to the relieved waiter. 'Can we have a round of drinks please? Whatever they were already drinking and add on three gin and tonics and a beer – any kind – for us.' The waiter was about to retreat gracefully when she added, 'And do you have any snacks? Pretzels? Chips? Anything at all. My hangover is about to break me and I can't do this on an empty stomach.'

'I'll bring an assortment of breads.'

'Yes!!!! You're a god and I want to have your babies.'

Aiden got the feeling this wasn't the usual customer conversation in a restaurant at the Bellagio. That's probably why the waiter was smiling as he retreated.

The prospect of sustenance must have invigorated Millie, because she stepped up to the position of chief investigator. 'Okay, clearly we've completely messed this whole thing up. How about we all sit down, take a breath, and try to sort this out. Now, we've told you how this little soiree came about and the good intentions – not to mention considerable expense that was behind it.' She scanned the parents' faces. 'So... and I'm sorry about the language, Mum – but can one of you four please tell us what the actual fuck is going on?'

20

EILEEN

Eileen felt a pressure on her chest and wondered if a heart attack was imminent. If there were two people she thought she'd never see again as long as she was on this earth, it was Brenda and Colin. And for it all to play out in front of Aiden made it so much more embarrassing. The worst moments of her life, dragged from the past to the present, and held up in front of her for the people that mattered to see.

She thought about getting up to leave, but what would that accomplish? It was all going to come out one way or another. May as well stay here to see the show, even though she was the clown that messed it all up at the end.

For a moment, she wondered if Brenda would leave, but she didn't, probably figuring the same thing – the lid was off the box and Pandora was about to spill her guts.

The Brenda that she saw in front of her wasn't the one she'd known in the nineties. This woman was... strong. In control. In those days, they were just young women who thought about nothing much more than having a good time and making their wages from the Beat House last from one week to another. Even when Brenda had started nursing, Eileen was doing secretarial temping, and Colin got a job in the accounts department at the council, they'd still needed their club money to supplement their wages.

Colin... she barely recognised him. In his twenties, he'd been Michael J. Fox cute, with his little round specs and a great line in chat. Now he was a middle-aged man and only the kind face and the serial geekiness remained.

The first trip to Vegas had been Gary's doing. The four of them were inseparable, so when he won a DJing contest organised by one of the big vodka brands, a transatlantic trip for two, with a guest gig at a Vegas club thrown in, they'd all chipped in to pay for the other two tickets so they could all come.

Yep, Gary had been a big deal. A bit of a local celebrity. He played in several clubs in Glasgow's city centre, but always did a Friday and Saturday night in the Beat House, because his flatmate, Colin, worked there too. When the club closed in the early hours of the morning, they'd all head out to one of the all-night cafés, then pile back to the lads' house, where they'd peel off into the two bedrooms and emerge again at noon the next day, ready to do it all again. It was the best of times. And it was all that had kept Eileen sane after her mum had passed away, suddenly and brutally at forty-two. Who'd been there for her? Brenda. Colin. And to an extent, Gary, but his priorities were always himself, his work, and the party. Some might say nothing had changed.

'Well?' That was Brenda's daughter again, the younger, more bolshy one, reminding them that they were still waiting to hear the background to the story. Eileen didn't want to be the one to tell it, but, well, maybe this was payback.

She took a breath, then exhaled, trying to steady the nerves that were making her hands shake, even though she'd tucked them under her thighs so the rest of the group wouldn't see them.

'The photo was taken on the day we arrived here. Thirty years ago yesterday, actually. I realised that last night. None of us had the money for that kind of holiday, but we came because Gary won a trip here, two tickets, and we all chipped in so the four of us could come.'

'So you *were* friends?' Zara asked, as if grasping at straws.

'We were,' Gary interjected. 'And I was a DJ. A good one,' he boasted. Eileen rolled her eyes as he went on, 'I won those tickets in a national competition. First place. The prize was to come over here and play a gig in one of the clubs just off the Strip. Don't even think it'll be there now, but it was a big deal at the time,' Gary emphasised, just in case everyone wasn't aware of his former superstar status. Thirty years and he still thought it made him his generation's equivalent of Fat Boy Slim and Calvin Harris rolled into one.

On the flight over Brenda and Eileen had been giddy. It was their first time out of the country, and it was Vegas! Even the loaded couple in Eileen's street, the ones who'd won ten thousand pounds on the premium bonds, hadn't been there yet.

When they'd arrived, they'd ditched their bags in their hotel, and then gone out sightseeing. They'd walked all the way up the Strip, following a map they'd picked up at hotel reception, and at the end, turned right and kept walking until they found the Vegas sign. It wasn't hard to miss. There were lines of people queuing to get their pictures taken, but they'd been happy to wait their turn. Eileen could visualise the photo, could remember the moment it was taken, could recall the feeling of the heat on her skin, the excitement of being there, the love she felt for everyone she was with. Sometimes, over the years, she'd wondered if, with the exception of the birth of her son, that sunny Vegas day was her last moment of true contentment and bliss.

The waiter came back with their drinks, giving Eileen time to order her thoughts, and for it to occur to her that she had to say everything in her mind out loud for the others to understand.

Her captive audience didn't make a sound as she began, 'The photograph was taken on the first day we got here. It was Colin's camera and we gave it to some stranger in the line behind us and asked her to take the pic. Afterwards, we walked back down the Strip, going into the lobby of every hotel just to look and see what it was like. There were not as many as there are now, but still we were gobsmacked, never seen anything like it. They don't do buildings like Caesars Palace, or fountains like those ones out there in Glasgow city centre.'

She ran her gaze around the table. Aiden was to her left, next to Zara. Gary was to her right. Colin, Brenda and their other girl – was it Millie? – were sitting across from them.

'If any of you want to fill in the blanks, go right ahead,' she said, addressing the others who'd been there a lifetime ago.

'Nope, I think you're doing just fine. Looking forward to the next bit,' Brenda said, with a distinct edge of a challenge.

'Mum!' Zara chided her, obviously embarrassed.

Eileen didn't comment because she knew she was only a few minutes away from losing the young woman's sympathy. She couldn't even make eye contact with Aiden. She wasn't sure if she'd ever be able to look at him again.

'The next day, we toured the city on foot, playing a few dollars here and there on the tables, and the craziest thing happened. I put two dollars on a roulette number at the Flamingo and it won. Then I doubled it up, and it won again. I kept going and within an hour I'd won over six hundred dollars, which was a fortune to us. That changed everything. Of course, we should have saved the cash for when we got back home, but we didn't. Brenda and I bought new frocks – I got a pink summer dress and yours was a white one – I still remember.' Brenda didn't break her hard stare, so Eileen just ploughed on. 'We went out on the town, partying, drinking, eating food we'd never even tried before. The guys got new outfits too, didn't you, Colin?'

Like Brenda, Colin didn't give her the courtesy of a reply.

Eileen felt something wet on her cheek and wiped away the tear with the back of her hand.

'That night, Gary had his gig, and along we all went...' Her gaze flicked to her husband, and he gave her a sad smile that almost made her feel sorry for him. He'd spent his whole life chasing that high he'd felt that night, but no amount of champagne and flash cars had ever delivered it. 'We were young, we were having the time of our lives, and we all thought we were indestructible. When the gig ended, the crowd went wild. Brenda, I remember you dancing on top of a table and Colin caught you when you toppled off...'

'And I shrugged him off and climbed back up by myself,' Brenda said quietly, finally speaking, almost to herself, staring into the middle distance as if she were right back there too, reliving it moment by moment.

Eileen noticed a look passing between Brenda's daughters, as if that surprised them. That was young Brenda. She was definitely the quietest of the group, but she was always fun, always happy, always the type to pick herself back up and keep going. Eileen wondered if she was still like that or if, like the rest of them, time had changed her.

'Anyone else want to take over?' Eileen asked, knowing what the answer would be.

Gary didn't have the bottle. Colin was staring at his shoes. Brenda was now glaring straight at her, eyes blazing. That was her answer, right there. Her punishment.

'Loud and clear,' she said, noting the unspoken slight that had passed between them.

Aiden still hadn't said a word and she wondered if he even recognised the woman she was describing.

'What happened next?' the younger sister asked.

'Hang on, Millie,' Zara chided her. 'Let Mrs Gregg speak in her own time.' So her name was Millie after all. She was so like the young Brenda, with her wild hair that no amount of gel would control, and the huge brown eyes that took everything in.

Eileen sighed, feeling her chest tighten again. *Right about now, please God. If you're going to strike me down, make it now.*

She was still breathing.

Damn.

'After the gig, someone suggested another club, and off we went there. It was packed, crazy busy, but I had money to burn, and we were determined to spend it. We drank too much, we danced until we ached, but the place was heaving and then, somehow, we all got split up. Gary and I found each other first, and we searched for the others for ages, but couldn't find them. To be honest, we were so tipsy that they could have been standing in front of us and we'd have missed them, and that's the truth.'

Eileen saw that Brenda was still watching her intently and realised this was probably the first time she'd heard this part of the story. The last time they'd spoken was just a short while later and there was no opportunity for a calm, informative exchange of information.

'In the end, Gary and I thought they might have gone on back to the hotel and we headed there, but nope, no sign of them. We didn't have mobile phones back then, and there was no internet, but it just wasn't in our minds to worry. It was a different time. People went out of communication and there was no panic. Besides, we figured they were probably together and searching for us too.'

Colin had finally raised his head and he was eyeing her with something that resembled contempt. Eileen wanted to shrivel, to stop, but she was right at the very edge of the precipice, there was no way back, and all she had to do was fall. All she could do was welcome the oblivion that the drop would bring her.

'Gary and I went back to our room, and, well, one thing led to another. I hate that cliché, but my son is here, and I want to spare him the details.'

'Appreciated.' Aiden spoke for the first time since she'd begun.

'I've no idea how much time passed, but we fell asleep and a while later, your parents came back and found us there. And that was the end of our friendship. We've never spoken since.' She stopped, praying that was enough, and that she wouldn't have to fill in any more blanks.

'Wait a minute, so that's it?' Millie was speaking up again, twirling her half-empty glass as she did so. 'Were you mad that they went home without you, Mum? Or did something happen to you while you were out and you were pissed off because she'd left you? I don't get it.'

'That's because, my love,' Brenda took over, 'what Eileen has omitted to mention so far, is that back then, she was your dad's girlfriend. And Gary was my boyfriend, not hers.'

21

THE SUNSET MOTEL, LAS VEGAS – 1993

The room was sticky hot and there was no air con, no fresh air, and no switches by the bedside to control the lights in the room, so when the door opened and the overhead light came on, there was nothing Eileen could do to hide her nudity except pull at the discarded sheet and try to cover as much of her body as possible.

Of course, it was too late.

Brenda had already seen everything, and so had Colin.

'Oh fuck,' Gary groaned, still drunk enough to slur, but sober enough to know that they'd just done something that was going to change their lives. 'Brenda, I... Fuck. Colin, mate...' He ran out of words, given that there were none that would make a damn bit of a difference in this situation.

'Don't you dare call me mate...' Colin seethed, and Brenda realised it was the first time she'd ever seen Colin angry. In all the years they'd been friends, he was always the peacemaker, the joker, the easy-going one with practical solutions. 'You're no fucking mate of mine now.'

Brenda just stared, and bizarrely the thought crossed her mind that when it came to Gary's panic, he'd mentioned her first. And she hated herself for being so bloody weak that she thought that way. So still she stared, waiting for the scene to change, for the alcohol to leave her system and for her mind to learn that this was just a really bad trip on some dodgy booze and it wasn't actually happening.

'Brenda, I'm so sorry...' Eileen's voice was higher than she'd ever heard it, a gush of strangled words. 'I didn't mean it. Didn't mean for this to happen. Didn't plan—'

'To have sex with my boyfriend?' Brenda didn't recognise her own voice. Just a few minutes ago, she'd fallen in the door giggling, and now her world had ended and she was someone else altogether. Someone she didn't want to be, in a place she didn't want to be in.

She picked up her bag, threw in everything that she could find. Grabbed her passport, her purse, her travellers' cheques...

'Brenda, please! Stay. Talk to me. Let me explain...' That came from Gary.

Brenda didn't even respond, just kept packing her stuff, then threw her bag over her shoulder. Gary had somehow managed to get his boxers on and he was on his feet now. Brenda still didn't look at him. She couldn't. He was the love of her life, the guy that she adored, the one who'd been her boyfriend for three years, no matter how strange people thought that was. Flash, overconfident, drop-dead gorgeous Gary, with little Brenda, the sweet girl who'd not long qualified as a nurse. Not a model. Not one of the sexy dancers in the club. Not even that stunner, Eileen, that worked in the ticket office.

Brenda. He'd been going out with her since before he'd started DJing, and they were still together, despite all sorts of rumours about what he got up to when she wasn't there. Brenda didn't believe them because she loved him, and because his best mate, Colin, who'd been seeing Eileen for even longer than she'd been with Gary, assured her they weren't true. That's why they'd always been such a great foursome. Eileen and Colin, madly in love for the last four years, despite the fact that she had a good couple of inches on him, and she was a total glamour girl, while he was a bit of a geek. That was her type, she always said. She liked them smart and funny, and Colin was both.

Eileen and Brenda were best friends, Colin and Gary were best mates, and it all worked out brilliantly. Sometimes, after a few drinks in the lock-in after work, they'd joke about how they should have a double wedding, then kids at the same time and raise them in a communal house... Brenda just hadn't realised she'd be sharing everything, including her boyfriend.

'Brenda, will you just stop a minute?' Gary begged her, but she blocked out the very sound of his voice, ominously sure that if he said another word, she'd throw up right there and then. Instead, she opened the door and walked out.

She'd made it to the pavement outside the hotel, when she realised that Colin had come after her and he looked just as shellshocked as she was. Yet another piece of her heart chipped off, this time for him. He was such a good guy. So sweet. And he adored Eileen. Sometimes, he joked that he couldn't believe he'd managed to land a girlfriend like her. Brenda could believe it. She saw his kindness, his intelligence, and was there night after night when he had them roaring with laughter at his daft jokes and funny chat. He was a catch. He just didn't realise it.

'I don't know where to go,' Brenda said, her whole body beginning to shiver as she slipped into shock, despite the heat of the May night.

Just at that, a taxi pulled into the hotel drive, and Colin ushered her in. 'The Flamingo please,' he said. Later he told her that it was the only place he could think of because that was where Eileen had won the money on the roulette. Turned out his mind was every bit as scrambled as hers.

At the hotel, she used her traveller's cheques to pay upfront for a room – two single beds – and they went upstairs.

He poured them two vodkas from the minibar, because they were the first drinks that came to hand. He topped the glasses up with a can of Coke, then brought Brenda's over to the bed. He pulled a blanket from the bottom of the bed around her shoulders, gave her the drink, then lay back on the other bed, staring at the ceiling.

Sometime later, Brenda had no idea how long, she spoke first. 'Are you okay?' Stupid question, but it was all she had, and it was in her nature to worry about everyone else. Just a shame Gary and Eileen hadn't been worried about her or Colin. That thought sent rivers of tears to her bottom lids and she blinked them back furiously.

Colin was still staring into space. 'No. Not okay.' He was deathly calm, and she almost wished he would get up and kick something. Punch a wall. Throw the telly out of the window. Anything. For once in her perfectly behaved, sensible life, she'd have joined him and caused an absolute riot. 'I... I loved her. I never thought she'd...' He couldn't finish and Brenda could see he was struggling to fight back tears too.

She had no idea what was happening in the other hotel room. She didn't know that Eileen was sobbing her heart out. She had no idea that Gary was pacing the floor, swearing constantly because he couldn't find any other words.

All she knew was that it was over for them all.

And she never wanted to see Gary Gregg or Eileen Smith again for as long as she lived.

22

ZARA

Millie drained her glass and then put it down on the glass table and gestured to the waiter to bring another round of drinks. 'I think I'm having an out-of-body experience. You know, one of those ones in sci-fi movies where you look down at yourself and you're robbing a post office, and you convince yourself it's true, even although you don't own a balaclava. Only that would be more believable than this.'

Zara eyed her sister with nothing but incredulity. 'Really? That's where you're going with this?' She leaned over and put her hand over her mother's. 'Mum, I'm so sorry. I had no idea. I feel awful, because you're having to relive all this and it's completely my fault.'

'It is definitely her fault and hers alone. She planned it all,' Millie said, the drinks she'd consumed removing all vestiges of solidarity with her sister.

Zara ignored her. 'And I'm so sorry about what happened back then too. Your reaction to our surprise is all making sense now. I'd never have brought you here if I'd known, I—'

'But that's the thing, love, you didn't know. The only people who ever knew the whole story were the four of us. And Gran Ada. She used to tell me that she'd bribed an old pal in border control to notify her if Gary ever re-entered the country, so she could settle the score.' Zara caught her mum's sad smile and knew that she would be missing gran more than ever right now. 'Thing is, I was never 100 per cent sure she was kidding.' Her mum's whole demeanour changed when she moved her stare to Aiden's dad. 'You probably had a lucky escape,' she told him, with no humour in her voice at all.

Gary Gregg didn't even make an attempt at a retort and Zara was the one who was staring at him now, feeling a whole bucket of emotions and not quite sure which one was going to rise to the top.

First of all, there was shock. Her mum and this guy? She just couldn't imagine them together. Her mum was so... well, reserved. Measured. Conventional. And she meant that in the nicest way. Her mum and dad went together, not this guy who, in fairness, looked like he'd just walked off a movie set. She could see where Aiden got the genes, the smile and the wide shoulders from. Picturing her mum with this guy was... Eurgh. That gave her the weirdest shiver right down her spine.

She felt exactly the same about her dad and Aiden's mum. First up, it was hard to believe that she'd given birth to the man on the other sofa, because this woman sitting here looked like she was closer to forty than over fifty. Wild guess, and yes, judgemental, but all Zara could think was that to maintain that level of self-preservation, she clearly had too much time, too much money, and not enough friends to hang out with. That level of maintenance was so far removed from the father that she knew. Her dad didn't even moisturise and he had a fit when Mum suggested paying thirty quid for a course of yoga classes at the community centre.

Next up on the emotional tombola was sorrow that her mum had to go through that. To lose her boyfriend and her best friend at the same time, and to deal with that level of betrayal must have been crushing for the young Brenda. Especially so far from home and at a time when she'd been so happy, so thrilled to be here. Zara had no idea how someone would come back from that kind of heartbreak. And for her dad to be gazumped by this bloke? Sure, he had the aftershave-advert jawline going on, but Zara would bet her Calvin Harris 2018 tour T-shirt that he didn't have the smarts or the capacity for care that their dad had shown them all their lives. Their dad was the most solid, reliable, dependable guy she'd ever known. In a lot of ways, her Kev reminded her of him. They both had the same quiet, low-maintenance approach to life. Gary Gregg was at the other end of the maintenance spectrum. There were definitely traces of hair dye in there. That tan was just a bit too perfect to be natural, the teeth a bit too white to be his own. And as for the clothes... Zara recognised the Hermès belt and the Prada symbol on the chest of his shirt. That lot probably cost more than her dad had paid for his new Flymo.

What did it say about a man that he had to put that much effort into his looks? Yes, she was being judgemental again, but if she met that guy in a bar, she'd think he was just a touch too fond of himself. Although, granted, Aiden seemed to have turned out pretty well and totally came off as humble and balanced. He must be a genetic blip.

Fury was also in her emotional melting pot. Right now, Zara could barely look at Aiden's mum and she felt utterly disgusted that one woman could do that to another, especially one she was supposed to love. And how could a bloke break Bro Code like that? He should be drummed out of the manhood.

And finally, there was confusion. She still had questions. If their mum and dad were the two who were betrayed, how did they end up married just a few days later? How could you go from devastation to getting hitched in forty-eight hours?

This wasn't making sense, but she wanted to talk to her mum on her own, and not ask her all these questions in front of the others. She'd been through enough and Zara had an overwhelming urge to protect her.

Drunk Millie didn't have the same level of restraint when it came to the founder members of Cheaters Anonymous. 'Can't believe you could have been my dad,' she was whittering now to Gary. Judas. 'Holy shit, my jaw would have been huge. I'd have looked like Buzz Lightyear.'

Zara was about to suggest that they go, when her mum beat her to it. With absolute elegance and class, Brenda stood up, smoothed down the skirt of her pale blue crepe dress, cleared her throat and spoke with utter serenity, even though she was perennially allergic to drama and Zara knew her heart must be thudding like a train.

'I think we're done here,' she said. 'Gary, Eileen, it seems like you have a very nice son, so at least you did something right. I wish you all well, but let's leave it another thirty years until we do this again.'

Her dad jumped out of his chair. Zara did likewise.

'Aiden, I'm sorry, I should never have dragged you into this.'

He shrugged, his whole body as slumped as that impressively solid core would allow. 'How could either of us have known? I'm sorry too.'

The poor guy. Zara was absolutely gutted. Somehow, in the process of trying to do something great, she'd inadvertently taken a bomb to his understanding of his parents and their history too. She felt terrible, even though the root cause of the problem definitely wasn't on her.

She took a couple of steps when she realised that Millie was still sitting there.

'Millie! Come on.'

'Shit, sorry,' her sister said, jumping up. 'I got a bit transfixed on his jaw there. I mean, no amount of contouring would make that work on me.'

Zara thought about saying something to Aiden's parents but couldn't think of anything on the spot.

Sorry you're both mad shaggers who devastated my parents' lives...

You two deserve each other...

And my parents deserve so much more than either of you...

Zara bit her bottom lip, knowing she'd come up with a killer line in about an hour and a half, and hate herself for not thinking of it in the moment. Maybe she could email them?

Millie was more focused on the practicalities. Zara saw her lean over to the waiter who had served them and speak loudly enough for Aiden's dad to hear every word. 'Thank you so much for the drinks. Big Tom Selleck here is going to pay, and he's going to leave a huge tip. Fricking gigantic.'

The waiter hot-footed it away to get the bill before someone changed their mind.

Zara slipped her arm through her mum's, and watched as she kept her head held high while they left the corner of the restaurant that they'd been sitting in. They'd only gone a few steps when her dad stopped.

'Hang on a minute, I forgot something.'

Zara sighed. This was not the time to be leaving your specs, your phone or your copy of *Landscapers Weekly* on a table in a restaurant in the bloody Bellagio. All she wanted to do was to get them all out of there, so they could go back to their hotel, climb into their comfy clothes, and spend the next few hours day drinking while finding out every single detail of what had happened here three decades ago.

Her dad passed them on his way back to the table, and as Zara turned to see what he'd forgotten, she saw Aiden, his mum and dad all rise from the table, clearly getting ready to leave, his dad clutching his credit card as he waited for the bill.

Zara, Millie and their mum kept an eye on Dad, just to make sure that he didn't get into any sort of further discussion with his old friend. He didn't. Instead, he walked right up to Gary Gregg, stretched up slightly on to the balls of his feet, and swung a right hook that would have taken down a tree.

'I've been waiting to do that for thirty years,' Colin told him, as Gary Gregg staggered and fell back down onto the seat he'd just left, clutching that admirable jawline.

Beside Zara, her mum gasped, while Millie let out a hoot of hilarity. 'Who invited Lennox Lewis to the party?'

Their dad didn't hear either of their reactions. Across at the other side of the room, he simply turned on the heel of his left loafer, spun round and marched back towards them, leaving a visibly stunned Gary clutching his face.

'You okay, Dad?' she asked, when he reached her.

'Fine, thank you, Zara. Now let's get out of here and get back to the room please.'

'Sore hand?' she asked, spotting the problem immediately.

'So bad I want to cry. Now, let's keep moving so I can get this in ice before it starts to swell.'

He strutted right past them, leaving the three women in the family going like speed walkers to keep up with him.

Zara didn't know whether to laugh or cry. She'd never been prouder of her parents. She'd never been more shocked by her father.

And she'd never been more concerned that she might not have enough bail money to keep her holiday companions out of a foreign jail.

23

BRENDA

Flanked by her daughters, and rushing to keep up with her husband, Brenda had walked back across to their own hotel, taken the elevator up to their floor, and made it to their room, all with considerable calm... right up until they got into the privacy of their own space, when her body shot a cannon of adrenaline around her bloodstream and she couldn't stop the trembling in her hands, her arms, her whole body.

Brenda had checked out Colin's hand in the lift, and she was fairly sure nothing was broken. She'd suggested going to A&E for an X-ray, just to be on the safe side, but he'd refused, saying it felt fine.

In the end, Zara went to help her dad sort out ice for his hand, while Millie came to the room with her, ostensibly to provide moral support, but more because Millie had the practical skills of a floor lamp, and at the first challenge, she'd abandon the ice for Colin's hand and just pop a few cubes in a gin and tonic instead.

These were all the thoughts that were going through Brenda's mind, while she somehow managed to get her shift dress off and pull on her comfy red cotton yoga pants and matching T-shirt – staples in her wardrobe despite the fact that Colin's tightness had put her right off actually going to yoga.

Millie had poured her a glass of wine from the minibar, and if Brenda ever needed it, it was right now. It was hard to say what had shaken her more: coming face to face with Gary Gregg or meeting Eileen again after all these years. She still wasn't sure that had really happened. Gary and Eileen. Even saying their names in her mind made her heart race and her stomach twist. She'd loved them both – more than she'd ever loved anyone else except her girls. Maybe even more than she'd ever loved Colin. Although, of course, the only person she would admit that to was herself.

She was mulling that over when there was a knock at the door and Millie opened it to let Zara in, face pale and an unopened bottle of wine in hand. 'I brought reinforcements,' she said, holding it up. 'Figured we might need this.'

'Sometimes I think we have nothing in common and then you bring vino,' Millie quipped, taking the bottle and putting it in the fridge, then pouring a glass from the open Prosecco for her sister.

'How is your dad?' Brenda asked, feeling guilty that she hadn't gone with Colin to take care of him, instead of letting Zara do it.

'All sorted. I got him the ice and he's taken it next door to our room. I went with him, but he says he wants to just take a minute to think things through, while he sorts out his hand. I think he's in shock. I'll go back in and check on him in a wee while and just make sure he's okay. Do you want to talk about what just happened, Mum? I'm so sorry,' Zara apologised yet again and Brenda's heart went out to her. She'd meant well. In fact, under different history and circumstances, Brenda could see that this would have been an incredible surprise.

'Zara, please don't apologise. I can totally understand how you thought this would be wonderful. And it would have been, only... well... you heard. Can you give me a minute before we talk about it anymore though? I just need the shaking to stop.'

Zara reached over and hugged her, while Millie went for changing the subject.

'Did you call Kev while you were next door too?' Millie asked, attempting to adopt her most innocent expression. It was a waste of time. Millie hadn't looked innocent in at least a decade.

'Yeah, I did...' Zara answered, and Brenda heard the twinge of emotion in her voice.

Millie, not usually particularly perceptive on matters of the heart – especially after a drink or four – heard it too. 'But?' she challenged her sister.

Zara immediately went on the defensive. 'But nothing.'

'So why are you off the phone already?'

'Because I wanted to come back and sit with Mum.'

Millie wasn't letting it go. 'And...? What are you not telling us? Don't make me torture you with a bendy straw.'

Zara caved. 'You really need to get out of my business and get a life. But since you insist, Kev was a bit busy with some online coding group he's a member of. Asked if I could give him a call back tomorrow.'

Millie handed the glass of Prosecco to Zara. 'Right, that's it. I keep my mouth shut all the time...'

'Millie, you never keep your mouth shut,' her sister countered, and Brenda wasn't getting in on this argument. She'd always made a point of letting them sort out their own squabbles, especially when, like today, it gave her a bit of breathing space to think. Right now, she had plenty of stuff to mull over.

'Well, this shouldn't be a surprise then. But honestly, Zar, this guy... I love him but he's not good enough for you. He makes zero effort.'

'Yeah, well, at least he sticks around long enough for breakfast,' Zara retorted, and Brenda knew it was a dig at Millie's enthusiastic fondness for a one-night stand. Brenda didn't get involved in that either. As long as Millie was being safe, she figured it was none of her business. 'Anyway, can we drop this? I don't want to talk about anything to do with me today, especially after this morning. All that matters is that Dad's fine, Mum's fine, and we can fight about trivial shit tomorrow,' Zara demanded, with uncharacteristic vehemence.

Even Millie got the message that it was time to change the subject.

Zara snapped out of the confrontation and joined Brenda at the chairs by the window. 'I still can't believe Dad punched that guy. I've never been so proud of you both, Mum. Or astonished, to be honest.'

Brenda knew her face had slipped into a sad smile. The truth was, she'd been pretty shocked herself. Not once, in the lifetime that she'd known him, had Colin Jones ever resorted to violence and it was both astounding and, in a strange way, encouraging to see him actually exhibit some emotion. She wasn't sure where that left them, but at least it showed he was capable of feelings, of being present, of having a shred of passion in that heart of his. Thing was, she wasn't sure if his outrage had been for her or for Eileen. And she wasn't even sure if that mattered.

Beside her, Zara let out a sigh and reached for her hand. 'I know I keep saying it, Mum, but I really am so sorry. I had no idea.'

'We!' Millie interjected indignantly.

'*We* had no idea,' Zara corrected herself.

They sat in peaceful silence for a few moments before Millie cracked first.

'Okay, if you won't ask her, I will. Mum, we need to know. What in the hell happened back then? How do you go from breaking up with your boyfriend and falling out with your trashy best friend...' Millie held her hand up, warning off her sister. 'Don't you dare correct me. The woman slept with her best pal's boyfriend. It's the very definition of trashy.'

Zara immediately jumped in with, 'Fine. But, Mum, I know it's none of our business, and please say if you're still not ready to talk or if you don't want to tell us. We completely understand.'

'No we don't,' Millie countered. 'Our dad just punched a man twice his size. I want to know exactly what happened to turn him into the accountant version of Rocky. Like the other Rocky, but this one is great with tax returns.'

Brenda sighed, knowing in her heart that they deserved the truth. 'Where do you want me to start?'

Zara sat forward in her chair. 'At where Aiden's mum left off. You found them together, you and Dad walked out, and then what...'

Brenda closed her eyes, right back there, living that moment again.

'We went to another hotel, got a room, and I cried for twenty-four hours straight. The whole time, I was throwing up, and I thought I was just overwrought, before I realised... my period was late. In all the excitement of the trip, I'd completely missed the dates.'

'Oh no, Mum...' Zara's voice was barely a whisper.

'Your dad went out and bought three tests, we did them all, and every one was positive.'

There was not one second of that morning that Brenda didn't remember. The fear. The horror. The unmitigated grief of knowing that she was having a baby by a man who'd just betrayed her in the worst way. And the hardest part of all was knowing that the one person she'd instinctively turn to in this situation, was the best friend who'd chosen Gary over her.

'Your dad was so lovely. He held my hand, made me drinks, talked to me until we were hoarse, trying to figure out what I should do.'

Brenda saw Zara's eyes were swimming with tears now. She had to clear her throat to shift the emotion that had lodged there before she went on, knowing that if she didn't get all this out right now, she'd never be able to tell them.

'We went out for a walk a couple of nights later, more to clear my head and get out of the room and that's when we walked past the marriage chapel. It was late. Dark. I'd been crying for days. I was a mess.'

'Marry me,' Colin had blurted.

Brenda had gazed at him like he'd lost his mind. Which he most certainly had.

'We don't need them, Brenda. Fuck them. We were always closer than they were anyway.' It had been a slight exaggeration, but only just. She and Colin had known each other the longest, had introduced the other two. 'I'll help with the baby, and you won't need to explain to everyone you meet for the rest of your life who the father is and what happened to him. Marry me. We'll do this together.'

Somehow, in that moment, the young, terrified, devastated Brenda had agreed. It was his point about Gary that had swung it. She never wanted to mention his name again, to explain where he'd gone, didn't want to think about him, and she really thought marrying Colin would make that happen. That was the naivety of youth right there.

'Your dad asked me to marry him, right there in the street. And just by sheer chance, I was already wearing the white sundress I'd bought when Eileen and I had gone shopping. We had no marriage licence, but we went into the chapel anyway and discovered that Elvis had a free slot. He married us there and then and I still can't listen to "Suspicious Minds". Then we flew home a day early so we wouldn't have to see them on the flight. Turns out, they didn't come back anyway, so we never saw them again.'

Zara jumped forward in her seat, spilling her drink. 'Wait, wait, wait, rewind, Mum – you were pregnant? And Dad wanted to marry you even though the baby wasn't his? Hang on... Oh shit. Were you pregnant with me? Oh my God, is Gary *my* dad?'

Brenda could see her first-born daughter trying to do the maths in her head, but before she could put her out of her misery, Zara got there first. 'No, what am I saying? I'm twenty-nine next month, so he can't be. So that means... Oh, Mum.'

Brenda nodded, feeling the pain of what she was about to say, the gut-wrenching travesty of a life lost before it even began. 'Sorry, sweetheart, I didn't mean to scare you and of course it wasn't you. I was pregnant with another baby. Your brother or sister. We'll never know because a couple of weeks after we got back home, out of the blue, I began to bleed and it was gone. I was maybe five or six weeks pregnant at the most.'

Not that the length of the pregnancy had mattered to her. It had been so much more than just a simple fact of life. Brenda had sobbed her heart out for weeks, slumped into a deep depression, until Colin and her mother became seriously worried and Ada had called in the doctor. He'd given her tablets to make her sleep at night, and it was slow progress, but after a few weeks they began to work. After a couple of months, she didn't need them anymore and in a moment of something – maybe gratitude or desperation to feel human again - she and Colin had somehow ended up in bed, seeking solace, closeness, attachment. By that time, she didn't know what she would do without him. He'd become the only person she could talk to, the only one who understood.

'Then, a month later, I found out I was pregnant again with you.'

Millie still wasn't satisfied with all the details. 'Wait – I'm back at the marriage license bit now. You said you didn't have one? So are you and Dad not actually legally married?'

That had been the most significant crossroads in her life. Her Sliding Doors moment. She and Colin could have respectfully separated, found a way to stay friends and to bring their daughter up together, or...

'We got married in the registry office in Glasgow three months later.

Just your dad, his parents, me and Gran Ada.' Colin had said he loved her, she'd said it too – they'd both known it was the friendship kind of love, but for them, back then, it had been enough. In fact, they were both so wounded, it had been all that either of them could bear. They had each other, and they had their baby on the way to make them whole –that had felt like all they needed.

'And you made it work,' Zara mused, tears sliding down her face.

'We made it work,' Brenda told her. She wasn't lying. For a huge chunk of their lives, they'd been happy, bringing up the girls, being the family that Brenda had loved. It was only in recent years, after the girls had left, that it had stopped being enough.

'Wait – so when is your actual wedding anniversary?'

'The twenty-fourth of October,' Brenda admitted ruefully. 'We just always told everyone that it was the nineteenth of May because that was the date of the Vegas wedding and well before I fell pregnant. Stopped any doubts and questions and it wasn't a complete lie.'

Zara pulled her knees up to her chest and rested her head on them. 'Nooooooo. All this and it isn't even the right fricking date. Next year I'm sending you flowers and a card. In October,' she wailed.

Brenda exhaled, glad that she'd finally told them the truth. She could have gone even further, explained why her lifetime of care and affection with Colin was no longer working, why she felt now that it was time for a different life, but she made the decision to leave the next chapter closed for now. This was enough for one day. It was a plan that held for about thirty seconds, until Millie, over on the bed, piped up with a question.

'Hang on, then, Mum. When you and Dad got married here, you weren't in love with each other. Is that right?'

Brenda felt a red rash of discomfort rise up her neck. This was way too close for comfort. This was a conversation for another time, but hadn't she vowed to be honest with them? There had been too many secrets in this family for too long.

'We loved each other,' she began, then saw from the quizzical expressions that greeted her reply, that it wasn't going to suffice. Full disclosure. 'But no, we weren't in love.'

'But you fell in love later, right?' Zara asked, and the hope in her words made tears spring to Brenda's eyes. She blinked them away. Truth. No lies.

'Honestly? I don't know that we ever did. We've been best friends for all of our married lives, but I'm not sure that we ever actually fell in love. I think Gary and Eileen left too many shadows for that.'

Her daughters were both staring at her now, Millie in something that seemed like horror, Zara with very obvious sympathy.

'Mum, can I ask you something? Do you think that's enough? The friendship and the love, but without all the bells and whistles of the head-over-heels stuff? Is it enough to make a great life together?' Of course that came from Zara. And Brenda had to think about her answer before she spoke, because she just couldn't shift the nagging worry that her daughter was following in her footsteps.

'I don't think so, my love. I really don't.'

24

AIDEN

His dad had been lying on his bed for a full ten minutes, and the
nosebleed that had started in the elevator had finally stopped. Still, he
howled as Aiden held a towel full of ice on his face. Aiden chose not to
point out that growing up, whenever he got injured playing sport, his dad
would just tell him to slap some ice on and work through the pain. Somehow, he didn't think that advice would go down too well right now with the
bloke lying on the bed making noises about potential concussion. Instead,
he went with a more reassuring, 'Dad, he punched you on the nose. I think
a concussion is pretty unlikely.'

Over in the corner, his mom had barely said a word, as if she'd slipped
into some kind of self-reflective trance. And no wonder. Aiden's brain was
still pretty close to exploding thanks to the events of the last couple of
hours. His mom and his dad, both cheating on their partners when they
got together? And getting caught in such a brutal way? It cast a whole new
light on their relationship, and he had no idea how he felt about it. The
one thing he did know was that he couldn't really blame Zara's dad for
trying to knock out his former pal. Thankfully, no one in the restaurant
other than their group had actually witnessed the blow, so they'd managed
to avoid a brush with the law. Small consolation.

'You okay over there, Mom?'

Eileen shrugged. 'Not really. Embarrassed. Sad. Regretful. It was the biggest mistake of my life...'

'Shanks vethy muth,' his dad murmured from under the ice pack. Aiden pressed down very slightly harder and got a howl of complaint which he ignored.

His mom went on, 'And I could make a dozen excuses for it, but the truth is, it was a moment of madness...'

They both ignored his dad's, 'Ppfffft,' of objection.

'...and my greatest shame. I've never stopped thinking about it, regretting it, wishing it were different. My only consolation, and I've reminded myself of it every single day since then, is that if all that stuff hadn't happened, then I wouldn't have you. If I could go back, I'd change it all, but not if it meant I didn't end up with you.'

Aiden exhaled, not really sure where to go with this, but knowing that no matter what had happened back then, he was responsible for bringing it all into their lives now. 'I can't believe that I opened you up to all this. I'm so sorry. I honestly thought I was doing something great for you, something that you'd love.'

'I know that, son, and you don't need to apologise to me. If anything, it should be the other way round. It must be pretty shocking to have found all this out about us. Especially on top of what you were already dealing with. Your opinion of us must have crashed and burned today.'

Aiden saw her eyes fill up and tried not to show his surprise. His mom wasn't a crier. She was the one who just took the hit, then got right back up again. In fact, before the conversation in the restaurant earlier, he couldn't remember ever seeing her cry, and that was unleashing a bit of a panic in his gut. He let go of the ice pack. 'Here, Dad, you do this yourself.'

The other wound in the room was far more important right now. He went to his mom and hugged her, letting her hang on until she was ready to release him.

'Thank you, son,' she said, brushing away more tears.

'Mom, I know this is crap, and I wish I could say the right thing to make you feel better, so here's how I see it... You were young. It was one mistake, and it was thirty years ago. Unless you've got some other dark secrets that I don't know about...'

That made the corners of her mouth turn up. 'None that I'm prepared to admit.'

Her sense of humour was still there. Hopefully that was a good sign.

'Okay, then you need to let this go and forgive yourself. And anyway, as you rightly pointed out, if that hadn't happened and you hadn't married Dad, then you wouldn't have a son who tries to do good shit and ends up breaking your heart and decimating your life. So, you know, there's always that bonus.'

Sniffing, trying to smile, she leaned over and hugged him again. 'So true.'

Weary, he got up and flicked on the coffee maker at the drinks bar. While he was there, he checked his phone. Two texts. The first from Zara.

OMFG. That's all. OH. MY. FUCKING. GOD. And I'm sorry. Again. Hope you haven't been disowned. Zx

He had a flashback to Zara's face when everything was revealed downstairs and the devastation was clear to see. All those months in the planning, all the thought she'd put into it, the anticipation of the big surprise, only to be crapped upon from a great height by his mum and dad. He felt an overwhelming urge to apologise, to make amends, to do something, anything to repair the damage. He texted back...

Not disowned yet. Apologies for our team wrecking your surprise. Hope you're all okay. Can I do anything to make this better? Ax

No immediate response. Okay. Understandable.

He opened the second text, this one from Trevon.

Hey, parents killed each other yet? Mom okay?

This text was a lot easier to write.

Shitshow. Dad got his lights punched out. Mom is struggling. Loads going on. Long story. Can't talk now, will call you later.

His dad was still licking his wounds on the bed, so he pulled a beer out of the minibar and took it over to him. 'Here you go, Pop,' he said, lifting the ice from his dad's face and trying not to wince. It didn't look great. As far as he could see, the nose wasn't broken, but it was definitely swollen and the bruising was already coming up and spreading under his eyes. The good-looking face would probably need dark glasses to cover two black eyes by the end of the day. It was always the little guys you had to watch. How many times had his dad told him that on the basketball court and the soccer pitch?

Gary took the beer, but instead of opening it, he ditched the ice and held the can against his face instead.

Aiden went back over to sit with his mom, when a thought occurred to him.

'Can I ask a question?'

'Sure,' his mom replied, at the same time as his dad said, 'Nope.'

Aiden went with the positive response. 'What happened next? I mean, how come you guys stayed here and didn't go home?'

His mum sighed long and hard before shrugging. 'Fate, I guess. That night, we waited for Colin and Brenda to come back, but there was no sign of them. We searched everywhere we could think of the next day, still nothing. We went back to the club your dad had played at, hoping they'd show up there, but of course they didn't. Then the owner asked your dad to do a set...'

'I wasn't going to turn that down. The place was jumping,' his dad mumbled.

Aiden's inner soul was shaking his head. It was getting tougher by the minute to have any sympathy for this guy.

The expression of shade that his mom threw to her ex-husband suggested she felt the same. There was no way on earth these two were ever going to find a way to come back together, especially now that their worst secrets were out and they were reliving them. His mum's disgust for his dad and for herself was in every word she spoke.

'Turns out, the guy had a load of venues and a new club opening in South Carolina. Asked your dad to do a gig there, said he'd pay for the flights. When the time came for our return flights to Scotland, we were going to go to the airport and beg Colin and Brenda to forgive us, but we changed our minds. Couldn't face it. We were such cowards. Instead, we flew to South Carolina the next day and never left.'

'And you stayed together.'

It was a statement, not a question.

'Yeah. Probably shouldn't have,' his mom conceded. 'But then you came along – we were pretty sure you were conceived that first night here. Maybe in another world we wouldn't have made it in those early years, but it was just the two of us with this perfect little guy, so we stuck together, and—'

'Wait, what?' That came from his dad, who winced as he pushed himself up on one shoulder and now looked even more pissed off. 'You don't think we'd have stayed together if we didn't have Aiden?'

Aiden was already regretting raising the subject.

His mom shook her head. 'Come on, Gary, you know it. I fell madly in love with you, convinced myself we would make it work, but you were never deserving of that because look how you behaved. Do you honestly think I'd have put up with how you treated me if I didn't have the best reason in the world to stay? Look, I'm not going to drag everything back up – no point now and Aiden has heard enough about his imperfect sodding parents for one day – but we both know it's true. We weren't right for each other, not then, not now, not ever. I just wish I'd found that out sooner than I did.'

'Ah, fuck this,' Gary exclaimed, pushing himself up off the bed. 'I'm out of here. No point staying now.'

'Woah, Dad. Wait a minute. You're in no state to fly.'

'Couldn't give a toss, I'm going. Not exactly the boys' trip you promised, son, is it?'

'What? Are you kidding me?' Aiden rarely got angry. Rarely lashed out. Rarely disrespected his parents. But, right now, he was building up to all three of those things in his father's direction. 'So because you're pissed off, you're just going to bail?'

'What's the point of staying?'

'Because maybe we can spend time as a family. Talk. Work out how to move forward, make this better?'

For a moment, he thought his dad was going to see his point, then...

'Look, son, I appreciate the thought, but this isn't working for me.' He headed over to the wardrobe, pulled his suitcase out from the bottom and opened it on the bed, talking while he threw things inside. 'When you called me about this trip, I agreed to come because I thought we could spend time together. Hit some bars. Do a bit of gambling. See where the night took us. Then you ambushed me with your mother...'

'Nice,' Eileen mumbled, but Gary ignored her.

"...but I still thought, ok, maybe we can work some stuff out and still have a good time. I don't want to sit and talk about my feelings. I'm too fucking old for that. I am who I am.'

Trousers in. Shoes in. Shirts off hanger and in. And still he was talking.

'Eileen, I love you. I do. I love what we had and I love our boy. But I'm not going to beg you to forgive me, or to love me back, and I'm not going to live my life trying to get your approval because I'm too fucking old for that too.'

Into the bathroom and then back out. Toiletries in.

'I understand I've been a dick, and a disappointment to you both. Eileen, I'm sorry, truly, for everything I did. You didn't deserve that and I'll always regret it. From now on, I'll be more respectful and I won't be an asshole when we meet. I hope that's good enough for you because it's all I've got.'

Case closed, zipped up. Pulled off the bed.

'Son, I apologise to you too. This was a good thing you tried to do this week and you're a credit to your mom, because I'm telling you, she's the one who raised you this way.'

Aiden unclenched his jaw. 'You don't need to tell me that.'

'You're right, but I want to, because your mom deserves to hear me say it. She's earned that. I'm proud of you, son. You're the best thing in my life and a better man than I'll ever be. Oh, and this face. I had that coming. But I'm not gonna cry over it, and I'm not going to sit here doing a post-mortem on everyone's feelings.'

'You don't want to go speak to Colin? Try to sort things out?'

'Nope. Because again, I'm too fucking old for that too. I love you both. Yep, you too, Eileen, whether you still believe that or not, it's true. I'll see you back in South Carolina. If you change your minds, you're welcome to join me. I'll be at the airport, in the bar, drinking until this face doesn't hurt any more.' He broke off to hug Aiden, then stormed out of the door, leaving them both open-mouthed and stunned.

'Do you think he does have concussion?' Aiden wondered aloud.

'If that's the case, he's had it since about 1989. He's not going to change, Aiden. He's flawed. He's an idiot. But he's generous and funny and there's some other good stuff in there too. Just don't have any expectations and you'll be fine.'

'What about you, Mom? Will you be fine?'

'Always,' she told him, but he could see the sadness. This had turned into one great big fricking nightmare and he felt awful that he'd caused it, all be it unwittingly. He couldn't bear to see his mum unhappy like this and right now his priority was taking care of her. He wasn't about to change how he felt about her because of a mistake she made thirty years ago and all he cared about was making sure she didn't let that mistake come back and consume her now either. She'd spent twenty years married to his dad. That was punishment enough.

'Do you want to go home? I can change our flights.'

She nodded and Aiden felt a pang of regret that they were about to walk away from the ashes of this trip with no progress or resolution.

'But not yet,' his mom added, surprising him. 'You said I need to forgive myself and you're right. But before I go, I need to ask someone else to forgive me too...'

25

EILEEN

Eileen knocked on the door, heart racing.

'Are you sure this is the right room?' she asked Aiden. His strength and decency never failed to impress her. He'd offered to come with her even though she had never felt more ashamed of herself. If he didn't resemble his father so much, she'd swear he'd been swapped at birth and she'd brought home the son of a decent, humble bloke with integrity and a healthy moral code, instead of, well, Gary.

Today had been a watershed moment for her and Gary. She'd always known who he was, but maybe for a long time, she'd refused to accept it. Maybe there had been hope – that he would see her, that he would change for her, that'd he'd realise she'd been the love of his life all along, that he needed her. The truth was, he never had. Gary only needed Gary. And today, when he'd gone off on his rant, a door had closed inside her. An acceptance. Both of him and of what they'd done. And with that came clarity. She had stayed with him for so much longer than she should have, because the guilt of how they'd got together had never left her. She'd convinced herself that the only justification for their one-night stand was that they had been meant to be together all along. It was the biggest lie she'd ever told and it was to herself. She'd made Gary her whole life because she'd already wrecked the one that she'd had with the person she'd loved most of all.

Her question about the room was answered when the door clicked, began to open, as a voice said, 'It'll just be room service, and... Oh.'

Eileen watched as Brenda's daughter, Zara, froze, eyes wide, first on her and then on Aiden.

'Hey...' the young woman managed.

'I'm sorry to bother you, and I know this must be a bit of a shock, but I wondered if I could speak to your mum.'

'Erm...'

Eileen's heart thudded even harder as she saw Zara bite her bottom lip, exactly the way Brenda used to do. It was like a step back in time and for a moment Eileen wanted to run, hide, block out what was going on. But wasn't that what she'd done before?

'I'll understand if she doesn't want to see me, but I'd appreciate you asking her. Maybe I could wait here?'

'Yeah, okay. Give me two mins,' Zara replied, not unkindly, before shooting an apologetic glance at Aiden and disappearing back inside and closing the door.

'She's not going to see me,' Eileen whispered, voice tight with anxiety.

'She will, Mom. Stay positive,' he replied, his big hand wrapping around her shaking fingers.

The door opened again. 'My mum says she'll see you, but only alone. Is that okay?'

'Yes,' Eileen replied instantly, flooded with relief, terrified at the same time.

'Okay, well,' Zara spoke to Aiden now. 'My dad and sister are in the next room, so we could go there, or maybe...'

'We could go downstairs for a drink?' Aiden suggested.

'Reading my mind,' the young woman said, before stepping aside, letting Eileen go past her and into the room.

'Thank you,' Eileen smiled at her, then glanced back to her son and Brenda's daughter. 'To both of you.'

'Good luck,' Zara said, with genuine kindness, as she stepped out to join Aiden in the corridor. The door closed behind her and Eileen took a deep breath and a few steps forward. That's when she spotted Brenda sitting in one of the chairs over by the window. The dress was gone, replaced by yoga pants and a T-shirt, exactly the same outfit Eileen would choose if she were home. Once upon a time, they'd had everything in common. They wore their hair the same way. Listened to the same music. Loved the same movies. Both swore they'd marry members of Duran Duran and, if they weren't available, Spandau Ballet would do. They were inseparable. The closest thing Eileen ever had to a sister. The only person, after her mum, who had loved her. Really loved her... And Eileen had sabotaged it all.

'Thank you for seeing me.'

'Did you expect me to say no?'

She heard the huskiness in Brenda's voice and wondered if she'd been crying too. Or maybe she was just finding it difficult to speak to the bitch who had destroyed her life and broken her heart.

'Can I sit down?' Eileen gestured to the other seat.

Brenda nodded. 'Sure.'

Okay. A tiny bit of progress.

Eileen took a seat before her legs collapsed beneath her.

To her surprise, Brenda took a wine bottle from an ice bucket on the table beside her, poured some into an empty glass and pushed it across the table to Eileen's side. Eileen was too scared to lift it in case her trembling hands tipped it all over her.

'Thank you.' A pause.

Brenda stared at her, understandably waiting for more.

'I don't have anything rehearsed, or know exactly what to say, but I just needed to tell you to your face how sorry I am. How sorry I've always been.' The tears were back, but she blinked them away. She wasn't the injured party here and Brenda deserved so much more than her tears. 'I said to Aiden earlier that it was a moment of madness and it was the only way I could describe it. I didn't plan it, neither of us did. It just happened, and I know how pathetic that sounds, but it's the truth and, well, I needed you to know that I didn't hurt you deliberately. I loved you. I truly did. I've spent my whole life ever since regretting what happened.'

Eileen ran out of words, and Brenda wasn't responding. She'd blown it.

And she had no right to expect any more than the other woman wanted to give her. She'd said what she needed to say and she'd lived with what she'd done for thirty years – she'd just have to live another thirty without Brenda's forgiveness.

'I'll go. Thank you for seeing me. For listening.'

She was about to stand when Brenda finally spoke. 'Have you had a great life?'

There was no anger in her voice, just the question.

Eileen opened her mouth to give the stock answer she'd give anyone who asked that. Of course. Great. Wonderful. But none of those things were true, so she stopped herself. They were way past superficial small talk.

'No.' she confessed. 'Not all of it. Some bits, maybe. Having Aiden, for sure. And perhaps some of the early years with Gary. I'm sorry, but I want to be honest. Have you? Had a great life?'

'Not all of it,' Brenda answered, with the same sad tone of resignation that Eileen had heard in her own voice a moment ago. 'Did you love him?'

Eileen exhaled, pushing all the clichés out of the way so she could get straight to the truth. 'Not at first. You know how much I loved... loved...' She couldn't say it. It was beyond inappropriate, and she'd done enough damage already.

'Colin,' Brenda finished for her, reading her mind just as she'd always done.

'Yep, Colin. I'd been in love with him for so long and had always imagined that's where my future would be, but then... well, I did what I did. Messed it up. Lost him. Gary and I just kind of stuck it out to start with, because we didn't really have an option. Over the next few months, well, I guess I did fall in love with Gary. I became besotted with him, I truly did. But looking back, I don't know how much of that was me trying to convince myself that everything had turned out the way it was supposed to. He was all I had. All my eggs in one basket. My mum was gone, I was in a new country, and the truth was that I was too ashamed to come home. I couldn't face you. Over here, I knew no one and then I was pregnant. Gary had that way of making me feel like I was the only person in the room, and I think I needed that, especially after I lost you. I just needed to belong to someone, so I told myself that he loved me and I loved him and we had our family and that it was all going to be okay. That sounds pretty pathetic too. Believe me, I've spent the last ten years since the divorce figuring that out.'

'Why did you divorce?' Brenda asked.

The big question and Eileen had figured it was coming.

'Lots of reasons. He was never faithful. Never. At first, I thought...' she hesitated, because she'd never vocalised this and she knew that when she said it, she couldn't take it back. 'I thought it was because I wasn't you.'

Brenda's brow furrowed in puzzlement when she said that. 'But he cheated on me too.'

'I know, but I blamed myself for that. Thought I must have somehow trapped him. And then – and my only excuse for this was everything I said before about being alone – but I decided that maybe it was just because I wasn't enough, so I tried to be beautiful, to be funny, to be cool. Nothing worked. Now I can look back and see that the problem was that he wasn't trying to be faithful. There's something in him: a drive and a need to get that attention, the thrills of the chase and the excitement of having his ego stroked.'

She stopped, suddenly aware that she might have said too much. This was the man Brenda had been in love with, the one she'd adored.

'I'm sorry. I'm running my mouth because I'm nervous. And grateful that you spoke to me. And a whole load of other emotions that I can't quite get a handle on yet. I don't expect you to forgive me, but I wanted you to know that I'm so sorry.'

Brenda picked up her wine, took a sip, and Eileen wondered if she was about to tell her that she should go. But no...

'I'm glad it didn't work out,' Brenda admitted calmly. 'I can hear myself and I don't even recognise something like that coming out of my mouth, but I'm glad. And I hate that I think that.'

'I'd probably think that too. I deserve it.'

Brenda sat forward, her words urgent. 'No, it's not revenge or some bitchy way to punish you. It's...' She hesitated, reframed. 'It's because I don't think that I could listen to what a wonderful life you'd had without feeling it should have been mine. There's some consolation in knowing that the other path didn't lead to a lifetime of bliss.'

Eileen felt her shoulders beginning to relax and there was a weird sense of familiarity. This was starting to feel like the old Eileen. Talking to the old Brenda. The one who was always so much smarter and kinder and wiser than them all.

Eileen's hands had stopped shaking enough now to sip the wine. 'Maybe it would have with you.'

Brenda shook her head. 'No.'

That surprised Eileen. 'You don't think so?'

'No. Even back then, if I'm really honest, I knew who he was and it made me nervous. I can say that now. I'd have lived a life with him, and I'd have been insecure for every day of it. For every heartbeat that adored him, there was always the feeling that I was waiting for him to choose someone else. I just didn't think it would be you.'

Eileen groaned. 'I owe you a lifetime of sorrys.'

Brenda nodded. 'Maybe. But I think we've had enough for now.'

'Not enough,' Eileen shook her head. 'Gary should be here apologising to you and Colin too, but he's left. Gone to the airport.'

'I'm not surprised. He never could face conflict. Urgh, what a prick. What did I see in that man?'

'It was the hair. The way he flicked his fringe,' Eileen immediately regretted the light-hearted joke, but to her relief, Brenda chuckled and added, 'And his music collection. I was a sucker for a bit of Simply Red.'

There was a pause as they both remembered nights in their old flat, singing at the top of their voices to 'Holding Back The Years'.

Eileen was the first to speak. 'You know, he still thought about you, even after we'd been married for years.'

Brenda's eyebrows raised in surprise. 'Really? How do you know that?'

Eileen could quite happily have wrapped gaffer tape over her own mouth. She shouldn't have said anything. Brenda might not take kindly to it. She might take it the wrong way and think it was a petty dig, but she was in too deep and there was no backing out now.

'Because it was the last straw for us – the thing that finally made me call it quits and divorce him. He'd been having affairs for years and I'd overlooked them. Aiden was in college, so it was just Gary and I at home. I think I had it in my mind that when I could give him my full attention, he'd stop, but if anything, the staying out and seeing other women got worse. And then he opened a Facebook account. Aiden mentioned earlier that your daughter had contacted Gary on Facebook, and Gary said he no longer used the account – that's because it was only set up all those years ago for one purpose. When I found out he'd opened it, I hacked in – he'd used a crap password – and saw that he'd written to a couple of women he'd known in the past, declaring his undying love for them. You were one of them.'

'But I didn't get a message…' Brenda said, puzzled.

'I know. He used your maiden name and sent it to someone called Brenda Fulton that didn't have a photo on her profile. She wrote back saying he was a jerk and he should go try scam someone else.'

'Noooooo. What a… what a…' At first, Eileen thought Brenda was sobbing and then she realised that she was laughing, great big howling sobs of laughter that spread right across the table, booting the tension away until they were both creased over, wiping away tears.

'I don't know why I'm laughing,' Brenda spluttered. 'It's utterly tragic.'

'Me either. It caused my divorce,' Eileen retorted, but the laughter kept coming until they both had no more left and fell into silence, a mood change that was as violent as it was unpredictable.

Eileen figured she'd outstayed her welcome. She didn't want to make Brenda sad or cause another iota of anguish to her. She began to stand up, hoping that they could part amicably, some kind of line drawn under their heartache.

That's when Branda said quietly, 'I was pregnant. With Gary's baby. Back then. I found out the day after I saw you two together.'

Eileen felt her legs give out beneath her and she slumped back down, the pain of the other woman's words ripping a hole in her chest.

'Oh, no, Brenda,' she wailed, her mind whirring. Brenda had been pregnant, and that line could never be drawn now that she knew she'd deprived a child of its father for the last thirty years. That was more than a twenty-something mistake. That was lifelong pain, lifelong grudges, lifelong resentments, wounds that never healed. 'So Zara…?'

'No, Zara is Colin's daughter. I lost the baby when I got back from Vegas.'

Eileen was still trying desperately not to cry. She had no right. None. 'I don't even have the words... I know you'll never forgive me for that, and you shouldn't. I'm sorry, Brenda. I deserve every ounce of blame that you put on me for that.'

She was shocked when Brenda shook her head. 'I don't blame you at all. I never have. I blamed me, because really, I knew what he was like. I blamed Gary, because he hurt me. But I'm a nurse, Eileen... I've come to terms with the fact that sometimes terrible things happen and it's no one's fault. It's life. Death. It's devastating and it will always make me sad, but hanging on to blame and anger would only have hurt me more, so I had to let it go. I'll always be heartbroken that it happened, and wish it were different, but I don't blame anyone. Besides, it showed me who Colin was. He was the decent man who was prepared to take care of us. That's why we got married. Here. Before we even went home. We discovered I was pregnant and he said we could raise the baby together.'

'So you got the good man,' Eileen whispered, and much as that twisted a knife, she was glad. Brenda deserved that and she didn't. It was only right. And that thought didn't come from a place of self-pity or martyrdom, just the sad truth that karma had doled out the correct result. 'You deserved him, deserved to have a happy life. I know I don't get to give an opinion, but I'm glad that you got that.'

There was a justice in that.

'Me too,' Brenda agreed.

Eileen decided that felt like the right note to leave this on. There didn't seem to be anything else to say and she was terrified that she'd mess up what felt like a resolution by saying something wrong.

'Thanks for listening to me, Brenda. You always meant the world to me, even though that night, I didn't show it. I know we loved those men, but I always thought we loved each other more. I'm glad we had that back then. I just wish we'd still had that for the lifetime we've lived since.'

It was time to go, even though there was nowhere else she'd rather be right now than sitting here with Brenda. It was as if she'd just found the sister that she'd been missing for thirty years. There was one question that was playing on her mind, that escaped before she could stop it. 'You've had thirty years with Colin and it's all worked out for you, so if you could go back, would you change it?'

Brenda raised her eyes to the ceiling, maybe thinking about the answer, or perhaps just sending up a prayer that Eileen would leave. Just when Eileen thought she was out of time and had pushed it too far, Brenda came back down to earth, reached over, lifted the bottle from the ice bucket, shook it, then dropped it back in.

'I'm not usually a day drinker,' she said, with a rueful sigh, 'but I think we're going to need more wine if we're going to discuss that question.'

26

ZARA

The daytime mood in the bar in the middle of the casino floor in Planet Hollywood wasn't quite as jubilant and exciting as it had been on that first night in the Chandelier Bar in the Cosmopolitan. Although, thankfully, it was also slightly less of a middleweight boxing match than the restaurant at the Bellagio that morning.

There were a few people at individual tables, but Zara and Aiden sat next to each other on stools at the bar counter, ignoring the other guests who were there. The guy staring into his bourbon a few seats along. The couple, giddy with love, snogging the faces off each other further around the bar top. The two elderly ladies giving their arms a rest after a few hours on the slots. And at least a dozen other people that Zara hadn't worked out a backstory for yet.

'Do you ever look at people and try to suss out what their lives are like?' she asked Aiden, while they were waiting for their beers.

'All the time. It's my favourite thing to do. Especially when a new client walks into the office. I like to see how much of their story I can guess before they tell me. It's deeply unprofessional.'

Zara smiled. 'Do you ever get it right?'

'Sometimes. I had a school teacher who'd just found out she'd married a quadruple bigamist last week. Didn't see that coming.'

'See, that's always my first guess when I meet someone,' Zara joked, laughing. 'Do you think anyone in here is looking at us and thinking, "There's two virtual strangers whose parents all slept with each other?"'

Aiden nodded. 'Most definitely. It's completely obvious. We can put it on billboards for anyone who doesn't spot it straight away.'

Zara let her head fall down on to her forearms on the bar. 'Aaaargh, what a disaster. How unlucky do you have to be to arrange an anniversary trip for your parents and then find out that not only did they not actually get legally married when you thought they did, but they weren't even in love and only did it because they'd both just had their hearts broken by other people.' That explanation would do for now – she wasn't going to tell him the whole story about her mom being pregnant because it wasn't her story to tell. She lifted her head and challenged him with, 'I mean, that has to be the unluckiest plan ever, right? Tell me one thing in your life that's unluckier than that.'

'I was supposed to get married three weeks ago and my fiancée, Layla, didn't show.'

'No. You're making that up to make me feel better.' Zara felt dread oozing from her pores. He was either a really good liar or she'd just come out with the most inappropriate, foot in mouth, stupid thing ever.

Aiden shook his head, shrugged. ''Fraid not. Beach wedding. Guests. String quartet. Free bar. Me in a suit at the end of the aisle. No Layla.'

Zara scrunched her eyes closed for a second, then opened them. Nope, still in the same place. Foot still in mouth. This was getting worse by the minute. 'I'm a nightmare. I'm sorry. Run while you can in case I say more stupid things. I'm clearly a jinx that just goes around unleashing people's most painful memories.' The dread had now elevated to full DEFCON 1 regret. 'I'm so sorry. Have you spoke to her since? Have you found out why she didn't show up? You see things like that in movies, but you never think it'll happen in real life.' In her head that sounded great, but as soon as it came out she realised... 'And yet it happened to you and I'm now pointing that out and making the situation even worse. I shouldn't be allowed out. Have I mentioned that I'm a jinx?'

Weirdly, he seemed amused by her lack of tact and general hopelessness. 'Could be worse. Most people I know just don't mention it because they're embarrassed and they don't know what to say. It's not the best look for a lawyer that specialises in divorce. Even the crappiest of relationship specialists usually manage to get married before their bride does a runner.'

Zara's hands were both over her mouth now, mostly because she didn't want to say anything else idiotic. What the hell was going on in this world? Her parents had a whole bucket of secrets. Her mum used to sleep with a bloke who looked like Tom Selleck in his prime. Her dad had just punched Mr Selleck in the face. Her boyfriend couldn't be arsed speaking to her. Her sister wanted to leave their partnership. And in among that whole bunch of crazy, someone made the absolutely moronic, unfathomable decision to jilt this gorgeous, sexy, successful sweetheart of a man at the altar. The universe had gone mad. It was official.

Aiden ordered two more beers for them. 'Okay, so your turn,' he told her. 'Tell me your most tragic love story. Make me feel better about being rejected and humiliated in front of everyone I've ever known.'

She could see he was teasing, but at the same time, he had a point.

'Okay... well...' She had to make this good. 'I've been going out with the same guy for eight years.'

'Really? That's the best you've got? That's supposed to make me feel better?' His grin gave the tease away, but nevertheless, she took a chug of beer, then put her hands up.

'Hang on, hang on. I'm not done. We've been together so long that sometimes I think we're only still hanging on out of habit.'

Her hand flew to her mouth again. Bugger. Had she really just said that out loud? This called for more beer.

He nodded slowly, as if he was giving that serious thought. 'Okay, I'm starting to feel slightly better. Need more than that though.'

'He hasn't called me once since I got here. I've called him a solid five times and he keeps telling me he's busy. We both know he just can't be bothered talking to me.'

'Ouch,' Aiden flinched. 'I felt that one right in the gut. Okay, definitely feeling a bit better about my crap existence. I appreciate the effort. I mean, it's not quite jilted on the wedding day but it's—'

'And we only have sex about twice a month and even then, only if there's nothing good on TV.'

Zara gasped, clamped her mouth shut and stared at him. He stared at her, nothing else on the face of the earth moved and she wondered if she could deploy some magical force to rewind the last ten seconds to when she hadn't blurted out the most intimate details of her life, stuff that she'd said to no one on earth, to a man who was a complete stranger three weeks ago.

Ten seconds passed. Thirty seconds. An hour. A fortnight. She had no idea. Time had stopped, their gaze was still locked, and her brain was on total shutdown, paralysed by days of over-emotion, stress, Budweiser, and... yep... attraction to this beautiful man who was still staring right back at her, his face so close she could see the muscle throb on the side of his jaw. What was this? It was like they were lost, frozen, cast in stone, or some other weird occurrence that had them sitting there, just staring at each other, while the whole world spun around them. Eventually, Aiden broke the silence.

'Zara...'

It was only one word, but it jump started her back to life, unleashed a full-scale panic. 'I know, I totally overshared. I'm sorry. I'm a complete liability. See, you were lucky you only got jilted. You could have a mouth like mine and be a daily source of embarrassment to yourself.'

'Zara—'

'Of course I don't mind if you bolt. Run like the wind. Like you're being chased by dragons.'

Dragons? What the actual f...?

'Zara, is it wrong that I want to kiss you?'

'Just go and... What?' She yelped, startled.

'Kiss you. I want to kiss you.' He was still staring. Still staring. She was still staring back.

'You want to...' She couldn't say it, because that would make it real and then her whole body would go into shock and there was the potential for a dislocated hip if she fell off this bar stool. 'Why?'

He was still staring. 'Because you're beautiful. And funny. And you might just be the nicest person I've ever met. Did I mention sexy? You're that too. Definitely that. And I don't usually do this – in fact I swear I've never done something so spontaneous in my life. I've no idea what's happening. But I'd really like, if it's okay with you, to lean over and—'

'No.' She shook her head, as if trying to exorcise some spirit – one that made her want to kiss him right back. 'You can't. Because I have a boyfriend and even if he can't be arsed speaking to me, that's not what I do. I couldn't live with myself and...' She was running out of words, but she was desperately trying to keep talking in the hope that a hole would suddenly open below her, allowing her to tumble to the earth's core.

That didn't happen. But the Gods of Oh Thank Fuck did interfere when Aiden's phone, sitting on the bar, sprang to life and began to ring. He didn't look away, completely ignored it, so she intervened.

'That might be your mum. You'd better answer it.'

That seemed to snap him back to the present and he picked it up, checked the screen, and suddenly the little muscle on the side of his jaw was pulsing again.

'It's not my mom. It's...' He turned the phone so that she could see it.

LAYLA. She tried to process. Layla. His ex. The one who'd left him at the altar. Wow, that was way too close. Did Layla have some psychic paranormal thing going on that alerted her to the fact that Aiden was talking to another woman? Had she hacked into the Planet Hollywood security system? Oceans 24 – the one where no-one steals anything but all the ex's track down their former loves using the Vegas camera networks. And why was she thinking nonsense like this when he was still staring at her, with a ringing phone in his hand?

'You have to go take that,' she told him.

'Do I?' he asked, and she felt like they both knew they were talking about something else. He had to go. Before they did something that she would definitely, absolutely regret.

'You do. I'm going to go back up and check on my mum anyway.'

His stare went from the phone, to her, back to the phone... 'Zara, I...'

'Go,' she cut him off, urgently this time. 'You're holding me back.'

This time, he did. He got up from the bar and answered the call as he walked away.

'Layla?'

Zara watched him leave, completely and utterly stunned, confused and generally gobsmacked about what had just happened.

She had no idea how long she sat there, staring straight ahead, thinking she'd rather be someone – anyone – else right now. Except maybe the bloke along the bar who was still glowering into his bourbon and very definitely tilting to the left, at an angle that suggested he'd be on the floor any second now.

'Hey gorgeous, do you come here often?' Thankfully it was a woman's voice, full of warmth and coming from the person who'd just climbed onto the stool that Aiden had vacated. 'Wait till I tell you... I fell asleep and when I woke up Dad was watching *Rocky*. I don't know what's happened to him. Anyway, I went back into the other room to check on Mum and holy fuck, guess who's there?' Millie gave her best dramatic pause.

'Aiden's mum,' Zara mumbled.

'Aiden's... Oh. You knew. They were in deep convo so I removed all sharp objects from the room and left. Mum said you were down here though. Why are you sitting drinking alone? That's my special talent.'

'Aiden was just here. He asked me if he could kiss me.' Zara felt like she was recounting what happened in a slow, robotic voice, brought to her by the powers of shock and a tickly attraction to a man who wasn't her boyfriend.

'Wait, what? Aw, bollocks. I was going to use him for no-strings sex. So what happened after you snogged the face off him?'

'I didn't. I said no. He left.'

'Great,' Millie announced. 'I mean, insane. But great for me. Did he happen to mention his standpoint on casual sex?'

27

BRENDA

They'd been talking for hours, and yet it still seemed that there was more to say. When Eileen had asked her if she would go back and change their lives, Brenda had thought about telling her the truth, about Colin, about their marriage, about her desperation to start a new life without him, but she hadn't. It just didn't feel right. It felt disloyal. Indiscreet. Like she was breaching a trust within the sanctity of their family. So instead, she'd avoided talking about their future and concentrated on the best bits about the past. That felt like a safer place to be, because she still didn't know how she felt about her old friend. It was difficult to unravel thirty years of resentment in the space of one day, even when there was a genuine apology from the other side, lots of wine and a bizarre feeling of comfort and familiarity with Eileen, so in the meantime, Brenda had been happy to settle for chatting about families and jobs and catching up on what they'd missed.

'What do you think our younger selves would say if they could see us now?' Eileen had asked. She'd kicked off her shoes and Brenda noticed the perfectly pedicured toes. No way she was taking her slippers off and showing the cracked heels that came with being on her feet on the ward all day.

'I think they'd say, "Bloody hell, Brenda, you've put on a few pounds and you look knackered."'

'That's not true! You look great,' Eileen had objected.

Brenda had decided she was just being kind. The physical difference between the two of them was stark, but then it always had been. Eileen had been the tall, willowy blonde, and Brenda had been the petite one with the crazy curls and the admittedly killer curves. It was just that those curves had got decidedly curvier over the years while Eileen's face seemed to be aging in reverse.

'If I could see myself, I'd probably say, "lay off the Botox and you're not kidding anyone with those hair extensions, doll,"' Eileen had declared.

'I did wonder...' Brenda had admitted.

Eileen had sighed. 'I'd love to say I do it all for me, but I'd be lying. I know it's shallow, but you've no idea, Brenda. The dating scene out there is a self-esteem-crushing nightmare. The men our age are all looking for women twenty years younger, so the pressure to look good is relentless. I'm exhausted with it all. What I wouldn't do for a reliable, decent, good-hearted man who didn't give a toss what direction my boobs were pointing in.'

The irony hadn't been lost on Brenda. Eileen's ideal life sounded like the one she herself had with Colin, whereas all Brenda wanted was the freedom to live like Eileen. The grass on the other side was neon emerald green.

Brenda had been pondering that when the door opened and Millie had walked in, stopping in her tracks when she saw their guest. 'Mum, am I hallucinating? Only it looks like Dad's old girlfriend, you know, the one that got caught shagging his pal, who, incidentally, was also your boyfriend – it's hard to keep up – is sitting in a bucket chair in our room.'

Brenda had turned to Eileen, with only a mildly apologetic shrug, for once secretly enjoying her daughter's fearlessness, loyalty and utter lack of tact.

'Eileen, I'd like you to properly meet our youngest, Millie. She was born completely devoid of any filter, but we've kept her anyway because she's endlessly amusing and, frankly, no one else would take her off our hands.'

Eileen obviously hadn't taken offence. 'Pleased to meet you again, Millie. And I'm sorry about all the chaos that I've caused. Can't be easy throwing two exes and a shitload of secrets into an anniversary trip.'

'At least you understand my pain,' Millie had said dryly, not quite letting her off the hook. She'd turned her attention back to Brenda. 'Are you okay, Mum? If this is a hostage situation and she has a weapon, blink twice and I'll get help.'

'I'm fine, thanks, love. But can you give us a little while longer to chat? Zara is down in the bar with Eileen's son if you want to go find them. They went there a while ago and she's not come back yet.'

'Okay, if you insist. I'll force myself to go to a bar and drink cocktails and it'll be terrible. What kind of mother are you?'

Brenda couldn't help but chuckle. This young woman made her heart sore with her antics, but there was no one who made her laugh like Millie did, or who inspired her more to make the most of her life.

'Talking of which...' Brenda had watched as Millie came over and checked the wine bottle in the ice bucket. Empty. She'd scanned the minibar and saw that it was running low on vino too.

'I'll send you up some more wine, Mum. Mrs Gregg, it was a pleasure meeting you,' she'd said as she made for the door. 'But try not to sleep with the room service waiter when he gets here.'

Eileen had dissolved into laughter as soon as the door closed. 'I know I should be offended, but bloody hell, I love her. She reminds me of your mum. I adored Ada but was also fairly terrified of her because she said what was on her mind no matter what it was.'

The mention of her mother and her daughter had made Brenda's heart swell. Trite as it was, she'd felt like there was a small victory in there. Eileen might have got the guy back in the day, but Brenda had landed two young women who were flipping spectacular. That was worth so much more than Gary bloody Gregg.

And while she was on her blessings, she'd had a lovely mum, one who'd loved her until the day she died, late last year. How lucky had she been to have a lifetime with her? Eileen had never got to share that with her mum and Brenda felt a genuine sympathy for her. It couldn't have been easy dealing with her life without support.

The perspective had softened her, given her a sense of empathy as they went back to sharing the stories of their lives.

The wine had been delivered and they were just about up to date, when the door opened again. Brenda expected it to be Zara or Millie. She held her breath when she saw that it was Colin. He looked older than he had this morning and the makeshift sling he'd made from a towel to support his hand was almost pitiful.

Like Millie, he stopped dead when he saw that Eileen was with her. 'I'll leave you to it,' he said, and Brenda could hear the uncharacteristic anger in his voice.

'No, stay. Please. Eileen just came to talk. I think maybe it might help.'

'How's your hand?' Eileen asked him, operating as a tag team to keep him engaged and stop him leaving. It was so bizarre. This was exactly the kind of telepathic communication they'd had when they were younger and now, after thirty years of estrangement and loathing, after devastating betrayals and unconscionable decisions, after heartbreak and disappointments on both sides, here they were, and Brenda wasn't sure how she should feel about it. For years, she'd wondered where Gary and Eileen were, if they'd stayed together, or if they'd gone their separate ways that night in Vegas. She hadn't had the courage to approach Gary's parents because she didn't know them very well, and Eileen had no family that she could have checked with. It was the days before social media was a thing. It still wasn't her thing. The girls were forever nagging her to get Facebook, or Instagram or the Twitter lark, but Brenda had never been particularly interested. Her world was her girls, her work and she preferred to see her friends in person. Yes, she knew that made her a dinosaur, but hadn't these last few days proven her point? Look at the chaos contacting a stranger on Facebook had brought them. A mortifying reunion, skeletons out of the closet and a badly bruised hand that was being supported by a Planet Hollywood bath towel.

'Come and sit, Colin,' Brenda encouraged him, knowing that he'd do the polite thing. She wasn't wrong.

'Is it broken?' Eileen asked, still trying to engage him in the conversation.

Years of working in A&E had given Brenda the skills to pick up on the micro signals that people gave off when they were in tough situations. Right now, she saw that the tightness around Eileen's eyes betrayed her nervousness.

'It'll heal,' Colin replied. 'Before you say anything, he deserved it and I'd do it again.'

'I'd hold your jacket,' Eileen offered, surprising him. 'He's gone, by the way. Back to South Carolina. Decided the notion for partying in Vegas had gone off him.'

This time it was Colin who was giving off signals, and it was a slight lowering of the shoulders, as if that news was a relief.

'The most surreal day ever,' he mused. 'I'm glad he's gone. I had nothing else to say to him. I'm surprised to see you here though.'

He didn't say it unkindly, just in that direct, honest way that he'd always had.

'I came to apologise to Brenda and she was kind enough to let me in and hear me out.'

'Without punching her in the face,' Brenda added with a cheeky glint in her eye, trying to make him relax a little. 'We're a bit more civilised over on this side of the gender line. By the way, before I forget, Millie says she's changing your name to Lennox Lewis by deed poll so you might want to have a word.'

That made him smile, and Brenda thought how attractive he still was when he did that. It had been so long since he was the funny, sweet, carefree guy who never stopped grinning. What had happened to him? What had happened to them all? Had their choices and the hands they were dealt robbed them all of the very core of their personalities? And was it too late for them to rewind the clock and make decisions that would restore their happiness, their enthusiasm and their curiosity about life? Brenda really believed that there was still time. She just had to convince him that they should do it separately.

Eileen was still talking. 'But I owe you an apology too, Colin. I treated you terribly. What I did... well, we all saw how that turned out. I know that we're thirty years down the line and it's too late to make amends, but for what it's worth, I just want to say again that I never meant it to happen. I didn't plan it. Brenda and I were just talking about how we honestly think that if that night hadn't gone like that, then our lives would have turned out very different. But we were also saying that we wouldn't want to go back and change it now, because look where we all are. You have your daughters, I've got Aiden. We've all managed to make it this far without too many heartbreaks. Maybe there's something to be said for that.'

'Maybe there is,' Colin said, with typically calm thoughtfulness. 'To be honest, Eileen, there's nothing I would go back and change either. We've had a good life, haven't we, Brenda?'

That one hit right in the heart and snapped a tiny piece off. 'We have,' she agreed. For the most part it was true, and she wasn't going to embarrass him by bringing up their problems in front of his first love. She owed him more than that.

'Tell me something – did you divorce Gary because he had a wandering eye, Eileen?' Colin asked, with the air of someone who had already guessed what the answer would be.

Eileen nodded, a sad smile confirming his question. 'I did. How did you know that?'

'Because he was always the same. I think it was in his genes. His father was married three times, last I heard, and went off with someone else every time.'

Brenda was stunned. 'When you say, "always the same", do you mean when we were going out together back then?'

She recognised the look on his face. He was deciding whether to be honest or kind, because whatever he was going to say couldn't be both.

'Be truthful,' she urged.

He went with her request. 'Yes.'

Brenda felt her chest deflate. 'I always suspected. Actually, more than that. I think on some level I definitely knew. Why didn't you ever tell me?'

'If I'd said that to you back then, you wouldn't have believed me,' he explained, and she knew he was right.

'And after we were married?'

'Then you were my wife, and I couldn't bring myself to hurt your feelings. I just figured his loss was my gain. I've never changed my mind about that.'

Brenda's throat tightened as she watched her quiet, dignified husband

show her his heart. The truth was, she'd changed her mind about him.
Now she wondered if it was too late to change it back.

28

AIDEN

Aiden hadn't been able to hear what Layla was saying on the phone. The noise in the casino was too loud, then, when he'd got out in the street, it was even busier, with car horns beeping and sirens blaring. Besides, this wasn't a conversation he wanted to have in a chaotic environment while he was straining to catch what she had to say. This was one he wanted to have when he was sitting down, when he was prepared and could think reasonably and logically and not be swayed by the fact that he'd just wanted to kiss another woman – one who wasn't the ex-fiancée on the other end of the phone right now.

'Layla, I can't hear you,' he shouted. 'Let me call you back in ten minutes when I get back to my room.'

'Your room? What are you talking about? Where are you?'

She was shouting too, so he couldn't be clear on the tone of her voice or get any sense of the reason for her call. This was why he needed to be somewhere quiet where he could concentrate on what she was saying.

'I'm in Vegas.'

The line went dead, and he couldn't be sure if she'd hung up or if he'd lost signal. Damn it.

He crossed the road, and made his way up the sloping drive, past the crowds outside the Valentino store and into the lobby, which was so busy that he had to swerve to avoid cliques of tourists who were either checking in or gazing in wonder at the stained-glass sculpture on the ceiling. Was it really only a couple of days ago that he'd arrived and seen that for the first time? How could so much have changed since then?

'Hey, buddy, got a spare couple of dollars for the slots?'

At first, Aiden barely registered the words, because he knew that they couldn't be directed at him, but then something clicked. The voice. It was as familiar as his own, yet it couldn't be...

'Trevon?' He said it aloud as he turned, and then immediately lost at least fifty per cent of his stress, because there, right in front of him, was his best mate.

'What the hell are you doing here, bud?' he exclaimed, pulling him into a hug.

'Ah, you know... just passing, thought I'd drop in. You sounded wired when you texted. Just wanted to check you were good, and an acquaintance of mine was headed this way, so I hitched a lift.'

Aiden shook his head, still laughing. 'You came on a private jet, didn't you? With some big shot client? You know, sometimes you're pretty hard to like.'

It was a source of much ribbing that Trevon and Aiden had been so skint when they met that Aiden used to take him to Eileen's on a Monday night, because she filled them with wings while they watched the football. Even then, he'd looked good though. Now he'd turned his love of fitness and the charisma of a born leader into a company and a lifestyle that those two younger dudes could only have dreamt about. Thing was, Trevon deserved every dollar of it, especially the ones that he funnelled into a non-profit that provided scholarships for inner-city kids. This was, hands down, the best guy Aiden knew. In a world of Gary Greggs, he'd much rather be a Trevon Anderson.

'How long are you here for? Are you staying?'

'Tonight anyway. Maybe a couple of nights.'

Aiden hugged him again. 'Man, you've no idea how much I needed to hear that. My dad packed up and left so there's a spare bed in my room if you're interested...'

'Sounds good. And what about your mom? Still here.'

'Yeah. Bud, I've got so much to tell you, but listen... Layla just called.'

It was Trevon's turn to be shocked. 'You're kidding.'

'Nope, but I couldn't hear what she was saying, so I need to call her back. Give me your bag and I'll take it up to my room, then I'll come back down and meet you at the bar when I'm done. That okay?'

'Sounds good. If I'm putting everything I own on red when you find me, save me, okay?'

Aiden nodded, laughing. 'I got you, don't worry.'

He picked up his buddy's bag and made his way to the elevator that took him up to his room. There he grabbed a bottle of water, opened it, and ten minutes later than he'd promised, he called Layla back. He almost choked with relief when she answered on the first ring.

'Sorry. I met Trevon in the lobby and got held up.'

'What are you doing in Vegas?'

Those were her first words and they immediately put the hackles on the back of his neck up, especially since she sounded none too pleased about his geographical location.

'Sorry, did you expect me still to be waiting at the beach?' It was a low blow, but it was out before he could stop himself. Still, he tried to smooth it over. He'd finally managed to speak to her and he didn't want her hanging up before he had answers to the questions that had been keeping him awake at night. There was a silence at the other end and for a moment he thought he'd lost her. Again.

'Aiden, I'm sorry. I'm so, so sorry.'

Her voice cracked with emotion and Aiden knew she was crying. He immediately dropped the challenge and softened his approach.

'I am too, Layla. But I need to know what happened? I just don't get it.'

There was a sniff, then a deep breath and he could picture exactly what she would look like right now. He couldn't hear any office buzz in the background so she must be working from home. In that case, her raven black hair would be pulled up in a high ponytail and her huge brown eyes would be framed with those flicks she did at the edges. She'd be wearing her glasses because she wouldn't want to get emotional if she were wearing contacts and she'd be on the cream sectional sofa at her mom's home in the city, the one with views right out over to Drum Island. She'd have been to Pilates this morning, so she'd still be wearing sports leggings and one of those crop top thingies, under a sports jacket that had those thumb holes in the cuffs. Oh, and there would be a pile of South Carolina trade and lifestyle magazines on the coffee table in front of her, because she was in travel and event marketing, so it was her job know every hotel, bar, restaurant, nightclub and venue on the east coast. And she'd be holding her phone in front of her because she'd have it on speaker as she answered his question.

'I panicked. I know that's a terrible excuse, but I did. I panicked. Derren called me the night before the wedding...'

Aiden closed his eyes. Derren, her ex-husband.

'I swear nothing happened, I promise, Aid. But he got in my head, told me this was a rebound, went on about how I'd only known you for a few months. And then I remembered how destroyed I was when we divorced and I know I couldn't handle that again.'

'You wouldn't have had to,' he said, quietly, knowing that was true. He'd loved her. He'd have married her, he'd have been faithful, and he'd have done everything he could to make her happy. He'd have trusted her. Adored her. Woke up every day and been glad she was lying there next to him... And he just realised that whole stream of consciousness was in the past tense. When had that happened? When had his mind shifted his feelings for her from present to past? Was that just some emotional defence mechanism or had there been a profound shift? And if so, had a fleeting meeting with someone else caused it? Chaos and confusion were usually on the other side of his desk – it was taking him a moment to absorb that they were now much closer to home.

'I see that now,' she said softly. 'I just needed time to think, to get everything straight in my head. I know I can't ask you to forgive me, but... well, forgive me. Please.'

He wanted to say yes, to tell her it was all going to be okay, that there was no harm done, nothing they couldn't fix. He just wasn't sure that was true.

'Look, I'll be back in a couple of days, Layla. This isn't something we can do on the phone. Let me call you when I get home and we can meet Sunday. We can talk properly then.' Yep, by then he'd have sorted his thoughts out. This strange apprehension in his gut would be gone and he'd know how he was feeling. Wouldn't he?

'Okay, I can do that. And Aiden...'

'Yeah?'

'I love you.'

She didn't wait to hear if he said it back, and he was glad, because he had no idea if he could. Fuck. Why now? If he'd got married last month, then this wouldn't be happening because he wouldn't be in Vegas, he wouldn't have met Zara, and he wouldn't be asking himself why he couldn't get her out of his mind.

It had to stop. Enough. This was crazy. He'd only met her in person this week and already some warped part of his brain was trying to convince him that he had feelings for her? She was a stranger. She lived in Glasgow. She had a boyfriend. It was ridiculous. This was the kind of situation he saw on his desk, when a couple filed for divorce a month after meeting and getting married in a moment of spontaneous derangement. That wasn't him. He wasn't his father. He made good decisions, decent, smart ones that he could live with and that were based on common sense. He had no idea if he could get back to that place of love and security with Layla, but this madness with Zara had to stop right now. And if this moment of self-castigation didn't make a difference, then his buddy downstairs at the bar would keep him right. Trevon was the most steady, the most focused guy he knew. He didn't sleep around, didn't get distracted by casual affairs or one-night stands. After Aiden had represented him in his divorce from the wife he had married straight out of college, Trevon had gone on to have a couple of long-term girlfriends, but nothing for over a year now, saying he didn't want distractions while he was building his company. Aiden respected that. He was beginning to wish he'd done the same.

He grabbed his room key, his phone, and his common fricking sense and headed back downstairs, checking out the bars on the ground floor for Trevon. He eventually found him in the Lily Bar, not far from the restaurant that had hosted the meeting with the Jones family, and smiled when he saw who Trevon was with.

'Hey, Mom,' he said, giving her a hug and thinking that she looked different from earlier. Lighter. And was he imagining it, or did her smile reach her eyes for the first time in as long as he could remember? 'How did it go with Brenda?'

'Better than I expected. Then there was the added bonus of bumping into this guy when I got back here. He flew in to check on you, so I've completely hijacked him and I've just been filling him in on everything that's happened.'

'You know, your half-assed texts didn't really capture the magnitude of the events I'm hearing about,' Trevon chided him, then pointed to a Modelo on the bar. 'I ordered you a beer.'

Aiden shrugged apologetically. 'Yeah, sorry about that. What bit are you up to?' he asked, pulling over a chair and lifting the bottle. He rarely drank at home. The odd beer while he was watching a game, maybe a glass of wine with dinner at the weekend. Yet, somehow he felt like he'd rarely been without a drink in his hand since he got here. This was clearly the effect that drama had on him.

His mom took over the conversation. 'I was just about to get to the bit where Colin punched your dad in the face.'

'No!' Trevon exclaimed, laughing. 'Okay, tell me this in every detail because I think I'll enjoy it.'

Aiden listened as his mom did just that, then moved on to the rest of the story. They shifted the conversation into the hotel's Prime Steakhouse restaurant and carried it on over dinner too. There was some obvious embarrassment when she told Trevon about her past, loads of reassurance and sympathy going the other way, a few tears, all of them his mum's and most of them when she was saying that she had a glimmer of hope that her friend might, in some way, forgive her.

Aiden was happy for her. She deserved this. Sure, she'd made a mistake, but he saw now that she'd spent thirty years paying for it in one way or another. No one deserved that.

He reached over and hugged her, just as the waiter brought the check. He and Trevon tussled over it and he won, signing it to his room.

'Okay, but if you're paying for dinner, I'm getting the nightcap. I know this pretty cool bar with views over the city. You down?' Trevon asked.

Aiden thought about it, but he couldn't do it. He had something else to sort out first.

'Much as I love you both, I've got some work stuff that I need to get done tonight...' Not strictly true, but he knew they wouldn't take it personally if he bailed on them because of work. 'So I'm going to turn in. Trevon, here's my dad's key to our room. I'll see you when you come up. He leaned down and kissed his mother. 'G'night, Mom.'

'Goodnight, son. Are you sure you're okay?'

'Yeah, I'm fine. Just a bit tired. It's been a long week, I guess.'

He hated lying to his mom, but he wasn't ready to tell her the truth. He was leaving them because he was desperate to make a call.

And was he okay?

That would depend on whether Zara answered the phone.

29

EILEEN

It was amazing how things could turn on a dime in this city, Eileen decided. The gambler who was down to his last pile of chips and put them all on one hand, only to win big. The whale – she knew that's what they called the high-stake gamblers – who was flown into town by one of the casinos in their private jet, saving the cost of an airfare only to drop two hundred grand in one night at the tables. The waiter or waitress who caught the eye of the wealthy business mogul and won his heart and his bank balance. The dancer who came to town with nothing and became a star.

And Eileen Gregg, who'd arrived here yesterday wearing a mask that covered the fact that she was broken. Carrying baggage that she'd been trailing for a lifetime. Only to be destroyed when her worst secrets were put under the spotlight. And yet now...? The behaviour of her ex-husband had closed a door in her mind, the time with her son had reminded her what a decent man he'd turned out to be, and the afternoon with Brenda and Colin had given her some hope of forgiveness. More than that, just being with her old friend had reminded Eileen who she used to be, had evoked a lightness and a familiarity that she barely recognised but that made her feel whole again. That feeling of talking to someone who knew who you were. Where you came from. Who had a real and deep connection to someone that you'd forgotten how to be.

It had been one of the worst days of her life and one of the best. Now she was in a club with a handsome man she adored, and they were drinking brandy and dancing, with the city lights twinkling in the windows that spanned the whole wall of the room. At least half a dozen ladies in the vicinity were blatantly watching the moves of the gorgeous man beside her, yet he was kind enough to pretend he hadn't noticed and to drink and dance with her and her alone. It was a little slice of heaven and she never wanted it to end.

The band played the last chords of 'Fly Me To The Moon', then settled into a ballad that was way too slow to suit her mood.

'Time for another drink?' she asked Trevon, who spun her around and then dipped her in the middle of the dance floor.

He was laughing as he pulled her back up. 'Okay, so how cheesy was that? On a scale of one to ten?'

'I think you pretty much slid right off the scale,' she teased him, slipping her arm through his as they crossed the few steps to their table. 'In fact, I'm beginning to understand why you're single.'

'I doubt that very much,' he countered a little sharply and Eileen thought for a second that she'd offended him. But no. Come on. This was Trevon. They trained together every week and they gave each other much harsher stick than that, all in the good-natured name of friendly competition. She'd known him for seven or eight years and never once in that time had she seen him be sensitive or touchy. She must have read his reaction wrong.

Yet... now he was staring into his drink like he had something on his mind. Ah, crap. Something was wrong. Aiden? Had something else happened that his friend felt the need to share now? Or was Trevon having problems of his own? In which case, she needed to hear about them because she wanted to help him fix them.

'Eileen, I need to talk to you.'

Again, ah crap. So much for never wanting this wonderful moment to end.

'Okay. I'm all ears.' She tried to keep it light, make him feel comfortable enough to tell her anything. Although, that had never been a problem before. How many times had they gone for coffee after a Sunday cross-fit session and still been sitting there four hours later? Trevon spent every holiday with her and Aiden too, and her son was always the lightweight that went to bed first and left the two of them to sit on the balcony, or by the fire, and chat until they'd solved all of the world's problems and a few of their own too. Now it seemed that there was a new one that needed attention.

'The reason I'm single has nothing to do with my skills on the dance floor,' he said, still staring down at the liquid in his glass.

'Trevon, I didn't mean to offend you and I'm sorry if I did. I was joking, honestly.' She tried to pull it back and thought maybe a quick apology and another spin round the dance floor would cheer him up and help him forget that she'd touched a raw nerve with a stupid joke.

'There is someone...'

'Really?' Okay, this was new. He hadn't mentioned having anyone in his life since he split with his last girlfriend and that was... Eileen tried to rack her brain... must be a year ago now, at least. Maybe longer. She must remember to ask Aiden in the morning.

'But it's complicated.'

Ah, now she was getting it. The poor man was in love and it wasn't working out for him. Okay, she'd had a lifetime of complicated relationships. This she could deal with. Instinctively, she put her hand over his. 'Okay, speaking as someone who is resolutely crap with straightforward relationships, who was married to a complete dickhead and who, since her divorce, has dated several absolute arses in Charleston, this is right in my wheelhouse, so let's do this. I need to know the problem with this person you like. Is she married? Is it Beyonce?'

His smile didn't match the frown on the rest of his handsome face. 'How did you get to Beyonce?'

'Don't know. Just reckoned there would be a couple of obstacles to overcome if you were seeing her.'

'Starting with her husband,' Trevon suggested.

'Ok, fair point. Right, well it usually falls into one of a few categories, so I'll shoot first and stop me when I get there.' She was on a roll now and the sooner they talked this out and came up with a solution, the sooner they could get back on that dance floor. 'Is she married?'

'Nope.'

Bugger. That was the one she'd thought most likely.

'Pregnant?'

'No. Look, Eileen—'

'Her family doesn't love you?'

'No, it's—'

The answer had struck her like a bolt of realisation. It wasn't a 'she'. It was a 'he'. And the 'he' was Aiden. That had to be it. The guy flew all the way here today, from the opposite side of the country, on the basis of a text that Aiden had sent him saying that there were problems here. That was more than friendship. That was love.

'It's a "he",' she finished for him. 'You're in love with Aiden.'

'Eileen! I'm not in love with Aiden. But I am beginning to understand why you're still single,' he blurted, mimicking her comment from earlier.

She was about to object when...

'It's complicated because the woman I'm in love with is older than me. She is the mom of my best friend. And she has no idea how completely amazing she is.'

Several things happened at once. Eileen's jaw froze, leaving her mouth stuck in the open position. She became absolutely incapable of speech. And she realised that her hand was still on top of his, but that he was now very gently rubbing her thumb with his.

As soon as she recovered her motor skills, she snatched her hand back and groaned, 'No. Trevon, you're not. This is something else. Something different.'

'Eileen, it isn't. It's exactly what I think it is.'

'But that's crazy.'

He visibly bristled at that. 'Why?'

'Because I'm twenty-five years older than you, for a start.' She felt herself starting to sweat, and her heart went into overdrive as it tried to fight against the lungs that were, right now, squeezing the air out of her chest.

'I'm thirty-eight. You're seventeen years older than me, and I've no idea why that matters.'

'Because I'm seventeen years older than you!' she repeated, with more emphasis on the 'seventeen'.

'Still don't get why that's a problem,' he shrugged, not buying into it at all. 'What was the age difference between Gary and his last girlfriend? Or the one before that? Or the one before that? A pretty solid twenty-five years for every one of them.'

'And holding my ex-husband's dating standards up to me as a reference point is not going to win you this argument,' she said sharply.

'Just pointing out the double standard,' he retorted, and she could see why he'd been so successful in his professional life. The guy just didn't back down.

She tried a different angle. 'Fine. But it definitely matters that you're my son's best friend. Trevon, that's just... not cool. For either of us.'

'Why? Because people will judge us?'

Eileen's irritation levels rose with that one. 'No. I don't give much of a toss what people think. But I care what Aiden thinks. And this...' She paused. What was she saying? There was no 'this'. It was ridiculous. Outlandish. She ploughed on anyway. 'This isn't going to be okay with him.'

'I disagree.' He leaned forward again, his body language emanating absolute confidence in what he was saying. 'Aiden loves you and he wants you to be happy. He feels the same about me. It might take him a minute, but he'll get this. I promise you. I just need to know that you get it too. I need to know that this isn't a one-way thing.'

Eileen sat back, stunned. Unable to process the question. Unable to give him an answer. She'd truly never considered this possibility. Why would she? He was her son's best mate and that was a boundary that it had never even occurred to her to cross.

And she wasn't ready to start doing that now, because the one thing in her life that she'd ever done right was Aiden and that wasn't a relationship that she would risk for anything.

'It's a one-way thing, Trevon. I'm sorry. And I think it's time I went back to the hotel.'

30

ZARA

On the anniversary of her parent's not-quite-legal wedding, Zara woke and, as with every morning that week, checked the bed next to her to see if her sister had made it home. Nope, no sign. Empty bed. Which would worry her, if she hadn't left Millie chatting to a very attractive off-duty police officer in a bar after the Celine Dion concert the night before, and then got a text two hours later with a photo of the guy, links to his social media accounts, his address, telephone number and a message saying...

Going home with Chad. These are his details. If I disappear, I'm tied up in his basement. Love you!

If anyone was making the most of this trip, it was her sister. Although, her parents seemed to be enjoying it now too. Yesterday, they'd all managed a full drama-free day, which was giddy relief after the debacle of the day before. They'd woken up early, taken a helicopter trip over the Grand Canyon, followed by lunch and a gondola ride at the Venetian. In the afternoon, her mum had shocked them all by saying she and her dad were going for drinks with Aiden's mum. Her parents had come back, both a little tipsy, just in time to go to the concert she'd bought tickets for weeks ago. Celine Dion had taken them through a two-hour emotional wringer that even had Millie filling up as she belted out 'All By Myself'.

And Zara hadn't thought about Aiden more than once... every fifteen minutes. He'd called her the night before last, late, but she hadn't picked up. And then there was a text yesterday:

I'm sorry. Can we talk?

She'd ignored that too, and yep, she knew that was a slide right down the greasy pole of maturity.

Pushing herself up in bed, the first thing she did was check her Find My iPhone. Yep, there was Millie, at the address she'd given in the text. Excellent. She typed out a reply.

Get your arse up! Mum and Dad's ceremony is in two hours. Don't DARE miss the whole point of the bloody trip. PS Hope you had a great night and are not locked in the basement. Love you xxxx

A reply came straight back.

Amazing night. I'm in love. Okay, maybe lust. I blame Celine Dion. Will meet you at the venue. Send me the address.

She texted back the details, then, groaning, she pushed herself out of bed and stumbled through to the shower, aware that this was definitely not how she was expecting to be feeling this morning.

Before she left home, a whole other range of emotions had been on the to-do list for today. Excitement. Giddiness. Anticipation. Gratitude. Romance. And the sheer joy of watching her parents renew their vows, reunited with the old friends they had sadly lost touch with, the four of them elated to have found each other again.

The reality?

She'd unleashed a domino effect of events that had pushed her father to violence, her mother to tears, dragged their most devastating secrets out into the open and put her in a position where just picturing a certain guy's face was making her hands sweat and her heart thud. And that guy wasn't the one who was back in Scotland, brushing off her calls because they'd both become too damn complacent with their relationship.

Thankfully, there was still time to salvage some of this, to get back on track with the original plan and at least give her parents the joy of celebrating thirty years together with their daughters by their side, grateful for every year that their mum and dad had been together because they'd given their family brilliant lives.

She showered, slapped on a bit of mascara, poured herself into the pale mint dress that she'd bought for the occasion, putting the grand total of beautiful dresses that she owned at a resounding two. The other one was a navy floaty frock that was her fall-back for all weddings, christenings, Christmas parties and, with the addition of a black blazer, funerals. She really did need to up her style game and stop living in sweats and jeans and spending her whole life at work or on the couch. If the last few days had achieved anything, other than a volcanic eruption of everything she thought to be true in life, it was that there was a big world out here and she had to get out of her rut, expand her horizons and start living in it. She added that to the list of things she wanted to talk to Kev about when they finally managed to have a proper conversation.

She'd asked her mum and dad to be ready for noon, so when she knocked on their door, it was opened straight away by her dad, who made punctuality his life's work.

All she'd told them was that they were going somewhere nice, and they'd both scrubbed up beautifully. There had been no need to get their dad a suit, because, they'd warned him he'd need something smart so naturally, he'd brought one of his own. Even if they hadn't briefed him, Zara knew the suit would have made it here, because Colin Jones didn't do casual unless it involved a garden or a golf course. Here he was, resplendent in a light beige linen jacket with matching trousers and a white short-sleeved shirt and blue tie. It was so smart, it almost drew the eye from the bandaged hand.

Her mum, meanwhile, was still in the hotel robe, but she had somehow managed to style her own hair in an elaborate up do that defied her usual time and talents. Her mum usually aimed for a 'stick it back in a bun' level of grooming.

'Do you like my hair?' she chirped. 'Eileen did it for me. My make-up too.'

That was when the bathroom door opened and out came Eileen, drying her hands with a towel. 'Och, that hairspray was making my hands so sticky.' She stopped when she saw Zara. 'Oh, hello. What do you think then? Doesn't your mum look lovely?'

'Yes, she does. She's gorgeous.' Heart racing and hands sweaty again. Oh, crap. This wasn't in the original plan, the revised plan, the emergency plan or any other fricking plan she'd managed to come up with in the last twenty-four hours.

'I just need to decide what to wear. Can you give me a hint as to where we're going? I was thinking the pale blue dress I had on the other day. Matches your dad's tie and I've got the handbag and shoes that look lovely with it. But I don't want to go for that if we're going back to the same place we were at last time. Although, I really hope it's not there, because your father is probably barred, and we don't want to cause a scene.'

While her mum flicked through her wardrobe, Zara caught Eileen's eye and saw a knowing glance there. She knew where they were going. Of course she did. Aiden would have told his mum all about the original reason for the trip by now, and she'd be well aware that, unbeknownst to her mum and dad, they were on their way to renew their vows. Zara wondered if that was why Eileen had volunteered to do her mum's make-up and hair, and she gave her a subtle nod and smile of gratitude. Whatever had happened in the past, Aiden's mum seemed like she was trying her best to make up for it and Zara was pleased about that. She just wished it didn't make her think about her son. Again. For the tenth time in the last hour. Arrrrgh.

'Don't worry, we're definitely not going there. It's somewhere way more special, Mum, and actually, I brought a dress I thought you might want to wear.' She gestured to the garment bag that was folded over her arm. 'We know the last few months have been tough with Gran gone, but we were thinking how much she would want to be a part of this... trip.' Zara swallowed a gobstopper that appeared to have lodged in her throat. 'And since we're going somewhere pretty special, we thought you might want to have a piece of Gran here with us too, so we brought this.'

Her mum stared at the bag for a full three seconds. 'Is that Gran's cream dress? The one she loved more than life?' she whispered.

'It is.' Zara held her breath, unable to gauge from her mum's tone whether that was a good thing or a bad thing. It wasn't like she'd got a single prediction right in the last week, so she felt it best to hedge her bets and wait for further developments – especially as her mum had now burst into tears.

'Oh Zara, it's perfect.'

'Mum, your make-up!' Zara cried, and her mum reacted instantly, her two index fingers flying up to her bottom lids to stop any more tears falling.

'Don't worry, I've got this,' Eileen promised, grabbing setting powder from the dresser and launching an attack on Brenda's cheeks.

It took many sniffs, some fanning of the face and dexterity with a setting powder sponge, but five minutes later her mum had calmed down and disappeared into the bathroom to put on her dress. When she returned, Zara gasped, but her dad got in first with the compliment.

'Brenda, you look beautiful, darling.'

Zara and Eileen stood behind him, both grinning at the happiness that was radiating from Brenda Jones.

However, they had a schedule to keep, so...

'Right, Mum, are we ready to go? Millie is going to meet us there.' There was no point being pissed off with Millie for ditching her and leaving her to do this bit on her own. It would be like getting mad at a cow for mooing. Or a cloud for raining. Or a Chippendale for stripping. It was just a fact of life and there was no sense in expecting it to change. She'd better be at the wedding chapel though, or Zara was disowning her.

Her mum nodded, pulling her powder blue handbag over her shoulder and slipping her feet into the matching shoes. 'Absolutely, let's go. Although...'

She stopped, as if she'd suddenly realised there was a problem. Zara sent up a weary *Oh dear god*. What now? She honestly didn't think she had the capacity to deal with any more hiccups.

'Eileen, would you come with us?' her mum asked her former friend slash make-up artist. She then turned to Zara. 'Is that okay, sweetheart? Can you change the reservation? Only, I'd really love Eileen to come.'

Thankfully, Eileen got right in there with the objections before Zara could even formulate a plausible rejection of the idea. The United Nations of Brenda and Eileen might have agreed to put past hostilities behind them and negotiated some kind of commendable peace deal, but any citizen on earth could see that given everything that had happened, it wasn't going to work to have the former girlfriend, former best friend, former fly in the great big jar of fucking ointment at the surprise renewal of her parents' vows.

'Oh Brenda, that's lovely, but I can't... I really wouldn't impose...'

'Nonsense. It's not an imposition. Is it, Zara?'

Zara's mouth was moving but nothing was coming out, so Eileen jumped right back in there.

'But I really need to get back to Aiden.'

Her mum shook her head and with all her trademark warmth and friendliness, shot that one down. 'Eileen! Didn't you say this morning that you were staying out of the way because Aiden had an unexpected visitor and you wanted to leave them to it?'

He had what, now? Zara tried desperately to compute. *A visitor. Layla. Shit. I mean, good. Definitely good. That solved that problem. Took it off the table. So great. Fantastic. Job done. Case closed. Why did she want to cry?*

'Yes, but...'

Zara saw that Eileen was running out of objections, but trying desperately not to be offensive, now that she'd somehow managed to build a tentative bridge with her old friend. Bollocks. Why wasn't Millie here? They needed some blatant rudeness to sort this out. Unfortunately, Zara just didn't have it in her.

'It's fine, really,' she told Eileen, giving the woman a look that she hoped said, 'Yep, we both know why this is a bad idea, but there's nothing we can do about it, so we'll just have to go along with it for now and figure something out later because neither of us want to upset my mum or hurt her feelings.'

Eileen must have got at least some of that, because she replied with a hesitant, 'Are you sure?'

What else could Zara say than, 'Definitely. It'll be fine. Great.'

As a last resort, maybe Eileen could fall out of the car and feign injury when they got there.

Downstairs, they all piled into the limo that Zara had booked, with plenty of ooohs and aaaaahs from her mum. She really was making the most of this trip now and it made Zara's heart soar because she didn't even know the best bit yet.

The Vegas traffic was heavy and chaotic, even at this time of the day, so that gave Zara way too much time to think.

This was going to be such a special moment for her parents.

Aiden's ex-fiancée was here.

Even if Eileen was with them and that was borderline inappropriate.

Aiden's ex-fiancée was here.

Dammit, she'd forgotten to call Kev yesterday or today.

Aiden's ex-fiancée was here.

They were turning into the street that the chapel was on.

Aiden's ex-fiancée was here.

Why the hell was Aiden's ex-fiancée here?

'Oh, there's Aiden,' Eileen blurted, as the limo began to slow.

Zara almost gave herself whiplash. Aiden was indeed there, standing in front of the white building, with someone who definitely wasn't his ex-fiancée.

Of course he would come. He'd been in on the plan from the start. He was invested and he'd tried so hard to help, so it made sense that...

'Wait.' Her mum's voice, and it didn't sound the same as it had five minutes ago, when it was gushing over the spectacle of the revolving tower at the top of the Stratosphere Hotel as they drove past it. 'I recognise this. Colin? Do you?'

'I do.' Bugger, he didn't sound thrilled either. 'This is where...' he began.

'I know exactly where it is,' her mum interjected, before switching straight to Zara, who felt herself wilting under an accusatory glare that she didn't understand. 'Zara, what are we doing here?'

Jesus, where was Millie? She needed an ally here right now to help her handle this. Faced with panic, she did the natural thing and went with unbridled enthusiasm.

'Mum, Dad, this is your anniversary gift from us. We've arranged for you to renew your vows in exactly the same place where you, erm, not quite technically, got married the first time. Isn't that amazing?'

They'd finally got here. The whole purpose of the trip. The climax of the whole idea. The cherry on top of the thirtieth anniversary cake.

So why did her mum look like she wanted to kick off her shoes and run for the hills?

She'd almost pulled it off. Almost. It had taken every bit of determination she had, layered with huge gratitude and appreciation for her daughters' efforts, and aided by a couple of unexpected surprises, but Brenda had almost managed to get into the swing of this trip and make the most of it.

After a rocky start, she'd thrown caution to the wind and just gone with the flow, vowing to leave all the complicated stuff – the problems with Colin, the decisions about her future, the conflicted but surprisingly amenable feelings for a former friend whom she would have to say goodbye to tomorrow – all of that, she'd just pushed to one side, suspended worry and negativity and decided that for once in her bloody life she was just going to think about nothing else but enjoying herself in the moment. And that's exactly what she'd done. She'd sung her heart out with Celine Dion. She'd made a pact with Eileen to take tentative steps to rebuilding a friendship, and she was so glad she had, because she'd laughed more in the last day and a half than she'd done in years. She'd even begun to see Colin in a different light, one that respected his integrity, his decency and his decision to take a swing at a man twice his size because he'd been a dick to Brenda all those years ago. Not that she'd ever condone violence, but she'd be lying if she denied there was something attractive about a middle-aged husband in comfortable slacks who was prepared to risk humiliation and a bodily injury to right a wrong that had been done to the people he loved.

If she were honest, another shift to her perspective had come from hearing how awfully Gary had treated Eileen. Brenda had spent all her life wondering what if, and now she was entirely sure that she'd dodged a bullet. There was a freedom that had accompanied that conclusion.

And now?

She'd just walked right back into a gilded cage. Renewing her vows. In front of the girls. To their father. The man she'd been planning to leave until just a few days ago, and with whom she still had an uncertain future.

'Mum!' That came from Millie, who was already waiting outside the chapel and gleefully threw her arms wide and hugged her as soon as she got out of the car. 'I'm soooooo excited! I may also still be slightly drunk. But if the Elvis bloke isn't up to scratch, I can belt out a couple of Celine's numbers from last night. By the way, this is Officer Chad. He's here to make sure Dad doesn't deck anyone.'

'I don't think that's necessary,' Brenda heard Colin reply, all full of embarrassment and indignation.

'Dad, I'm kidding,' Millie told him, wrapping Colin in a huge hug and squeezing him. 'He's here because he can't bear to be parted from the new love of his life. That's me. We met after the Celine Dion concert last night, after you, Dad and Eileen had gone off into the dusk singing "The Power Of Love". We've had the most amazing night and I had to bring him because he's besotted with me already. Chad, don't deny it,' she jested, nudging him with her shoulder.

Brenda closed her eyes for a second, begging her mind to accept the ludicrousness of this whole situation, then opened them when she heard Officer Chad say, 'Pleased to meet you, sir, ma'am,' and realised his hand was waiting for her to shake.

She and Colin both took turns to greet him, almost apologetically. 'Good to meet you too, Chad.' This polite, respectful man didn't know what he'd let himself in for with their Millie.

At the moment, though, Brenda had other problems to deal with.

'Right, if we can all go inside, please,' she heard Zara say, 'because Elvis hasn't got all day and we've only got a half-hour slot before the next devoted couple does the happy ever after stuff.'

Everyone began to troop in, and Eileen gave her hand a squeeze on the way past. 'Are you okay? Only...' she didn't need to finish. Thirty years may have passed but these two could read each other like a book. Only, much as she was enjoying the reconnection, this book was none of Eileen's business.

Smile on. Happy voice on. Act one. 'Of course. Yes. Thank you.'

Her latest Meryl Streep performance lasted until she watched Eileen's back go ahead in front of her into the chapel. That's when something inside her broke as she realised that for the last twenty-four hours there had been no acting. For the first time in years, she'd just enjoyed herself, had a great time, made the most of it. Yet now, once again, she was back in the land of making other people believe she was happy.

And she had absolutely no choice.

She wasn't going to hurt her daughters, or embarrass Colin, or make a scene. Obedient, middle-of-the-road, make-nice Brenda was back and there was nothing she could do about it.

'This is fantastic, isn't it?' Colin prompted, although she could hear the uncertainty in his words. Poor Colin. He'd done his best. 'I mean, look at those roses. From a distance they look like the real thing.'

She could run. She could hitch up the skirt of her mother's dress and just bloody run. If Ada was here, that was exactly what she'd be telling her to do. Her mother had a fondness for Colin because he was a good man, but only once, when the girls were small, had she hinted that Brenda didn't need to be anywhere she didn't want to be. They'd been at her mum's kitchen table, having a cup of tea while Colin played with the girls in the garden. 'He's a lovely lad, that one,' Ada had said, immediately putting Brenda on alert because if her wonderfully warm but achingly blunt mum was giving out a random compliment, there was probably about to be a 'but' at the end of the sentence. She wasn't wrong. 'But...' Ada had gone on, 'I'm not sure he sets yer knickers alight, ma love. And that's important in a marriage. I mean, yer dad still...'

Brenda had blurted, 'Don't finish that sentence, Mum, I beg you.'

'Fine. But I'm just saying... You need to be happy and... what's that word they're all using now? I heard Oprah say it on the telly. *Fulfilled*. Aye, that's it. You need to be fulfilled too and if yer not, then you know I'll support you in whatever choices you make, m'love. You and the girls will always have a home here.'

Of course, Brenda had immediately snapped into contented wife mode and insisted she was perfectly happy exactly where she was. Her mother never raised it again.

'Brenda?' Colin was staring at her now and she couldn't respond. Her throat was closed. Her brain screaming inside. 'Brenda... shall I get the girls?' He was panicking, she could hear it and the mention of the girls was enough to jump-start her words.

'I don't know if I can do this, Colin.'

The sadness that swept right across his face told her that he knew exactly what she was talking about.

'But I thought things were so much better... the last couple of days...'

She nodded, words run out. They had been better. Last night, after the Celine concert, they'd even had a fumble under the sheets, and he hadn't got up afterwards to put his pyjamas back on.

'They were, but not...' She couldn't finish the sentence, but she could see that he knew what she was about to say. Not enough. This. This wasn't enough.

'Mum, Elvis is waiting!' That was Zara, her amazing Zara, who'd popped her head back out of the door and who was gesturing them inside, her frown a sure-fire indication that she was worried something would go wrong. Brenda couldn't be the one to make that happen. Not now. Not here. Not after all the love that had been put into arranging this.

Big girl pants on. Deep breath. She'd been acting since the day she left this place the last time and she could do it for another day for her daughters.

'Coming, love,' she assured her, with a beaming grin, before holding her arms up for Colin. 'Shall we?'

He frowned. 'But...'

'Colin, our girls are waiting for us. Time to go.'

The frown disappeared and he understood. She saw it. He pulled his shoulders back, cleared his throat, and took her arm and together, they walked inside, to the profound, emotional, classical sounds of Elvis Presley belting out 'It's Now Or Never'.

Inside, Brenda cast a glance around the room. In the front row to the right, Zara, Millie, and an officer of the law. To the left, Eileen, Aiden, and a very handsome man whose smile indicated that he was happy to be here. He must be Aiden's unexpected visitor, the one Eileen had mentioned earlier.

Brenda took a few more steps to the front of the aisle.

Last time, their witnesses had been two cleaners who'd been kind enough to stop vacuuming and stand for the two strangers who'd wandered in in the middle of the night. They weren't here, but the rest of the cast were ready for action.

Straight ahead, Elvis. And Brenda had a sneaking suspicious mind that it was the same one as before, because he was in his eighties if he was a day, and his zimmer was parked over beside the Chapelettes, who'd clearly stopped into work on their way back from collecting their pensions at the post office.

Out of nowhere, Brenda felt herself begin to laugh. And laugh. Everything was exactly the same. Time hadn't moved on, and as Elvis got started, she heard that the script hadn't either. Not one bit of it. As Elvis got to work, she wasn't sure if she was right here or right back there...

Elvis threw his arms out to the side, making the tassels that dangled from his white leather jacket quiver. The Love Me Tender Elvis Chapel of Las Vegas was his white-walled, plastic-flower-draped stage, and the people standing in front of him were his audience.

'Do you, Brenda,' he sang, still in a slightly less impressive voice than the man who had actually been Elvis Aaron Presley, '...take this man, Colin...' That set off a flurry of tambourines from the three pink-clad backing singers the advertising billboard called the Chapelettes, standing to the left of Elvis. 'To be your hunka hunka burning love and husband until your last day on earth?"

'I do,' Brenda whispered, tears falling. Once again, her response set the tambourines off again, and exclamations of 'Praise be,' from the Chapelettes.

'And do you, Colin, take this woman, Brenda, to be your wife and promise to love her tender until the day you die?'

Colin stared into her eyes, and Brenda could see so many things there. Love. Fear. Uncertainty.

'I...' he began.

A pause. Everything stopped. Suddenly, Brenda was right back in the present moment, and couldn't quite understand why proceedings had ground to a halt. Had Colin fainted? No. He was still standing in front of her, staring at her, his mouth open but forming no more words. She was about to run through the stroke protocols that she used every day at work, when he finally spoke.

'I... don't.'

Brenda met his gaze, then saw his sad smile, his resolute nod of the head.

'I don't,' he repeated, stronger this time.

Elvis was beginning to quiver in his blue suede shoes.

'Dad!' Zara yelped.

Colin glanced over to her with an apologetic grimace, then came back to Brenda.

'I don't, because I think it's time that Brenda got to choose her own life.' He was speaking right to her now, and every other person had faded away, so it was only her and her husband, just like the last time. 'You've been a wonderful wife and a wonderful mother. Now, if you want to be, I think you should just be a wonderful you.'

Brenda heard a whisper from Millie of, 'I thought I was the day drinker in the family,' but she ignored it, eyes still locked on her husband, as she threw out a question to Elvis.

'Can I change my mind?'

Stunned, but going with the flow, Elvis nodded, 'Ma'am, your dime, your time.'

'Okay, thank you. In that case, I don't either. Because, Colin Jones, you've stood by my side for thirty years and you've never wavered. You've been the best father our daughters could ever have hoped for, and I love you dearly. But now, we can close this chapter and know that we both did our best.' The tears were still rolling down her cheeks but she could feel the sadness mingle with the joy of this moment. 'And I think you should also go and do exactly as you please now, and just be wonderful you too.'

'They've lost the plot. Do you think someone spiked their drinks?' Millie again.

Brenda turned to her daughters, saw Millie's wide-eyed astonishment and the tears in Zara's eyes. 'Girls, we both love you so much. and we're sorry. I hope you can forgive us. But there's a time when you just have to live your lives exactly the way you want to and for us that's now. I hope you both have the heart and the courage to do that too.'

Still holding Colin's hand, Brenda held out her other arm, and Millie and Zara slipped out of their row and came into their fold. The four of them hugged, while over in the corner, the Chapelettes, unprepared to go off script, broke into a hesitant but perfectly pitched first verse of the 'Wonder of You'.

Zara was the first to speak, breaking the circle, kissing her mum on the cheek, then her dad. 'You two are amazing. Unexpected but amazing. All we want is for you to be happy. If you can excuse me, though, I need to go make a phone call.'

32

AIDEN

Aiden watched Zara rush out, staring straight ahead, without even a glance in his direction. No wonder. The last fifteen minutes might have been the most bizarre of his life, and he was a lawyer who'd once represented a couple who were getting their fifth divorce. From each other. He'd heard that they had remarried yet again a year later, and after that, he'd stopped taking their calls.

Beside him, Trevon was watching the whole thing with wide-eyed interest, which pleased him because his mate had been in a total funk for the last day or so. Aiden didn't get it. His mom had been pretty much absent the whole time, hanging out with Zara's parents, so he'd been pretty sure Trevon would be up for hitting the town hard, but instead, he'd been as low as he'd ever seen him. He'd even listened to Aiden spilling his guts about Layla, about Zara, and about his general confusion in life for two hours last night without complaint. Trevon had just fed him beer, commiserated, and then tracked down a Charlotte Hornets basketball game on ESPN to take his mind off it. That was true friendship right there.

'I'm sorry, bud,' Aiden had said at half-time. 'We should be out making the most of being here. I'm officially the most pathetic wingman in the world right now.'

Trevon had just shrugged, put his feet up on the coffee table in their suite and opened another beer. 'Nah, you're fine. Got our whole lives to tear it up. Some other stuff is more important.'

Aiden had nudged him, gesturing to the screen. 'Like the Hornets making the play offs.'

'Yep, nothing's more important than that.'

They'd spent the rest of the night watching games and reruns, but by midnight, Aiden was beginning to wonder if something really was wrong with his mate because he'd barely said a word all evening. Normally, Trevon would be shouting at the TV, calling the plays, living every moment of the game in real time. Instead, his ass stayed parked on the couch, his shoulders slumped and he just kept checking his phone.

'Trev, is there something you're not telling me? Shit, sorry. I've spent half the night telling you about my problems. What's going on with you? Troubles?'

Trevon shrugged. 'Work stuff.'

Aiden wasn't buying it. Trevon was the most proactive, switched-on guy he knew. If he had work problems, he'd be in there sorting them out, not slouched on a couch in Vegas with his pissed off mate. No, this had to be about a woman, but Trevon kept things close to his chest so there was no point probing. He'd tell him when he was ready.

This morning, he'd still been preoccupied.

'Okay, I've made a decision and feel free to tell me I'm an idiot, but I'm going to go along to this thing today,' Aiden had announced.

'You're going to go to some second wedding thing, for the parents of the girl you're crushing on, even though she's not taking your calls and the whole reunion with your parents plan was a bust?'

'Yeah, that's about it. Wanna come?'

Trevon had laughed, shaking his head. 'Man, I love you, but not that much.'

Aiden had got dressed, shaved, fully aware that this was probably a bad idea, but Zara was leaving tomorrow and this could be the last chance he'd have to speak to her, even if it was only to say goodbye. And sorry. If nothing else, he definitely owed her an apology for putting her in that position the other night.

He'd been about to leave when his mom had texted to say she was heading there too.

'Okay, I don't feel like so much of a loser now turning up on my own. My mom is going, so at least it'll look like I'm just there to keep her company. Last chance to change your mind. You may get to see me make a complete dick of myself, for the second time in a month.'

To his surprise, Trevon had pushed himself up from the bed. 'You know what? I don't think I want to miss that. You being a dick makes me feel better about myself.'

Ten minutes later, Trevon was out of the shower, pale grey shirt and black trousers on, ready to come support them. Or bear witness to his idiocy. Either way, Aiden was glad he was here now to see all this, because re-telling the story of what had just happened in this chapel could never quite capture the surprise of it all.

His mom had left her chair and gone over to hug Zara's parents, leaving the seat at the aisle empty and a clear route to slip out without causing a fuss. Aiden took it.

Outside the chapel, he scanned the street searching for Zara. He'd almost given up, figuring she'd bolted, when he spotted her. Looking like some kind of gorgeous paradox in a Banksy painting, she was sitting on the grubby sidewalk beside the run-down pawn shop along the street, her head resting on the knees that were pulled up to the chest of her beautiful mint green dress. Feeling a relief that he could barely explain or justify, he wandered over.

'Hey,' he began softly, so that he didn't startle her. 'You waiting for someone or can anyone sit here?'

She lifted her head and brought her hand up to her eyes, shielding them as she squinted against the afternoon sun.

'To be honest, I'm kinda hoping for a serial killer to put me out of my misery, but there's no sign of one.'

Aiden cast his gaze around the street. 'In this part of town, one could show up at any minute.'

He watched her gorgeous face find a way to a half-smile and took that as an acceptance of his offer. He slid down the wall, not caring that he was about to wreck a five hundred dollar pair of Tom Ford pants by sitting on a sidewalk that hadn't been cleaned since the beginning of time. He rolled up the sleeves on his black shirt and pulled his sunglasses out of his pants pocket. He offered them to her first, but she declined.

'I'm Scottish. I see the sun about three times a year so I could do with the Vitamin D. But thanks.'

He slipped one of the arms of the sunglasses into his mouth, figuring that if he chewed it, it might cover up the fact that he had no idea what to say. Nothing. He spent half his life discussing cases with clients, taking depositions, arguing in court. He practically spoke for a living. Yet here he was, on a Vegas sidewalk, with no idea how to formulate a decent sentence.

'Tough gig in there.'

'Yep,' she replied, sighing with weariness. 'I told you I was a jinx. I don't even know where to start with what they just did. I guess they had another whole thing going on that we didn't understand. I'm pleased for them though, truly. Whatever makes them happy is cool with me, because it's their lives to live, not mine. But I'm now officially done with surprises for any kind of celebration. From now on, everyone is getting wine for birthdays, Christmas, anniversaries and every other special occasion. At least if it all goes tits up, we can drown our sorrows.'

Another silence. That's when the universe threw him a break and he spotted the phone in her hand. Okay, he could work with that.

'Waiting for a call?' It wasn't exactly oratory genius, but it would do.

'Just made one,' she replied, obviously finding this as awkward as him. 'Wasn't great.'

He had no idea what the call was about, but her monosyllabic attitude was making it pretty clear she didn't want him here. He took the hint. Fuck-up made. Time to apologise and get out of there and hope the memory faded real fast. He felt his palms begin to sweat and it wasn't just down to the heat. Nor was the dry throat, the swirling guts or the inability to make his thoughts turn into anything more than basic words.

'I'm sorry.'

'Not your fault.'

'No, I mean, about the other night. I'm so sorry. I put you in a position and I shouldn't have done that. It's not my usual style and I apologise.'

Okay, he'd finally managed to plead his case. He'd thought maybe she'd shrug his apology off, and then, crushed but still breathing, he could go and do something unusual but therapeutic with the rest of his day. Maybe drink until he fell down and forgot about this.

'Did you mean it?'

'Mean what?'

'Oh, for God's sake, it's like we've lost the power of communication! I'm dying here, and not just of bloody sunstroke. Did. You. Mean. That. You. Wanted. To. Kiss. Me?'

He was astonished that she had to ask. 'Of course I did. I don't just go saying stuff like that to...'

'Aaaargh!' Her frustration came out in a low strangled groan, just as her hand shot out and covered his mouth. 'Don't speak. Not a word. Because I'm so bloody fed up with guessing what everyone is thinking and feeling, and what would make everyone else fricking happy and then getting it wrong. I'm sick of it! Look where it's got me!'

He'd have chipped in there, but she still had him gagged.

'So here's the thing, Romeo. The call I just made was to my boyfriend and I informed him that I don't want to be in a relationship with him anymore because we were in a rut and only still hanging in there out of habit and we've made absolutely zero bloody effort to make the most of our lives or to make each other happy. And he proved that point by asking me if I could call back because he was in the middle of something important at work. So we're done. Finished. And one of the reasons that I did the first rash and unpredictable thing in my entire well-behaved, sensible life was because the other night, when you, you big bloody lovely man, asked if you could kiss me, I really, really, really wanted to say yes. But I couldn't, because I had a fricking boyfriend and I'd have hated myself forever if I did something awful to him. And then, you blew it all by taking a call from the woman who broke your heart, so you've probably realised that you're still in love with her because I bet she's all sexy and smart and has a manicured bikini line and doesn't do half the crazy shit that you've seen me do since I hijacked your life and coerced you into one of my daft plans. And if that's the case, then tell me now, because I might have mentioned I'm FRICKING OVER GUESSING WHAT IS GOING ON IN THE MINDS OF

OTHER PEOPLE. And in case you need me to wrap that all up in a nice little bloody bow, here it is. You make me feel a way I've never felt before. I don't know if I like it or not, but it's making me do stuff like break up with my boyfriend, so that's done, and now I'm single. And it felt like someone was taking a baseball bat to my heart earlier, when I thought your ex might have showed up, but now I realise that she hasn't. However that doesn't mean you haven't gone back to your fiancée, the invisible bloody woman, and if you have, then say it now and then walk away. But if you haven't, then I'm going to stop talking in a minute because this is the longest rant I've ever spouted in my life. I'm going to take my hand off your mouth and you're going to lean over, and put your thumb on my chin, and then my cheek – because I see that in movies and it looks so bloody sexy – and then you're going to kiss me and I'm going to let you and we're going to see how that goes. Do you understand? Nod once for yes.'

He nodded.

And then, as she removed her hand, he leaned over and touched the chin of the most spectacular, funny, gorgeous, intoxicating woman he'd ever met, then slowly, so, so slowly, never once breaking her gaze, he moved his hand to her cheek, and then he edged closer. Then stopped. But just for a second. Because he wanted to remember how totally incredible this felt. Then he moved closer again, until his lips grazed hers, then pressed a little harder, until their breaths joined and became one, until his heart couldn't stand it, until he wanted to punch the air because he had never felt anything even close to the giddy, ecstatic, earth-shifting joy that he was feeling right now.

He kissed her again. Then kissed her again. Then kissed her some more. Then kissed her until she pulled back and he could see her face again. He watched as her natural shyness kicked in and she laughed, then checked around them to see if anyone was watching because she wasn't really a kissing-in-public kind of girl. Until now.

'Aiden, can I ask you something a bit random?'

'Anything. Especially if it means we can get off this sidewalk before we pick up some bacteria that could kill us, and go somewhere that I can do that to you again. For a long, long time.'

'No, not that. I mean, yes, that too. But something else...'

'Anything.'

She was squinting off into the distance again, so he figured it must be something pretty profound.

'Is that your mum over there snogging your best mate?'

33

EILEEN

It was only 6 a.m., but already the departure lounge at Las Vegas airport was busy. Some of the Saturday morning crowd were heading home after coming up here for shows the night before. Some had been at conferences all week and tagged on an extra night so they could have one last blowout before returning to the responsibilities of families and everyday life. Some were gamblers who'd arrived yesterday, lost every penny they had on the tables and were now cutting their weekend short because they'd just learned the lesson that the house always wins.

And some were, like them, a mixed bag of family and friends.

Aiden and Zara were sitting across the table from her, holding hands, both of them staring at the floor until Aiden got up and wandered off. Eileen's heart broke for them. It was obvious to them all that Aiden and Zara had found something in each other. When they'd come back from the wedding chapel yesterday, they'd been wrapped up in each other and Eileen had never seen her son look at anyone, not even Layla, the way that he was looking at Brenda's daughter. This was something very new and very wonderful, yet already they were having to say goodbye.

Brenda and Colin were sitting beside her, although Colin was already engrossed in a gardening magazine. Brenda said he'd brought it with him, which told them all they needed to know about how exciting he thought this anniversary trip was going to be.

Next to Colin, Millie was sitting on the knee of Chad, her off-duty cop, who had barely left her side since the moment he met her.

And finally, beside Aiden's empty chair, Trevon was deliberately avoiding eye contact with Eileen, because he still couldn't work out what was going on in her head. That made two of them.

It struck her that every one of them had come here expecting one thing, only to discover that this city was full of surprises.

And no one had surprised Eileen more than herself.

Spontaneously kissing Trevon yesterday when they'd left the chapel – that had all been on her, but it had been inspired by Brenda.

She'd heard the words Brenda had spoken to her daughters after Colin had ripped up their vows and, together, they'd chosen another path. Smart, quiet, caring Brenda, who, even back in their twenties when they were just all figuring life out, had always been the wisest of them all.

'There's a time when you just have to live your lives exactly the way you want to and for us that's now. I hope you both have the heart and the courage to do that too.'

In the thirty seconds after Eileen had left that church with Trevon, she'd had the heart and the courage, but the old doubts had swept right back in again and she'd jumped into a cab on her own and made her way to the fancy big late lunch that Zara and Millie had organised in Spago, Wolfgang Puck's restaurant in the Bellagio, overlooking the fountains and one of the most romantic experiences of her life. At least, it would have been if she hadn't avoided all opportunities to be alone with the one man that she was suddenly desperate to stare at, to speak to, to touch. The feelings had ambushed her, and she needed time to process them. This was Aiden's friend. He was too young. Too gorgeous. Too special. So close to her heart that he would almost certainly break it. And that wasn't a path she could even contemplate going down in case it hurt her, hurt him, hurt her son.

She'd been grateful, then, when the late lunch had turned into group drinks in Aiden's suite, which had then evolved into a party. There had been dancing. There had been singing. There had been much laughter and the kind of banter that was great for the soul. At Millie's insistence, they'd all continued the revelry through the night and come straight here at 5 a.m. for the British contingent's flights. There had been safety in numbers, no chance to be alone with Trevon. She knew she was going to have to discuss what had happened with him at some point, but not yet. Not when she still had no idea what to say.

'Is it just me or does everyone look totally depressed?' Zara asked dolefully, watching Aiden, who was on his way back to them carrying a tray of coffees. The London flight, then on to Glasgow, was going to be the first to leave, with the South Carolina one not going until the afternoon, but of course they'd come along to say goodbye to Colin, Brenda and their girls.

'It's the whole "what happens in Vegas stays in Vegas thing."' That came from Millie. 'Which sounds like it should be great, but it's not.'

'Okay, that's enough,' Brenda this time, and so forceful her daughters' eyes widened with surprise. She still had on last night's make-up, although she'd swapped her beautiful non-wedding dress for jeans and a sparkly jacket with 'Planet Hollywood' on the back. Eileen wasn't sure how it had happened, but Brenda looked ten years younger than she had a few days ago. Especially now, when she was sitting forward, eyes blazing. 'Did none of you listen to a word I said yesterday?'

There were mumblings, but those might just have been thank you's to Aiden for putting down the tray of coffees. Everyone reached in for their beverage except Brenda, who was still on a roll.

'Millie Ada Jones.'

Her daughter swung her head round, eyebrows raised, mumbling, 'Full name. Am I getting grounded and sent to my room?'

Brenda ignored the sarcasm and instead went straight to the point. 'What is it that you want? Truly. It's clear to me that you've been restless for a while now. Are you not happy? Because there is no one bolder than you on this earth, my love, and if you can't claim your best life, then the rest of us are lost. So tell me, what is it that you want right here and now?'

Eileen watched as Millie glanced around the table, until she eventually focused in on Zara.

'I want to stay here.'

Zara's coffee never made it to her mouth. 'What? Millie, don't be ridiculous. We have the shop, we have lives, we have—'

'But you know it's not the life I want.'

'Then stay here, sweetheart,' Brenda said. 'Just stay. For as long as you
want or until your money or your visa runs out. And, Zara, we'll sort out
the shop. Your dad and I will help and if you need to take on more staff,
then we'll pitch in until you do.'

For a moment Eileen thought Zara was going to cry, but after a long
pause and a deep, weary sigh, she finally shrugged. 'I suppose we could
make it work,' she admitted, and Eileen watched the conflicting thoughts
show on her face. She'd already sussed that Zara was a woman who always
chose to do the right thing. After Aiden's last experience with romance,
Eileen couldn't be happier for him that he'd now found someone like that,
even if she had no idea how they were going to handle a transatlantic relationship.

Eileen recognised a forehead free of Botox, as Millie raised a sceptical
eyebrow. 'Sis, is this one of those trick scenarios, or do you really mean
that because I'm about to sprint for the door before you change your
mind.'

'I mean it,' Zara replied, with a sad smile. 'I'll miss you every minute –
apart from your hungover ones – but I want you to be happy. So stay.'

Millie was off Officer Chad's knee now and launching herself at her
sister, landing on top of her with a ferocity that threatened to tilt the chair.
'Thank you, thank you, thank you. I love you. And I promise Chad will bail
me out if I get into any trouble. Won't you, baby?'

Millie's new man spoke for the first time, with a very cute, 'I sure
will.' He was a man of few words and many muscles, so Eileen had a
feeling that this might be more of a Mr Right Now than a Mister Right.
Millie climbed back onto his knee when she'd finished crushing her
sister.

'What about you then, Zara?' Brenda questioned her eldest daughter.
'What do you want?'

Zara looked at Aiden, held his gaze. 'I want to go home.'

Oh no. Eileen's stomach lurched. How could she have got this so
wrong? She was sure that those two had made more than just some

fleeting connection. And she could see from Aiden's surprised reaction that he was thinking the same thing.

'I'm sorry, I do,' she went on. 'But it's not what you think,' she took Aiden's hand while she rushed to explain. 'I want to go home and sort out my shop, especially now that Millie won't be there. Then I want to come visit you in South Carolina and I'd like you to come and see me in Scotland, because I want us to get to know each other properly. I want to see how that goes before we make any huge decisions or put any pressure on each other. I really hope that's okay with you, because I think maybe this could be really good, you and me, but you need to know who I am and I'm the person that likes to take my time and give things a lot of thought before I jump. Do you think you can handle that?'

Before Aiden said a word, Eileen could tell from the way he was smiling at this girl that the answer would be yes. How could it not be? He'd grown up seeing what life was like when you were in the orbit of someone who made rash and impulsive decisions about relationships. If that, and his job, and the disastrous ending to his rushed romance with Layla hadn't given him an appreciation of taking his time, then nothing would. He would be fine, her son, because he and Zara were both the kind of people that were worth waiting for.

The sound of a tannoy sliced through the atmosphere, and the announcement came over that the gate for their flight to London had now been allocated. Time to go.

Brenda, Colin and Zara stood up first, then the others followed. Eileen leaned in to hug the woman that she'd once thought she would never see again. The friend she'd loved and lost, and that she might just have back again. They'd already planned a trip home for Eileen next month and she was counting the days until she saw Brenda again.

'You take care of yourself,' Eileen murmured in Brenda's ear. 'And of Colin too.' She'd already said all the sorrys that she'd owed, and given all the thanks for forgiveness, so for now, she just had to say her goodbyes.

'I will,' Brenda whispered. 'And, Eileen, maybe you need to take back your life too. That man over there loves you,' she nodded subtly in Trevon's direction.

Eileen gasped, murmured, 'But how do you know...?'

Brenda winked. 'I've got my sources. Not that I need them. It's so obvious and you'd be a fool to ignore it.'

Eileen felt her face begin to burn. How did Brenda have even an inkling of the situation with Trevon? And how could she say Eileen should go for it when there were so many perfectly clear bloody reasons why this wasn't a good idea. But, of course, she said none of that. Instead, she kissed Brenda, kissed Colin and Zara, then stepped back and let everyone else say their farewells.

There was a minor panic when Millie realised she'd already checked in a suitcase, until Zara reminded her that they'd checked it in under her name, so they wouldn't have to offload it. All Millie had to do was live off the stuff in her hand luggage until she bought new clothes. Tears flowed, as Millie hugged her parents and sister goodbye, and Eileen wasn't sure, but she thought she heard Millie telling Zara to remember to clean an air fryer. Or maybe she imagined that. After more hugs for all of them, Millie went off, Chad in tow, to let the airline know she wouldn't be boarding.

When Brenda, Colin and Zara finally managed to tear themselves away, Eileen stood between Aiden and Trevon, and slipped her arm through her son's as they watched them go.

'She'll be back,' she told him. 'I think she's one of the good ones. She's a keeper.'

Aiden gave a final wave to Zara, who'd turned around to blow him a kiss right before disappearing through security. 'I know she will. It's weird because I don't even feel sad, just excited about what will come next. She's special.'

'She is,' Trevon agreed, but before he could say anything else, Aiden cut him off.

'But so are you two,' he said, so calmly that at first Eileen thought she'd misheard him.

Trevon clearly hadn't. 'What are you saying, Aid?' he asked tentatively.

Aiden shrugged. 'I'm saying I'm going to go grab another coffee. I'm saying that I'm going to leave you guys here and maybe you want to talk some stuff out. I'm also saying Zara and I saw you outside the chapel yesterday...'

So that was how Brenda knew. Zara must have relayed that little nugget of information to her mum.

'...and if there's any part of you,' Aiden went on, 'that's backing off starting something because of me, then I'm saying please don't, because all I want for you both is everything good. And I'm biased, but I think you two would be pretty damn good together.'

He walked away, smiling, leaving her and Trevon staring at each other, astonished.

Even with Aiden's blessing, there were still way too many problems with this. The seventeen-year age gap terrified her and she was scared of the judgement. Physically, he was perhaps the most beautiful man she'd ever seen so she was consumed with anxiety because she was a fifty-five-year-old who'd given birth, lived a life, who was now dealing with the vagaries of the menopause, and who couldn't compete with the bodies of women half her age, although she bloody well tried. More than that, he was someone who was important to her, and she didn't want to risk a romantic relationship in case it went wrong and she lost him.

But Brenda, wise, smart, enlightened Brenda, was still in her head.

'There's a time when you just have to live your lives exactly the way you want to and for us that's now. I hope you both have the heart and the courage to do that too.'

Sod the problems.

Eileen stepped forward, put her hands on Trevon's chest, leaned up and kissed him for the second time, feeling the heat of his skin and the tender, heart-bursting touch of his lips.

'I'll go there if you will,' she told him.

He pulled back, stared at her, smiled. 'Baby, I'm already there.'

EPILOGUE

SEVEN MONTHS LATER

The snow had come early, right on time for a white Christmas that thrilled the American visitors.

Brenda threw a couple of logs on the fire and asked Colin to fetch some more from the garden. Bernadette's garden. Her fabulous friend had moved to Dublin to live with the man she'd marry next year, and Brenda had rented this sweet, riverside cottage from her. It now had the most beautiful garden in the street too, thanks to the man who was once her husband, but who was now... What did Millie call them? She flushed as she remembered. 'Friends with benefits.' There was something to be said for it as far as Brenda was concerned. Freedom to live their own lives, to make their own choices, to go where they pleased, and to see other people. Colin had met a lovely lady down at the garden centre and had taken her out a few times, and Brenda was having a flirtation with one of the consultants on the elderly ward. She had no idea if either of the relationships would go anywhere, but the important thing was that they could. And both she and Colin were happy to throw the dice and see where they fell.

He was so much more interested in the world now that he'd retired from the council and spent his days working with Zara. He did all the run-of-the-mill stuff, while she concentrated on the flowers for special events and it was working out perfectly. For now.

Her daughter certainly seemed to be loving her new life. Brenda took a tray of mulled wine over to the dining table, where Zara and Aiden and Millie were playing cards, Millie howling in outrage because she hated to get beat. Some things never changed.

Actually, everything had changed. Millie had stayed for three weeks in Vegas, until her fling with Chad had run its course, then spent a month travelling across the country, ending up in South Carolina, where she'd lived with Eileen for a few weeks. It was there that she'd heard about the job on the cruise ship out of Florida – a resident florist on an exclusive, very expensive ship that sailed the Caribbean. It was wild, it was exotic, every day was different and Millie loved it. For now. Brenda had no doubt that her irrepressible lover of life would need more adventures in her future.

Eileen had developed a bit of a thirst for adventure too. At work, she had sold some big house and pocketed a healthy commission, so she'd used that to visit Scotland just a few weeks after the Vegas trip. Brenda had taken her on a tour of their old haunts: the club they'd worked in – now turned into flats. The house they'd all shared – now knocked down and a petrol station in its place. They'd laughed, they'd sang, they'd danced, and they'd hung on to each other as they'd sobbed at Eileen's mum's grave and then at Ada's too. And they'd vowed they would see each other again soon.

They'd made good on that promise. Brenda had gone over to Charleston for a fortnight in October, and now Eileen had come to Scotland for Christmas with Aiden and her boyfriend, the gorgeous Trevon. He'd asked her to move in with him and she was thinking about it. She was hopelessly, gloriously head over heels in love with him and the best bit was that he felt the same. Eileen had gleefully revealed that she was over her reservations now, having the best time of her life, and they didn't give a toss what anyone thought about them. Especially her ex-husband, Gary the Gob, who was at home in South Carolina, recovering from a facelift and liposuction.

He'd had the cheek to call Brenda when he heard that she'd separated from Colin. He'd told her he'd always loved her, that he wanted her back, then he'd asked her to go to America and let him sweep her off her feet. Instead, she'd told him about losing his child back in the nineties, and her motivations for marrying Colin. She'd then informed him that much as she was embarking on a new, adventurous stage of life, she'd rather go without sex until the end of time than go anywhere near him because she saw now that he'd been a pretentious dickhead back then, and he was still one now. Then she'd hung up, popped open a bottle of wine and invited Colin over for a naked fumble. And yes, her mules had trembled.

Brenda went over and joined them on the sofa. 'So what are we thinking – will it be tonight?' she asked in a low whisper.

Trevon nodded. 'Definitely. He's not going to be able to hold off much longer.'

Eileen seemed to agree. 'I think so. Look, his leg is shaking. He's done that since he was a kid when he's nervous. He didn't even do that when he got ditched at the altar by that horror.' Eileen had made no secret of her dislike for Leah. Or Lila. Or... Layla, yep, that was it. A few days after they'd all returned from Vegas back in May, Eileen had called to report that she'd spent a whole day immersed in retail therapy to take her mind off Aiden's meeting with Layla to discuss their future. It had cost her a spontaneous purchase of a Valentino bag that she returned the next day when, to the relief of them all, Aiden had called Zara to let her know that he'd told Layla they didn't have a future. His heart had found a new home. With her.

As far as Eileen and Trevon were concerned, Aiden had dodged a bullet there, and judging by the way that handsome big fella was looking at Brenda's daughter now, he obviously felt the same.

Over at the table, Millie had abandoned the game and gone off to get another drink.

Aiden reached for Zara's hand. 'Fancy some fresh air?'

'It's flipping freezing out there,' Zara objected, but only half-heartedly. Brenda knew Aiden could suggest a wander, barefoot in the snow and Zara would go because they were utterly besotted with each other.

Eileen dug Brenda in the ribs, and gestured over to them. 'It's happening,' she hissed. 'Look! It's definitely now.' She could barely contain her excitement.

Trevon was already on his feet as Aiden and Zara went out the back door.

Millie clocked the activity. 'What's going on?'

'They've gone outside. We think it's now,' Brenda whispered urgently.

The whole lot of them – Brenda, Eileen, Colin, Trevon and Millie – crept over to the kitchen window and crowded around it, holding their breath as Brenda opened it slowly and silently, so they could hear what was being said. It was a gross invasion of privacy, but that was overruled by the sight in front of them, as, outside, they saw Aiden stop, turn, go down on one knee.

Brenda had to clap her hand over her own mouth to stop the yelp of delight. It had only been a feeling, a hunch, and a report from Trevon that he'd spotted a small square box in Aiden's apartment. The combination of all those things had been enough for the mothers to get ten steps ahead of themselves and start scouting wedding venues and shopping for big hats.

Out in the snow, Aiden was looking up at Zara.

'Zara, since the moment you didn't let me kiss you in a Vegas hotel, I've known that I was in love with you. You're everything and I'd very much love you to be mine and for me to be yours.'

At the kitchen window, Brenda was crying, Eileen was holding her breath, Millie was knocking back the mulled wine, Trevon watched knowing he'd be next, and Colin wondered whether he should take a few inches off the leylandiis that bordered the garden.

'Zara Jones, will you marry me?'

They heard the intoxicating sound of Zara laughing, then, 'Can I think about it?'

Several gasps from the kitchen window, then...

'Definitely not.' Aiden replied, sounding amused.

'Then absolutely yes,' Zara exclaimed gleefully, as he pushed the ring on to her finger and then stood up, touched her chin with his thumb, then her cheek, then leaned down and kissed her.

The kitchen window spy team cracked and began clapping and cheering, until the newly engaged couple came back inside, to a roar of congratulations.

'Dad, would you take over the shop so I can go live in America with my husband?'

'I think I can manage that,' Colin chuckled, hugging her. That set off another round of cheers.

'Hang on, hang on,' Zara stopped them. 'We do have one condition.'

The others waited, frozen in suspense until she laid it out.

'If we make it to our thirtieth anniversary, can we just celebrate at home?'

ACKNOWLEDGMENT

My endless gratitude to every single person in my brilliant publishing family at Boldwood Books. As always, this book wouldn't exist without my inspiring, encouraging and miracle-working editor and friend, Caroline Ridding. I'm immensely thankful to copy editor, Jade Craddock and proof reader, Rose Fox, who make everything I write so much better, and head of marketing, Claire Fenby-Warren and her awesome team, who do a fantastic job of spreading the word far and wide.

Huge thanks to Rachel Gilbey and the book bloggers who participate in my blog tours, for all the wonderful words and support for every new release.

And to the readers who buy my stories, thank you from the bottom of my heart. I am beyond grateful that you continue to allow me to share my imaginary worlds.

Much love,

Shari xx

MORE FROM SHARI LOW

We hope you enjoyed reading *One Moment in Time*. If you did, please leave a review.

If you'd like to gift a copy, this book is also available as an ebook, large print, paperback, digital audio download and audiobook CD.

Sign up to Shari Low's mailing list for news, competitions and updates on future books.

http://bit.ly/ShariLowNewsletter

Explore more from wonderfully uplifting novels from Shari Low...

ABOUT THE AUTHOR

Shari Low is the #1 bestselling author of over 20 novels, including *My One Month Marriage* and *One Day In Summer,* and a collection of parenthood memories called *Because Mummy Said So*. She lives near Glasgow.

Visit Shari's website: www.sharilow.com

Follow Shari on social media:

f facebook.com/sharilowbooks

𝕐 twitter.com/sharilow

⃝ instagram.com/sharilowbooks

BB bookbub.com/authors/shari-low

Boldwood

Boldwood Books is an award-winning fiction publishing company seeking out the best stories from around the world.

Find out more at www.boldwoodbooks.com

Join our reader community for brilliant books, competitions and offers!

Follow us

@BoldwoodBooks

@BookandTonic

Sign up to our weekly deals newsletter

https://bit.ly/BoldwoodBNewsletter

Printed in the USA
CPSIA information can be obtained
at www.ICGtesting.com
LVHW031745180923
758542LV00008B/58

9 781804 268742